WE ALL HAVE TEETH

WE ALL HAVE

TEETH

A collection of stories and assorted nonsense

by C.A. Yates

For Paul, always

... and to the old me who lost faith. Told you so.

www.foxspirit.co.uk

We All Have Teeth copyright © 2021 C.A. Yates

Cover art and design by Vincent Holland-Keen and C.A. Yates

Book layout and typesetting by handebooks.co.uk

ISBN: 978-1-910462-35-5

Published by:
Fox Spirit Books
www.foxspirit.co.uk
adele@foxspirit.co.uk

Extended copyright and publishing information at rear

Contents

WE ALL HAVE TEETH

We all have teeth, dear… and oh! Such teeth we have! All the better to eat you with, wouldn't you say? Wouldn't you like that dear? To be useful, to be part of things? It's a ritual, nothing fancy, just a little something to bring about the End of the World, dear. You look like you're tasty, like you take care of yourself, like you eat well. Do you smoke, dear? I didn't think so. Your teeth are far too white, healthy looking. You don't smell of it either and that's good because around here we make our own marinade.

GO FORTH IN THE DANCE
OF THE MERRYMAKERS

Tranced out, jacked up, and very much *on one*, the fist pumpers work clenched hands above their heads to the heavy bounce of the bassline. Their eyes are closed; they're communing. Others are communing with a bit more of the old flesh-on-flesh, if you know what I mean, right out there in the open while others are crying and laughing beside them, everyone letting it all hang out and indulging in whatever floats their particular boat. Heaven on Earth some are calling it, Elijah certainly is, but with the Harbinger casting its bloodlight across the crowds it looks more like a snapshot of that other place, the one my grandmother papered pictures of all over my old bedroom walls.

Love ya, Grandma.

The end is nigh. They've been saying it for what seems like forever, over and over, and I'm still not sure if most folk truly believe it, certainly not in the West. Punch drunk in their bubbles of Reality TV and online shopping, most people still think it's nothing more than a story on the goggle box and it's certainly not going to happen to them. I guess there's comfort in denial. It ain't just a river and all that.

Not that everyone's been pretending it's not coming, far from it. Governments squabbled about it for months, nobly taking a diplomatic time out from the business of killing each other. Eventually they banded together and came up with a plan. For all the good it did. They flew all their rockets and science into the Harbinger but to no avail. In an epic twist of human stupidity, and predictability, the despondency at their failure just made the juice of conflict tastier for the warmongers and that meant another round of tribulations went on the docket. Sure, others have gone into the forests and mountains, dug deep, and are hoping for the best. Maybe they'll be all right. Others still have turned to people like Elijah. To find meaning they say; to make their last days *matter*. They matter to Elijah. He's been feeding off their desperation like a starving man, gobbling down the morally dubious offerings his followers make so they can get in on the straight fire deal he's promising. Who wouldn't want to party on for divine redemption? I was one of those offerings. When it came down to it, my pious grandmother was only too willing to offer me up to the golden boy, despite always having preached at us about how drinking and dancing were the work of the devil. Goose and gander, am I right? I guess it got me off her hands so she could go relive her glory days, before she'd got zealously inclined, with the other olds in the group.

Speaking of Grandma...

Hot warmth trickles down my arm and I raise it, licking off the blood responsible without thinking. It's from both the knife in my right hand and my grandmother, for whom the knife had become that long-feared demon she'd prayed so hard against and ended her twisted life. By my *righteous* hand.

'How'd ya like them apples, grandma?' I'd asked as she had clutched at me, begging for mercy. 'My, grandmother, what big eyes you have,' I'd said as I plunged the blade into the old woman's chest over and over. She was what you'd call a fire and brimstone type, worse when she'd been on the whiskey. It was all unnecessary bluster, of course, to cover the fact that underneath it all she was a frightened hypocrite. When I was younger she despised all frivolity but Elijah had eventually changed her mind with all his glamour and fame – I mentioned she was a hypocrite, right? To be fair, she hadn't realised how debauched his – what do they call it? – 'doctrine' was, not at first, not before it was too late. *Not before it was too late.* Huh. Here's my problem with that; there's simply no excuse for such egregious ignorance. Be faithful but be smart. Hells bells and buckets of blood, old sport!

These losers think they're going to heaven? That they are going to be raised up to sit at God's right hand on high or whatever? Not because of listening to Elijah they're not. He's a liar, a fraud, and so much worse than that. So much worse. Hundreds, thousands, have heard his words, have heard him preaching that while this might be the end of humanity's time on Earth it's really just the beginning of the next step, the path to Paradise, to everything they have ever wanted. The Harbinger is not a force of evil, he has told them, it is a messenger sent straight from God and, oh, see how it lights up the sky with His glory! Behold as it shows us the way! A cosmic disco ball telling us to party hard as the righteous are resurrected and so, I guess, the plan is we all neck bob with the zombies right into the world to come. Revelatory.

It's the most messed up excuse for a party there's ever been and that it's worked so well shows just how much we need the Harbinger to wipe us all out, if you ask me. Not that anyone has.

Ever since he got the approval of that late night talk show host, John or James, something or other, Elijah notched it up a level. He took the surge in popularity that followed as permission to embark on a spree of righteous wickedness. Yeah, that is an oxymoron, heavy on the moron. Suddenly it was like the end of the world meant he could do whatever he wanted and he did. As far as his 'church' is concerned, as long as you celebrate, anything is allowed.

'Such tribulations we have seen,' yep, that's the way he speaks these days, 'and now we are ready for another life, for the next world. God is joy and joy is hope and hope is faith and faith is celebration.' I mean, forget the deadly sins or them classic Ten Commandments, right? 'God is showing us the way.' Yeah. I asked him how once but even here, at the end of the world, the questions of young women go unheard. Nothing has really changed. All the war and violence, all the famine and the crying orphaned babies, the scarred lands and polluted waters, the sacrifices and the spilled blood have been for nothing.

We deserve this but, more importantly, Elijah deserves to be robbed of what he has persuaded himself this is. He's bought his own bullshit hook, line, and sinker, just like his lemmings. I'd feel sorry for him but the fact is abusers like him shouldn't get what they want, no matter if it's the end of the world. Fair is fair and he's getting what's coming to him.

Right here, Right now.

I watch the masses cavort as the music takes them on and on. I feel so detached from them it seems impossible we're the same species and for a moment I feel panic flutter in the pit of my stomach, like I'm not real or, perhaps, I'm going to float away before I can finish it. A couple of deep breaths help to steady me. I count slowly to ten. I am here, I am present, I will get this done.

The congregation, the members of The Source, are in full flow. That's what they call it, this cult. Officially they don't have a name, but when the newspapers first caught wind of one of the new End of Days cults becoming so popular they were more of a movement, they hadn't been able to resist. Some nineties dance group or something; Elijah thought it was hilarious – he had been a pretty famous DJ before, not so long ago really, banging out tunes at clubs all over the world, hits in the charts, celebrity and everyday followers flocking to hear him spin. And then the Harbinger had suddenly appeared, and I mean *literally* appeared, by the way. It happened while he was playing in Ibiza, some big mad festival, where everyone was out of their heads on who knew what and then some, and Elijah had been thrown off his game. Even with all the technology in his expensively slim silver laptop, his distraction had led to silence. At a rave. The crowd got restless fast, but Elijah had simply raised his arm and pointed. *And so, brethren, they beheld the Harbinger* – Elijah's word for it, and how quickly that caught on because, oh lah dee dah, people are such sheep – and he had seized his moment. It was his destiny he told me once, after yet another molestation for my salvation. He began to claim to have received visitations from an angel – not just one of course, he's all about the multiples. He had been laughed at but not by everyone. Many, too many, quickly followed the thirsty crowd from that first rave and listened to him. *Listened* to the bigmouthed bellend. You couldn't make it up. Except you could and Elijah did. And they believed him. Still do.

I know he's not going to be out in the crowds yet. You'd think he might want to be amongst his people, but Elijah will be somewhere getting high and grabbing pussy to get himself hyped up for his set. He's that kind of guy right to the end, baby. In the name of the Lord, of course. No decent god I know of, if any even exist, would welcome a classic wasteman like Elijah Street, DJ E-Z Street in his previous incarnation (I know, right?), and one who would accept him wouldn't be the sort of god anyone decent should be doing anything for, least of all dancing here at the end of time.

I know exactly where he'll be.

'Hey Matty!' Damn. I quickly hide my right arm, still holding the knife, behind my back. The Harbinger's light will hopefully disguise the spatters of blood peppering the front of my dress. Maybe he'll think it's a pattern. 'Come and dance.'

Ezra is a sweet boy, good-looking too if you like the sharply creased trousers and side-parting type. He's always looked at me in a way that makes me know he likes me but, for starters, he's one of them. He's bought the shady bullshit, the whole shebang, because he wants to be important, to feel like he matters. That's all anyone wants, I guess, but I don't think you should get it at someone else's expense. Common decency, y'know? And then there's the fact he's a bloke. Never been into them. Yes, I'm old enough to know for sure.

'Not yet, Ezra, I've got to see the Prophet.' That's what Elijah likes us to call him, no, not likes, he *insists* upon it. The self-aggrandizing sad sac. I hope if there is a god He gives him a punishment for all eternity like that guy Sisyphus. Rolling a rock up a hill doesn't seem enough though. Maybe if they banged nails into it first... or into his balls.

I throw Ezra a cheery wave, remembering to do so with my left arm, and head off towards the cabins, pretending not to see his face fall as if to say 'Not even our last day on Earth, huh?' Yeah, I feel real bad for you, son. Another cadaver for the Suck It Up pyre, buttercup.

Elijah's... sorry, my mistake, the *Prophet's* place is in the centre of the compound and is the biggest by far, naturally. Almost everyone is out in the field dancing or debauching so it's deserted here. According to the scientists, we've got a few more hours until we all burn up when the planet gets royally smooshed, so he's not supposed to be spinning for a while yet. I've got time so I walk slowly, appreciating the breeze that tries to cool my skin from the now incessant heat of the

Harbinger. It's slowly been getting hotter for days. No one knows what exactly *it* is, maybe that's why it's been so easy for Elijah and others like him to get away with all this. The scientific community called it an asteroid at first, then they said it was a comet, then they couldn't decide and it was like nerd warfare for a while, and then there was a whole hella bunch of crazy shit spouted by all kinds of pseudo-science types, while the homeopaths were jerking themselves off to the sight and sound of science being mystified, but it all amounts to the same thing in the end: sixty or seventy miles of something big and heavy that's clearly on fire and careening towards us at something like thirty thousand miles per hour is going to destroy the planet.

So let's dance, right?

Suddenly, I'm at his door. I'm sorry, my brain's a bit sketchy at the moment and I'm only just holding onto my train of thought. I guess when you finally reach your limit, when you simply can't process anymore and it's time to take matters into your own hands, your brain has trouble keeping everything in order except your main objective. That's what it feels like. As long as I get this done though it doesn't matter. It's not like I'm going to be around long enough to find out this is Alzheimer's or some such brain muncher. All I need is to see justice done. Just a small dose, just enough to wind things up down here on Earth. I don't hold much stock in an afterlife, but I really hope there's a hell waiting for Elijah and his squad. Maybe I'll join them because of what I've done already and for what I'm about to do. Nothing would give me more pleasure than to toast their marshmallows in Old Nick's diabolical fire pits. Nothing.

I don't knock. Why would I? I'm one of the chosen few, a handmaid to the Prophet they call me, and I am trusted. They've all forgotten you can only kick a dog so many times before it bites you. They've all been drunk on this delusion of the End Times for too long and they're no longer big on paying attention to details like that. No security needed backstage anymore, boys. All the better to blow the house down…

Opening the door lets out a waft of cannabis and sex… and something else. Something metallic, coppery. I check quickly to make sure it's not just me, but this is freaky fresh and it's definitely blood. Recent experience has taught me that much. Candles complicate the Harbinger's light inside the cabin for a moment but, as my eyes adjust, I see the splashes of dark scarlet up the walls and across the floor. It's everywhere and its epicentre is on the bed.

Elijah is still holding her, crying softly, bleating sorry over and over to the lifeless body in his arms. Naked, except for all the blood splashed over him (ain't we a pair? The Psycho Siblings. Good band name that. Punk, for sure), he rocks gently as though keeping time with the beat of the music in the distance. He doesn't look up but I know he's aware of me because he starts talking to me almost straight away. Like he's been waiting for me.

'I couldn't help it, Matty, it just happened, Matty, God forgive me, Matty, I never meant her harm, Matty, she tempted me, Matty, she made me, Matty.' Matty Matty Matty. On and on he goes, a monotony of self-pity and excuses, round and round. If I hadn't already been sick to my stomach after offing Grandma and contemplating the reality of mass extinction, I'd be hurling my last meal at him. *Vomitus iudicium.* The Judgement of Vomit. I just made that up. It's probably not even Latin. Maybe I'm having a psychotic break. If it wasn't for the red heat of the Harbinger at my back, I'd quite happily believe it. I mean, look at me. I look like I've escaped from an asylum, hair all wild, splotchy dress, and a nice big bloody knife in my hand.

The End is definitely nigh.

Elijah, the Prophet so false he couldn't foresee he'd mutilate yet another girl, looks up at me and I watch as tears run down his face. If there's one thing I can't stand more than a liar, or indeed a rapist, it's a drama queen. I mean, spare me the theatrics, sweetheart. He's killed so many girls *by accident* I don't know why he's so surprised. No one knows about his little mishaps of course, only the Brethren, who are really just cronies who jumped on his bandwagon early doors and not the 'Appointed' like he says. It's all been hushed up. Not good for the flock to know, not good for keeping those high times a-rolling. I don't know why he hasn't gone overboard with me; I guess everyone has a line they don't cross. At this point I'm mainly glad he hasn't because it means I can serve him something nice and hot for his last earthly meal.

'Say something.' Now he's looking at me a bit more carefully, the indulgence in his self-induced tragedy starting to wane. 'Matty?' I step forward, not wanting to lose my chance, but I slip on a puddle of the girl's blood and fling out my arms to steady myself. He sees the knife. How could he not?

'Matty, what the actual fuck?' He's shifted her off him now, letting her body roll off the bed and onto the floor with the callous slap of dead meat. Hate fires through me even more, I didn't think it was possible, and I feel my fingers gripping the knife tighter, my feet stepping forward regardless of me having lost the element of surprise. Just call me Harry Hotspur.

He is bigger than me and stronger. Gallingly, it doesn't take him much effort before he knocks the knife from my hand and me to the floor. I barely notice the motions my own body makes as I fall, still fighting him as he tries to straddle me. Everything is red, redder than the blood I'm laying in, scarlet with sacrament for the false prophet. He slaps me hard across the cheek, the sudden blossoming pain making me see stars for a moment, and I stare up at him, all thoughts of resistance abruptly gone. My programming kicks in… but it's nothing more than an automatic response, a crapplet, I've finally knocked through it. It's useless. I wait. I plan.

He prefers it when I struggle.

So I don't.

'Matty, what are you thinking, you little fool? The hour is at hand, our time is come, I…'

'Oh for fuck's sake, spare me the sermon.' The sound of my voice, the first time, apart from the recent rushing at him with a knife thing, I've ever shown defiance, seems to wound him. It's a surprise to me too and I won't lie; I get a kick out of it.

'Oh no, Matty, no. Not you. Not this.' His fingers bite into the flesh of my wrists where he's gripping them either side of my head, my knuckles pressed against the blood-soaked floor. 'I thought you would want to be with me at the end as we are raised up, together. I love you, little sister; you must not lose faith now. Soon we will be on our way to our Lord, to our salvation. Isn't that what we've wished for all this time?'

'I wish I'd killed you sooner.' He is aghast at my words, visibly shaken. For the first time I notice the wink of genuine crazy in his eyes. It's a flash of something loose, something that's broken free and is careening across his mind like a dog on ice. I've often thought he must be mad for doing all this, but there was always something about him that reeked of control. He'd meant to do all those things, thought he was righteous in doing them, but now... now something – perhaps the very real prospect he's remembered he made all this shit up? That if there is an afterlife he's almost certainly headed down rather than up - has shaken his hinges loose.

'Would you deny me my Ascension, Matty? Would you deny the Lord his partner in this battle at the end of all things here on Earth? Would you allow the Antichrist to seize power, allow what has been writ to be unwrit?'

Like I said: Dog. On. Ice.

'The Kingdom of Heaven is at hand, my child, my Matty. We must go to him with love in our hearts, our souls afire with our faith, as one.' He's practically foaming at the mouth with zealousness. He's a true believer in himself.

'What happened to her?' He closes his eyes against my question for a moment. When he opens them again the crazy is still alive and well. Thriving.

'I don't know. She must have been unworthy.' His tone is uncertain, his voice wobbles, but just for a moment. 'So many are. And the power of the Lord came upon me and rent her asunder. We will not take those who are not worthy, Matty, He will not allow it. He has shown me so and I must not bow now, not in these final hours. Are you worthy, Matty? Show me you are worthy. Show me now.' Quick as a flash his mouth is on mine, his hot breath scourges my skin, and I react. I can't help it. Strength surprises me out of nowhere. I've been so tired for so long I thought the cupboard was bare; that me lying here exhausted from my exertions this afternoon would be my grandmother's final revenge instead of mine.

Only for a moment.

Hot white fire fills me. It is righteous anger and I feel it in every atom of my being. I am powerful and I use it. I bring my knee up sharply and lay it right into his nuts. Hard.

Bullseye.

His teeth take a chunk out of my lip, in surprise more than anything, and he collapses on top of me. Blood fills my mouth but at this point it could be anyone's – the girl's, his, mine, Grandma's, Grandma's lover who was being led around by her on a dog lead when I tanked him too. I almost felt bad about that.

Elijah is a whining weight holding me down but the strength is still there, I can feel it humming inside me. Bucking my hips wildly, I manage to shove him off me and look around for the knife. Of course he grabs my leg as I scramble away from him to get it, but I'm not done, the tank's not empty, and I kick him square in the face. His nose explodes at the contact, and I suddenly have the knife in my hand again. Good.

'I forgive you, Matty.' His muffled sanction gives me pause. Does he think I will show him mercy? That he can trick me? Doesn't he realise yet? I am steadfast. I know what has to be done. He has to be denied what he so desperately believes is his by right. I can't allow him to die thinking his precious salvation has come, not after what he's done. Those three little words, not the ones every girl supposedly wants to hear, are barbs in my soul and, when it comes to the crunch, and this is the crunch, they are petrol on the flame of my purpose. Forgive me? *He* forgives *me*? Oh, Hell no.

Stabbing him is easy. Like passing a knife through butter, if the butter is made of gristle and fat and muscle.

I rob him of his Ascension, making sure I roll him over and see the anguish in his eyes as I do it too.

'Please Matty…' are his last clear words as he reaches out to me. The life leaches out of him, his outstretched arms fall to the floor with a meaty thunk and it is done. I feel no guilt. My family is dead, the world is ending, and I feel only relief.

'You got the love, brother.'

I drop the knife, slip and slide my way back to my feet,

and leave the bodies and the cabin behind me. I walk to the edge of the cliff just beyond the encampment and turn to face the Harbinger, welcoming its approaching heat.

So here it is.

My name is Matty Street, my first name means 'mighty in battle', and I am sixteen years old.

I will soon be stardust.

I'm okay with that.

TUNA SURPRISE!

The singing fish was not convincing anyone. In her prime she'd been a Diva in every sense of the word. Now, years of adulation – others' – and pomposity – hers – had turned theatrical glamour into shrewishness, while her drinking habit and a penchant for Piccard's Porphrya cigars had lashed her vocal chords into a brittle reef knot of mediocrity. You can't pass off lumpsucker eggs as caviar, kids, no matter how hard you try. Silence fell as she clipped off the agonising high note she'd been clinging to. Grongo Congridae had been praying for a miracle but all he had was damp squid. Admittedly, she was better than she'd been even yesterday, better than a week or a month ago, but her voice was still as rough as a razorfish's arse.

The fish stared down at him from the stage.

Grongo stared back.

Impasse.

The fact was Grongo was on the edge of losing it all. Once world renowned and respected, the Grand Neptunian Operatic Company was on the skids, it had been haemorrhaging money for months. *He* had been haemorrhaging money for months. Since the death of his father, the great Cinereus Congridae, audiences had been in decline. They'd never even given him a chance. The son was a shadow of the father, they said, his productions a weak echo of the great man's successes. Once upon a time, shoals had flocked to performances night after night, the auditorium filled to the rafters with eager fish, pelagic and deep sea alike, but now the company was barely able to cover costs. He needed something special, a surefire success, something to pull in the crowds, and for that he needed a star. The creditors – Scavengers! Fiends! – were baying for his blood and he was desperate. Grongo was sinking fast. He'd sell his soul for a single flash of the inspiration that had oozed unbidden from his father's pores. Alas, Miss Ceto Albacore was all he had. He'd coaxed her, coddled her, had specialists look at her, given her anything she wanted and anything he could think of. And still, here they were.

Even at the bottom of the sea, there was somewhere to sink.

'Thank you, Miss Albacore, that will be all for today. Get plenty of rest and hopefully there will be an improvement by the morning.' He rubbed the back of his head with the tip of his tail and sighed wearily. He was out of ideas.

The tuna turned with a sneer and a thrust of her caudal fins to stalk from the stage, her dark blue skin shimmering under the stage lights. Even if her voice wasn't improving, her body certainly was, Grongo noticed. She seemed younger, more vital than the tired bloated puffer that had turned up all those weeks ago. Grongo could see the raving beauty she had once been, and that made it all so much worse. If he had more time to push her maybe her voice would follow her lateral line and shape up. More time. The one thing he most certainly did not have. He stared after her for a long moment before resting his head on the seat in front of him and making every effort not to cry.

From the wings, Bonita Tunny watched her beloved Grongo despair. It hurt to see him like that. She would do anything to help him. She loved him with a fierceness that burned, had done so ever since she'd first set eyes on him, a primal pulse inside her insisting they belonged together… but he barely knew she existed. Not like that. She was just a chorus girl, a backline Betty with a pretty face. One more late replacement in a dwindling cast. People didn't understand loyalty anymore, that's why so many of the other girls had disappeared without so much as a by-your-leave. Well, she wasn't faint of heart, her love made her strong. Whether he noticed her or not, she would find a way to help him – but the question was how?

As far as she could see, that fossil of a tuna was the biggest threat to Grongo's great comeback with her faded talent and supercilious attitude, but what could she do? Doubt suffused her for a moment. She was nothing but a little Tunny. A shadow of the diva who had just left the stage.

Just left the stage.

A kernel of a plan began to form in the back of her mind. Turning away from the wretched sight of her beloved, she flitted into the darkness of backstage in pursuit of the tuna.

Bonita had noticed Ceto slip behind the Above-Sea tapestry hanging backstage several times before, but only because she liked to hang around after rehearsals. She was one of the few company members, cast or crew, who could bear to spend time in what was essentially a sinking ship. She slipped her hand behind the fabric to pull it away from the wall, and quickly realised it wasn't somewhere the tuna hid to take a surreptitious nip of whatever ichthyic hooch she'd got her hands on, as she'd assumed. There was something else afoot here. A dark breeze from a dim passageway beyond made her shiver. What was Ceto up to? Bonita decided to follow her; with any luck she would find a lead that could help Grongo. She felt like Yessica Flounder from *Piscicide She Wrote*. If she hadn't been terrified, she would have been excited.

The passageway was a channel of smooth rock that seemed to shine despite the darkness. As she got further down, sporadic pockets of light began to appear. Some kind of bio-luminescent bacteria, she guessed, but she didn't stop to find out because a familiar shadow loomed ahead of her. Carefully, Bonita swam on, nervously glancing back the way she had come. The spooky light and the narrow passageway were zapping her tenuous bravado with acute anxiety. If it hadn't been for Grongo and the idea of being able to help him, she would never have ventured past the tapestry. Her small heart was pumping so hard she was afraid that Ceto would feel the vibrations through the water. She took a moment to steady herself, taking a deep breath and letting the water wash over her, soothe her, and then she bravely pushed on.

Eventually the passage came to an end and Bonita arrived at the mouth of a great cave. Any thought of giving it the once over was burned in a flash of blinding light that flared from inside it. The split second that it took for her lenses to adjust around her retinas was her undoing. From nowhere, something struck her on the top of the head and she didn't have to deal with the brightness anymore.

'Ah, you're awake at last.' Ceto Albacore's face swam into view. Bonita's eyes were hazy and her head was ringing but she would know those over-rouged cheeks and that gravelly croak anywhere. She tried to flex her fins, but she was tied tightly to something and there was no give in her bonds. 'No time to talk, I'm afraid, we really must get on.' Bonita wished she were one of those rare fish with eyelids so she could blink away the obscuring fog the light and the blow to the head had wrought on her.

A low hum pulsed through the water, growing swiftly, as though one was swelling into many at breakneck speed. Bonita squinted into the depths, her eyes beginning to focus at last, and what she saw almost made her forget her predicament. A glittering rainbow of sea anemones – from brightest red to seaweed green and indigo – lined the walls of the cave, their tentacles swaying in unison. She'd never heard them make noise before but they were the only other creatures in the cave. Ceto stepped away from her, swaying along with the anemones, chanting words she didn't understand. The light stalled intermittently – maybe the anemones were as scared as she was – but each time, with a sharp flick of Ceto's tail to the nearest brightly coloured actinaria, they were quickly back again. Bonita had never seen anything like it.

As she watched the performance in front of her, the tuna chanting louder and louder, the anemones swaying hypnotically towards a crescendo, Bonita realised that the humming was actually coming from a huge hole in the floor. So fascinated had she been by the anemones and their odd presence there she hadn't noticed the water positively thrumming from that direction. The water became somehow thicker with every pulse, breathing became harder and, as she watched in horror, a dark mass began to rise from the depths of the hole.

A thousand bright eyes seemed to open at once, dazzling Bonita once more. By the time her sight was anything other than spots and flashes, Ceto had returned to her side. Light glinted off the obscenely oversized teeth that she was exposing with a wicked looking grin. She lifted her fins as though in supplication, but kept her eyes on Bonita, not yet looking at the being she had summoned from the darkest fathoms. Perhaps it was bad luck. Bonita almost giggled. Almost.

'Old One, we salute and welcome you. We thank you for your presence here. With this sacrifice, we beseech your aid. Take this Tunny's young blood, her scales and fins, and give me in return her voice so that I may sing your praises ever-more. I beg you, Mighty One of the Deep, hear my plea.' She smiled at Bonita almost kindly for a moment. 'Sorry kid, but needs must. It's for the greater good. Think of Grongo and what he needs. Your voice is the last piece. I'm so near, I can taste it. You'll never know what it's like to be adored as I once was and to lose it, so dark, so hopeless. Trust me when I tell you that because of that I'll appreciate it more than you ever could. I'll appreciate it for you, child.'

Bonita wanted to shout that she wasn't making a sacrifice, that Ceto was making one of her, and that maybe she wasn't so sure anymore that she would do anything in the name of love – but all that came out of her mouth was a single large bubble. In that moment she knew she was going to die, trussed up and at the mercy of this lunatic has-been, whose only hope was Bonita's death.

(The circle turns)

Ceto thrust her face at Bonita, those bizarre teeth bared and ready. As she felt them sink into her flesh, a scream erupted from her but any sound rushed straight into her assailant's mouth and down her greedy, gulping throat. Ceto fed from her, on her, ripping into her vocal chords, suck-ing them down into her bloated silvery white belly, leaving Bonita to watch as her life force seeped agonizingly into the water, her blood winding its way towards the thousand-eyed monstrosity from the deep.

And then all was darkness.

Grongo's chin nearly hit the floor. The tuna was nailing it! It was incredible. Every note was pure and sweet, the torturous bellowing of the previous day gone. He sat transfixed as she ran through the aria, not missing a single note. Could it be? Had his miracle happened? It must have because those lump-sucker eggs were suddenly looking pretty damned good... so why did it feel so wrong?

It was only as she came to the end of the piece that he realised what was niggling at him. Her voice was different. Of course, it was in tune and didn't pierce the eardrums like a rusty needle, but it was also different in tone. It reminded him of... of Bonita. The little Tunny who he had been trying so very hard to ignore for the past few weeks. She was fresh, an innocent, and not for the likes of a jaded palate such as his, but her quick smile and that sexy dorsal fin kept him awake at night when the prospect of bankruptcy did not. It was her voice he heard when Ceto sang.

Grongo looked around at the shoal of chorus girls hanging around in the front row, clearly as astounded as he was at the grand dame's sudden transformation. All of them, the ones that had stayed, were there. All of them except Bonita. That wasn't like her. She was always around for rehearsals, taking notes on other people's performances, doing everything to learn and improve, to impress him. He smiled at the thought of her and let himself drift as his ears tuned back into Ceto Albacore's final note, this time as clear as a bell and as sweet as stealing lobsters from a fisherman's pot. In his reverie, it was Bonita's lips that formed the note, her face radiating the joy of a job well done.

Grongo came to with a start. It *was* Bonita's voice. He was sure. It couldn't be and yet it was. Anger rose in his breast. What had that wicked old tuna done? By Neptune's tit, he would... he would...

The endless note worked its dark magic, the sweetest kind, and his concern began to fade as he was reminded of what this all meant. He had never fully dared to hope before, but the creditors could go hang. Here, right here in this theatre, he had a star again. He was going to have a success on his hands. He knew it with the certainty that only the blackest witchery can assure.

The satisfied smile that spread his conger jaw wide was the final betrayal of sweet Bonita Tunny.

TONIGHT, YOU BELONG TO ME

In the end, I'm always alone. At least I think I am and that's what counts. This time though, I've got a head in a bag and I'm not giving it up for anyone. There ain't nothing those chittering imps sitting in my periphery can do about it either. Tittering and cavorting and pulling at my mind like they can get in there and sew it up nice and tight for themselves. Well, you can't, you gang of tiny fucking hooligans. So get with it and pipe down. If I don't get some goddamned sleep my human skin is going to blow right off my bone house.

I slip off my shoes and haul my legs up onto the bed. I'm so tired I could sleep for a week but I've only time for a nap, and as I close my eyes to do just that the chittering starts up again. I scrunch my eyes up tight, frowning into oblivion, the tiny galaxies that swirl behind my lids a dizzying sight, but those little shits just keep on going, nag, nag, nag, and I snap.

'God damn it, you little freaks! Can't you just shut up?' I swing myself off the bed, grab my shoes, and throw them in one pretty smooth move… except one goes through the window. What kind of window breaks from the impact of a shoe? I realise too late it was the bag I'd picked up. That human head weight gets through anything, apparently. So now I'm going to have to book because surely no one can ignore that sort of ruckus and I'm not exactly what you'd call inconspicuous. Cloven hooves come as standard with my kind and there's no amount of your Balearics or your Manilows, or whatever they call those fancy shoes, can hide them. The Victorians knew what was up with their crinolines sweeping up the crumbs. Hippies, too, with their flares. Man, I miss the Sixties. I do what I can though and I get by for the most part. Pity is, when I was severing the head, there was a not inconsiderable amount of blood to go around and I got more than my share, you might say. So my good old bell bottom denims, the ones Zappa gave me, finally had to be sacked and now I'm just hoping everyone notices my generous backside in these black leggings before they notice the hooves.

Enough spinning my wheels, let's go. The ritual's got to be done in a couple of hours anyway, so I might as well get out of here right now.

I do my best to ignore the chittering little shitcakes who seem to have multiplied in the last five, and grab my stuff lickety spit. Running out the door, I grab the head from the pavement out front, shoving it back in its bag as I go. Well, how'd you like that? All that worrying and no one's noticed a damned thing! I mean, come on, humans, what the Hell? I know this place is, by necessity, a blow in the hole shit pile, someplace where you don't look and you certainly don't tell, not unless you pay or are paid to, but a human head bursting through a window at speed?! Honestly, I'm the foul one? You'd never think it some days in this cesspit of a realm. It's rotten with debauchery and lies, full of manipulation and cruelty, both low and high stakes, not to mention all those Mister In-betweens. Cole Porter had it right, y'know; anything goes. All the blind eyes and brass polish in the world doesn't change the facts. Humankind has The Stench and it ain't never going to wash it out. And yes, you can take that to the bank.

In my car, if you can call a rusted bucket of mismatched parts held together largely with duct tape and demon-will 'a car', I throw the bag with the head in it onto the backseat and pull my keys out of my jacket's inside pocket. When I look up ready to stick that sucker in the ignition, they're there. Aren't they darned tootin' always?

An angel. *The* angel.

My whorespit shadow sent straight from God.

A being, celestial or otherwise, more full of shit and umbrage you will never meet. Liar liar, pants on fucking fire.

Let's call them Wormwood. Nobhead is more apt, but bear with me.

No wonder the chitterers were getting all worked up. Makes sense now – now it's too late. I never learn.

The angel's hands are planted on my hood and I'm not

going anywhere. No wonder no one noticed anything. I'm not entirely sure, although I have a theory, how I got behind the wheel because old Wormwood can warp time on this plane. Fancy shit, so they are. So they think they are. They can't keep it up for more than a few minutes at a time, but it always feels like just enough, y'know?

I close my eyes tight for a moment. I say the words. See now, while angels have the big obvious tricks, we demons? We're not exactly shabby with that magic shit either, especially when we've got the coin to pay for it. In fact… any time now…

The car starts shaking and it throws Wormwood back a step or two. It's enough. They look up at me, surprised, and the sweet kick of triumph is almost too much for me. In your face, angelic horde. I flip them the bird, thrust the key in the ignition, and I am backing my shit-can out of there before they can change direction. One thing you ought to know is angels are slow. Being all pure and stuff makes you a by-the-book type by nature and they never really lose it. Not even Lucifer really breaks the rules. He just gobbles them up and shits them out again. They're still the rules in essence, if not style, you might say. I might have lost you. Suffice it to say that with such major league sticks up their arses, they don't roll so well with the punches. And so I punch the accelerator hard. Literally, figuratively, whatever damned adjective you please.

For my part, I know exactly where I'm headed. I might have barely enough time now Wormwood's arrived earlier than expected, but I'll be damned if I'm going to let them mess this up without a fight. Besides I'm demon-born stubborn and I'll hightail it until…

Right on cue, that ape-humping dog's spleen is on the roof of my car and I'm reminded of that urban legend the humans have about a lunatic with a hook. I wonder what celestial weapon Wormwood is wielding, other than their dickface of course. I slam my foot on the brake and the celestial prick shoots off the top of my rig, bumps on the hood, and disappears. I back up a short way, slam my foot on the accelerator, and… nothing, I just speed forward.

'Thanks for that, friend.' They're sitting in my passenger seat, smug as smug can be.

'Fuck you.'

'That's not very nice, Sal. You're always so hostile. Why is that? Do you need to talk about it? Get it off your chest?'

My fingers itch to punch their stupid face in. Every one of my basest demonic qualities is sounding off siren-style and I want so much to indulge in at least six of them right this second, but I know I can't. The ritual is all. It's my way out. The ritual must be completed.

'I can help you, you know.'

Their voice is so soft that I don't quite catch it. Or don't think I have. I look at Wormwood for a moment and they nod back at me. After all these millennia, this is a new tack. Who'd a thunk?

'Why the Hell would you help me? You've been chasing me since Gehenna and I don't think it's because you wanted to get to know me better.' I sound whiny rather than defiant and the silence that follows is uncomfortable, so I keep my eyes on the road. Usually I feed off this kind of tension, it fuels me, but if I could see my face properly right now I know I'd be blushing. This fucking angel, man. Always getting under my skin. Never quite catching me, but always there, niggling. An itch I can't scratch, the tack inside my shoe, the fly in the ever-loving ointment.

My headlights, such as they are, brush over a sign and I turn. My reactions, despite the exhaustion, the frustration, and the five thousand years walking this godforsaken dust bowl, are still en pointe.

'I know where you're going, Sal.'

'Mate, you're not going all HAL9000 on me, are you? I could do without that on top of everything else.'

'Well now, *that* was almost polite. I'd almost given up hope.' Angels, most of them anyway, don't give up hope; they just channel all that nasty negative energy into something else. Vengeance, politics, owning a newspaper, whatever.

'Like I said already, fuck you.' They're smiling as I turn back to the trail ahead. It's pretty dark, my headlights barely work for shit, and I need to concentrate.

'We go way back, don't we?' Angels never take the hint. Obstinate pricks. 'Do you remember when I disembowelled you in Lyon? That was a fun time, wasn't it? Or when I had that rancid old sea captain keelhaul you off the Barbary coast? Good times, buddy. We should do something like that again. It's been too long.'

I squint out at the darkness. It's not much further now; I can feel it in my entrails. Let them keep talking. It's true, they've done me up like the proverbial kipper more than once or twice, but the circumstances were different. I was different. I still had respect for them back then, we once were brothers or whatever the shit we were, and whether I wanted to or not I stubbornly held to that for too long. Old habits die hard. It's a cliché but clichés are most often based in truth and that's a God-given fact. Good old Wormwood thinks they're in control here and I don't mind them thinking so. Bigger fish to fry, mate, much bigger.

'Do you remember Grace? She was a beauty, wasn't she? You liked her, loved her maybe, although your kind spit on that sort of thing, don't they?' It's not true. Demons can love. We have free will. Not like these shitkicking angels who, even after millennia beyond imagining, are still just doing whatever Daddy tells them. And I did love Grace. Loved her with every fibre of my infernal being. Losing her was hard and losing her to this bucket of piss was even harder. They're forgetting something with this corny old shit though – I mean, come on, man, *do* better – I'm five thousand years old. Even if I wasn't a demon, I'd know. I lose any human I get close to; I've been through it more times than you'd be able to comprehend, so I'm used to it. It hurts at the time, you get a bit melancholy now and then, but I'm not human and they can't bait me with that sort of base emotional manipulation. They're not doing anything but pissing me off even more.

'She was nice without her skin too, you know. So vibrant, so… FUCKING JESUS…!' The last words are shouted as they plough through the windscreen. Even the angelic host need to clunk click, kids. I'd slammed the brakes hard as soon as I'd seen the Will-o-the-Wisp. Ancient little gloomies they are, but handy when you need them. I'm in the right place, and although I hadn't needed to stop so sharply, who could get tired of watching a sanctimonious angel defenestrating onto a filthy car bonnet and sliding onto the floor? No one, that's who.

I grab the bag with the head in it from the back seat, and then I'm sliding out of the car, my feet feeling like they're on fire. Come to think of it, the whole of me feels like I'm on fire. I'm so close to getting this done and every ounce of me, corporeal and unearthly, knows it, is on fire for it.

Of course they get up. They're an angel. Traffic accidents don't generally kill them. Unless you've got a couple tankers full of demonfire and the spark from Lucifer's left nut sac maybe. That's a joke. Lucifer doesn't have nuts or sacs. No angels do. Anyway, they've clearly taken a decent hit and I can thank dear old Ma Vickers for that. Witch has an arsenal of quality sigils, not to mention some fine curses, and I paid handsomely for the one she scratched into my windscreen. I could do worse to them at a push, but I don't have time. I plough on. The wisp is up ahead and I can see where I need to be. And then miraculously, of course, they're in front of me, hands on hips, eyes burning with a fire of their own.

'STOP.' Oh yeah, they're angry now, real angry. Capitalisation time angry. The fire bubbling forth from my marrow responds to it, loves it, and suddenly I'm hurtling at them like a steam train, ready for impact. I've been waiting for this for a hundred years and... A hundred million pieces of angel burst apart in the night, firework bright, and I'll be wearing the stain of it for the rest of my days. Another scar to add to the collection. It'll take them time to pull themselves back together. Being blown to bits tends to put them in a terrible mood and they're vindictive bitches, so I've only tried it once before, but by the time they've rejiggered their mainframe the ritual will have begun, so no repercussions. Besides, ain't no stopping Granny when Granny wants to get fed. It's a saying. No, not where you're from.

I slide to the ground, dumping the head out onto the dirt in front of me. The wisp is right above us, and its luminescence is throbbing, reaching down, intent on the head. It slips into it, lighting up the pallid skin, punching radiantly through every pore, every orifice. It's greedy and it's not what it seems. See, we demons? We don't tell everyone everything. The All-Mighty doesn't either, doesn't let his arse gobbling legions in on the full skinny. He's playing with them, always has been, they just don't seem to get it. Before you take umbrage with that, just think how bored you'd be if you were that old. Right? The wisp is a conduit, there's something on the other side, that something is hungry for entertainment, and that something is God her damned, his damned, their damned self.

The ground is shaking, the air throbbing with burgeoning power. It's so potent the scratchy grass around me seems to get greener, thicker, even in the dark. The trees sigh with pleasure. If I had a dick it'd be straight up and pointing at the moon. The night's got lighter without me realising it, I'm too caught up in watching and feeling, like it's the rapture and I've got a first class ticket. I remember myself just in time and the incantation springs to my lips. It's an indecipherable litany of demon tongue to human ears; you'd likely perceive it as something between a dog whistle and child farts. I'm not even sure of the meaning, it flows out of me like piss and it's just as golden, just as rank, filling the night air with a thousand million droplets of brightly fetid power.

The pain doesn't hit me until the angel is standing in front of me, the point of its righteous weapon of God sticking out of my chest. I have the answer to my earlier question: a spear. Quel cliché. Even then, I don't really feel it to be honest; it's more the knowledge that I should be feeling it, because all I do feel is the pleasure of the power that is coming. They're standing in front of me, their face a rictus grin. They couldn't do their time hokum and they don't ask why, they're too busy thinking they've won, too busy focussing on me, and I start to laugh. They've got their back to the rent that is slicing the air open behind them. Impossible golden light is spewing out of it and even this pain-in-my-arse-for-an-eternity angel can't fail to notice it now. They blink, turning slowly as they finally realise. Comprehend. Falling to their knees, they cannot take their eyes off the light as it beats and bends the earthly night air around it. Their hands rise in supplication, a soft moan of surrender, of obedience, and I know they know.

Behold your God, bitch.

They forgot I am pestilence and fear, the rot in your gut, the undetected cancer in your ball sac. I am the fury that raises your fist, and the hate that will one day blot out the sun. I can get into places no one remembers are there and I can negotiate deals with bored gods. I care but I forget, live long enough and you'll see.

I watch as the head of the man I loved for a while turns in the dirt. That's some John Carpenter shit right there. I think for a moment it'll sprout legs and let loose an unholy scream, but I have a habit of tending to the dramatic. You might have noticed. His eyes blink open like he's not the one responsible for all that light, and he smiles slowly, sorrowfully, at the angel.

'Oh, Wormwood. How sad you have made me, fiddling about with this grubby demon...'

'Hey!' I'm not having that.

'What? You *are* a demon and those leggings *are* covered in filth. Sort yourself out. Damned demon nitpickery. Now, where was I?' The head frowns for a moment. 'Ah yes, you were once my greatest delight, child, although I would never say it in front of the others. Far too sensitive. I set you into this world with such hopes, such excitement, but you've let everything become so much the same! There's no originality, Wormwood, no novelty, no *innovation*. It's all become so bloody boring.'

'But I am War, I am Chaos, I am...' Wormwood sounds like he's going to cry, like maybe he already is, and I'm not going to lie about the little frisson it's giving me in the under bits.

'Do shut up, dear. Just the sound of your voice gives me the shits. This little demon here – ' Rude ' – has been an amusement at least and for that I won't smite them, for now.' Reassuring. 'You, however, have become tedious, Wormwood. God cannot forgive tediousness. It looks bad in the brochures.' He chuckles. Did God just make a joke?

'Please, Father, please, I can make it right, I can do better, I can...'

'Wormwood, my love, you said the same thing last time, and the time before that, and the time before that... I could go on, it's kind of pleasing, but needs must when the devil drives. I'm joking, the devil is still flapping about in his ice block down in the Ninth Circle. You never know though, one day he might nibble his way through. Let's get on with it, shall we? Suffice it to say I'm bored, you're redundant, so, like the kids no longer say, more's the pity, let's boogie.'

The light suddenly drains of all colour and the bright white of its absence burns into my eyes. My human eyes. If my demon eyes were exposed they'd have been crisped in a heartbeat. The God-light saturates the night, ripping the darkness in twain as it pours forth from the tear in reality. Wormwood screams as it sears through them, severing them, inch by inch, molecule by molecule, then it seems to suck every tiny piece of them in, breathing them all sharply into the rent until, with a pop, it is sealed, and the night is dark again. God don't mess.

The head is just a head once more.

In the end we are all alone.

Of course I am a fool. Of course I assume. I don't check. I'm a demon and that means I'm basically an ass. Besides, the game is stacked. Still blinking from the scourge of brightness, I stumble to my car in the dark and get the Hell out of there, pardon the pun. I drive through the night and only stop when I get the taste of smote angel out of the back of my throat.

The truth only hits me when a brand spanking new angelic arsehole lands on my motel bed, coughing and spluttering like a newborn turd, just as I'm finally getting to sleep. You'd think I'd have got the message when the foul imps that plague me started getting their chitter full on again. See, I must have blinked. The Godlight flared just before it was snuffed out, and I did not see the shape slip from the rent as the light finally died; I did not see the new angel, my new *friend*, my other, birthed into the world. God is a slippery bastard, whatever they say. 'Because you can't have one without the other' isn't an explanation, it's going back on the deal. I was supposed to be free. I never learn.

In the end, we are never alone.

A TREACHEROUS THING

Classified Location, April 1997.

The barking girls were vicious, frothing at the mouth behind the thick paint and fabric concoctions plastered over their faces, nightmare jowls stretched as they yapped and growled their malice. Demented acolytes of a false god. Murderers of the innocent. All around Lynx Ruffieux lay the bodies of those she was supposed to protect. Betrayal sprayed across the walls and puddled on the floor in crimson accusation. She tried not to look, holding her ground, her face set in grim determination. The frenzied canine wannabes danced around her, their feet kicking up small storms of blood as they waved their knives and empty guns over their heads, a conga line of corruption, delighting in the knowledge that their work was having its desired effect, no matter the loaded gun pointed at them.

It had all happened so fast, Lynx could barely make sense of it. One minute she and her partner had been shuttling their charges into the safe house, the next the shooting had started and the world was in chaos. All because of these masked, bewigged jumping jacks. Suspicion niggled at the base of her skull, something she was overlooking, *had* over-looked, but she shrugged it off. Lynx jutted her chin at the girls, fighting back incipient nausea, every muscle tensed; she was getting out of there and she was taking whatever casualties had anything resembling a pulse with her. She'd had her rabies jab. It was time to finish this.

'Stand down or I will shoot you in the face, one by one.' The words came out through gritted teeth; their yapping was sorely testing her patience. Howls of laughter filled the air and the pounding echo from the gunshots that had killed so many people so quickly grew exponentially inside Lynx's head. She wanted to close her eyes and sink to the floor with the corpses – she already knew everyone was dead, knew it with every one of her senses – but sheer bloody-mindedness kept her upright, her trigger finger still and ready.

'Hey Mama Cat, what's up with you?' The blue-faced dog-girl had stopped her dancing and was staring at Lynx, head tilted to one side as though something was confusing her. 'Why so sad?'

Three little words, a throwaway sentence. Nothing to lose your head over…

Lynx lost it. Completely. Later, she would tell herself over and over that she should have remembered her training, her years of experience, berate herself for shrugging her self-control off so easily, for folding when the chips were down, really down, with barely a thought… but with the smell of blood and death in her nose, and that noise, the yapping and yipping that would drive a sane person mad, filled her mind with such red hate – *red as blood* – that it coloured every synapse, every nerve ending. Suddenly she hated dogs. Hated them.

'You'll be last then. You can watch your friends bleed out.' Her voice was low and she wasn't sure if the faux-dog girl had heard her. A twitch started to tug at Lynx's right eye. Blue watched her for a moment, assessing her, that grin still plastered across her face, right from ear to ear. Lynx imagined shooting her right in that stupid mouth.

'Big talk, pussy cat, I'd like to see…' The first shot silenced the leader of the pack, the biggest one, the back of her head blowing out across the face of one of her comrades, the bullet downing them both. The two on either side were blinking blood out of their eyes before they even knew what had happened. A split second later, hackles raised, Lynx took out the next one. As her target hit the ground, three of the remaining dog-girls turned tail and ran. She shot all three in the back, one after the other, one, two, three, down on their knees. That left one. Blue. By no means the biggest, but certainly the smartest. Smarts were relative. She was already turning, going low and reaching toward the ground where Lynx's dead partner's gun lay discarded, still loaded. However clever Blue was, Lynx was smarter. Even in her fugue-like state, she had done her maths, her mind on autopilot. She aimed, wanting it done quickly and the shot rang in her ears before she'd even pulled the trigger.

Before.

No smoke curled from the barrel, her finger hadn't squeezed, her shoulder… her shoulder was somehow numb and hot with vicious pain at the same time. It hadn't been her gun that fired. The thought was sluggish at best, but the truth of it was fast-becoming all too evident. *It hadn't been her gun.* Blue stepped towards her and Lynx tried to fire her weapon, but what had been almost numb pain suddenly blossomed into excruciating and she dropped it. The sound of the impact echoed around the suddenly quiet room, making her cringe as though she'd sworn in church. It seemed as though her mistakes were still racking up. Trying to make sense of what had happened, her mind plunged through the molasses of shock that came with being shot unexpectedly. From behind. It wasn't karma that hit her, it was realisation and the impact was every bit as hard as the bullet's had been. Slowly, every move an agony, she turned to look behind her.

One look was enough. She closed her eyes, scarcely able to believe what they had shown her even as the stench of betrayal pervaded the room like ammonia. The man had the decency to look chagrined at least. She had made it so easy, so damned easy. You trust once in your life, for the first time, and the rat bastard shoots you in the back. She started to laugh, the sound wrenching at the bullet hole in her shoulder, trying to persuade her to stop but, if you thought about it for too long, it was just so damned funny. Her, the consummate loner, left to fend for herself early, recruited by the service because no one could control the troubled cub she had been… shot in the back by the man she'd trusted. The man she loved.

As Lynx sank to the floor, the pain radiating through her body even as the blood exited it, she tried to say something. The words bubbled to her lips and she hoped they were offensive enough to cause at least some irritation, before letting the darkness claim her, happy for the oblivion it offered.

Break ups were the worst.

Somewhere in the Swiss Alps, 18 months later…

Barely clinging to the ledge, claws wedged into whatever gaps the rock offered, Lynx was buffeted by the merciless mountain winds that seemed to be trying their hardest to dislodge her from their territory. Any minute they might muster a mighty enough blow to dislodge her, but she clung on doggedly. The irony was not lost.

She reflected, and not for the first time, that her life would be immeasurably better with the addition of a sidekick, maybe even a friend. The thought was quickly anaesthetised, also not for the first time, by the memory of how trusting someone had left her high and dry with a bullet in her back and a black mark on her service record. Connections were a liability and not just in her line of work. Shaking off the intense bitterness that seemed to have been stalking her since *then…* Lynx swallowed hard, trying to block the details out, like they hadn't taken up residence in every corner of her mind. There was no escape. She felt the claustrophobia of her thoughts closing in on her, narrowing her thought processes into that most primal of reactions: panic. If she panicked now, she'd be dashed to pieces against the mountain's stoic face in moments. Her claws weren't the only things that needed to get a grip.

Bare tacks, she reminded herself, tick the boxes, do the job. Mechanically, she checked the sheer rock face above her. Sheer except for her ledge; a ledge that was slowly crumbling. Once the jeopardy would have been exhilarating, she'd been as hungry for it as she'd been for… god, she'd been an idiot, she'd been so hungry for love it had blinded her, made a fool of her.

'Stop it!'

Things were bad enough as they were, and slipping back *there* every five minutes was not an option. Right now she needed to not fall from the mountain and end up a faint smear across its rocky roots, barely a memory, so she needed to stop wool-gathering and get her backside up onto and then off said ledge before it crumbled to nothing and her chance was gone.

Taking a deep breath and then another, repeating the

simple exercise over and over until her breath became everything and not even the mountain winds could claim her attention, Lynx centred herself, focussed on her desired landing spot, and prepared to leap. Her muscles bunched and released, pushing her straight up into the air, her front claws flexing as they made ready to hook into the rock face above her. It was over in moments, chips of rock falling as she scrambled for purchase briefly with her back feet. Resting her face against the unyielding surface she took a deep breath, feeling for the vulnerability in the rock with her mind as she did so. Lynx could get into anything, anywhere in the world, but that didn't mean it was simple or explicable. Sometimes you just had to go with what worked. Dutch Babs, her handler back at HQ, who she had been forced to mute on their audio link after yet another diatribe about inferior British stroopwafeln, said it was her natural cat-instincts, but that wasn't it. Lynx *wanted* to get into things; she desired it with every fibre of her being. It was what she was made to do, it was coded right into her DNA, into her soul, and she often wondered if she'd been some sort of wraith in her past life, able to slip through solid...

The rock face in front of her suddenly opened up and Lynx fell forward onto the newly revealed floor. Luckily, she'd stowed her human clothes in her backpack to climb up to the hidden lair and her tail was at liberty to balance her before she could sprawl unceremoniously across the cold rock. So much for having been a wraith.

Scrambling up onto her hind legs, she stretched her body into a more human-like frame and pasted herself against the wall of the passage she had uncovered, edging her way along it carefully. The place was musty as hell, but with only a few metres gained it became obvious something was terribly wrong. Lynx could smell something metallic on the otherwise stale air and there was no mistaking what it was. Blood. Fresh blood. No one was supposed to have been in this network of caves for twenty years or more, at least that's what the suits had insisted on in the briefing. So, what a surprise, here she was on a mission that, despite the tricky logistics, was supposed to be a simple retrieval and instead it was very clear her superiors knew jack. *Comme d'habitude.* Technically she was out on a limb, with only Babs in her ear for back up, so it was a good job she'd known all this before she'd set out. Her lessons had been hard learned. She would not forget them.

Something was very wrong up ahead, even if her sense of smell hadn't been as sharp as it was she would have known it because she had reached the part of the cave with the bloody handprint smeared across the wall. Remote mountain? Check. Creepy caves? Of course. A blood trail? Standard.

Taking a deep breath, although she could feel in her marrow that she already knew the answer, Lynx tried to place the blood. The scent of human in it was unmistakeable, but the underlying stink of canine was too strong to ignore. For some reason she still wanted to be wrong, even after all this time and effort. Wasn't that a kicker? Of course it was dog blood. Lynx closed her eyes and the smell intensified in her nostrils. Oh god, it really was, wasn't it? She whimpered against the certainty forcing its way in but, even as she tried to dismiss the memories that leapt straight to mind, she knew it was him.

Him.

She hadn't thought about him in… Lynx could barely contain the mirthless laugh that bubbled in her throat at the abject lie. She thought about him constantly. Once she had thought about him like that because she had been more in love than she had ever thought herself capable, more in love than she had thought it possible for anyone to be. Now, however, he was on her mind night and day because he had become her purpose, her reason for being in none of the ways poets lionised. She had stayed alive and in the service despite misgivings from pretty much everyone involved. She had completed her rehab in record time, stunning the doctors and confounding the shrinks, had said all the right words and nodded in all the right places, doing as she was told while all the time working to find him. Against orders. Her country be damned, this was personal and, although she hadn't been sure she'd been right about the tip off she had kept from her superiors, the thrill of the confirmation of being on the right track was electric. Her hackles rose along her back, tickling her spine with exhilaration. Her shoulder, where *his* bullet had pierced her flesh and lodged itself so intimately inside her, ached with the force of the memories that suddenly assailed her.

'God, Lynx, I need you, need to taste you.' His voice, enough to make her come on its own, rolled across her skin like melting chocolate as he kissed his way down her stomach. She burned with impatient desire, urging him to move faster with the desperate press of her body against his. His low chuckle nearly sent her over the edge.

'Impatient, little one?' No one had ever called her 'little' anything before him; no one had ever used endearments of any kind for her. It gave her a feeling low in her stomach that had nothing to do with the way he was touching her, well not much, his strong hands pawing gently at her thighs, pushing them open, sliding down between them, that long thick tongue of his ready to...

Lynx shook herself back to the present. It was exactly that kind of obsessive thinking that had got her shot and left for dead in the first place. Nose turned up high in the air, sniffing at the all too obvious signs that her quarry was within her reach, Lynx knew it was a set up. She had also known this from the moment the information had been handed to her. He had left her a trail of crumbs and she had devoured them, gone straight to him when he'd finally decided it was time, as though he was in control of the situation even now. It surprised her how little that mattered to her. All that mattered was that he was within her grasp and this time it would be him who paid the price. After months of planning – after months of agony and confusion – she was ready.

Padding softly along the passage, she came to a large antechamber filled with archaic machinery and dust. Cobwebs decorated the surfaces merrily, spinning and twisting between the rusting edifices of clunky, long dead technology. The only sign that anyone had been here were the distinctive footprints. Four of them, every time. He obviously wanted her to know it was him. He only ever walked on two legs when it was necessary to blend in... or to shoot her in the back.

Cautiously, Lynx followed the tracks. It was obvious he knew she'd come, and he must have known she would know it. Lynx laughed at the ridiculousness of her train of thought. If she had known so damned much she would have brought a rocket launcher. Despite everything, she'd still listened, just a little, just enough, to the cautions of her doctors and her superiors - white men in suits, saturated in privilege, good backgrounds and costly educations, with a helping hand from Daddy's golfing buddies here and there for good measure. Not a one of them had any more working knowledge of the real world than she had of how to button one of those expensive suits they liked so much. Still not trusting your gut, Ruffieux, she thought to herself, still listening to men.

His scent was getting stronger and Lynx knew she was close. She headed down another passage that ran off the antechamber, leading her deeper under the mountains. Eighteen months of hard work, of scheming, lying, trekking, nightmares, night sweats, panic attacks, and flashbacks; all of it would be worth it once she had him where she wanted him. Once she had payback.

'Lynx.' The sound of her name breaking the near-silence made her jump so hard she almost peed right then and there. Behind her. Again. Lynx whirled around, but the passage was empty. Blinking, she started back towards the antechamber, but there were no prints in the dust other than her own. Not even the ones she'd found in the antechamber. She realised the dirt covering the floor hadn't been disturbed until she'd done the disturbing. The prints she was sure she'd seen hadn't been there. Had the voice been his? Or had it been hers? Had she unconsciously corrected herself, called herself back? She shook her head but suddenly the thoughts that had plagued her for so long, that she was barely able to control at the best of times, flew at her from every corner of her mind, free to bombard her with anxieties and doubts. Her head throbbed with all the old rhetoric. *Idiot! You've walked into a trap! Again! Not good enough! Another mistake! Always you! Always a loser! Always wrong! Always the common denominator! No one wants you here! He never loved you. No one has. They all know the truth about you, all of them. They all know what you are! Impostor! Stupid! Wrong!*

Lynx cried out against the bombardment, falling to her

knees, clutching at her head with shaking hands, trying to keep the thoughts from rattling her teeth, from shaking her to pieces from the marrow out. Her heart was racing; rivulets of sweat trickling down her back, beads of it across her brow, her upper lip, on her palms. She felt the old madness heating up in the depths of her veins, felt it coming ever closer, ready to consume her.

I love little kitty...

The familiar song came into her mind suddenly; a whisper at first, but with every line the voice in her head became stronger.

Her coat is so warm,
And if I don't hurt her,
She'll do me no harm.

Lynx mouthed the words, only sounding the last word of every line at first, then growing in strength as the song became everything, drowning out the thoughts, and slowing her heart. The repetition might not have been as soothing as it had been in the safe confines of her doctor's office, but it worked enough to take the edge off the fury that had threatened to engulf her. The fury that had been born in the cold realisation of *his* betrayal.

She stayed on the floor for long moments, her breathing less ragged with every passing minute, but she still felt too shaky to stand. She hadn't had one that bad for a while. Even the night terrors had all but stopped and yet here she was almost out of control again. She wanted to howl against the injustice of it. *He* was the one to blame and yet it was she who carried his scars on her body and her mind, weighing her down with what should have been his guilt to bear. Only his. He needed to feel what he had caused her, really feel how much she had borne because of him. She wanted to shove it in his mouth and make him choke on it. The sudden conflagration of hate threatened to overwhelm her again...

I love little kitty...

Not like this. Did she want him to see her like this? Let him see how far he had driven her down? A ragged mess, no longer the clearheaded agent she had been before him? Ruled by what he had done to her?

That drove her to her feet. There were days when pride was the only thing that kept her together. She clung to it now like a lifeline, straightening her spine, testing her haunches. Time to pay the piper and the piper didn't accept cheques from beat down pussycats.

His scent trail was still strong and she made her way back through to the antechamber and down a different passageway. She trusted her nose more than her eyesight, so ignored the fact of no footprints and kept on going. Her fur prickled as she got closer. She knew he was there, knew she would find him at last. Locking down her excitement, Lynx sang her song in her head, murmuring gently to herself, comforting, encouraging. She had this and she would win, one way or another.

The sound of running water caught her attention, getting louder with every step Lynx took. Someone was down there – *he* was down there – taking a shower. A bloody shower! The passage led to another chamber, but this one had clearly been someone's living quarters. A perfectly made bed sat in the middle of the room, incongruous in its neatness beneath a thick layer of dust. No other furniture cluttered the room, and Lynx guessed that wardrobes and cupboards were hidden behind the walls. Evil genius chic. Without thinking too much about it, she pulled back the coverlet carefully so as not to provoke too much of the dust into the air, bundled it up in her arms, and stowed it safely in a corner of the room. She removed the pillows just as carefully and then sat down on the side of the bed, folding her legs beneath her comfortably. She would wait.

After fewer minutes than she would have liked, however, impatience got the better of her. Lynx got to her feet and headed for the bathroom. She slipped through the door, not wanting to alert him to her presence before she was ready. Splashes of blood sat garish on the cold stone of the floor. The puddles grew the closer she got to the opaque cubicle. The air was thick with the coppery smell of blood, so thick she could taste it. The urge to sup at one of the puddles was almost too strong to fight. When had she last eaten?

The water was still running and, even though she could

not see through the glass of the cubicle, she knew he was in there. On the floor. What was he doing down there?

It only took her a moment, a flash of realisation. Suddenly she knew.

'No, no, no, you bastard, no!' Lynx grabbed at the door handle and threw it open, water rushing over her paws, washing through the blood, turning the floor into a swirling pink mess. She didn't think about why anyone would design a shower with a door that opened outwards, all she knew was that she had to get to him before... she cried out with the pain of expectant loss, slipping and sliding on the slippery mess beneath her as she crossed the cubicle. To him, she had to get to him. She knelt down beside the body of the large furry man. His powerful canine hind legs curled beneath him, his more obviously human chin slumped down to his chest. Propped against the wall of the cubicle, his arms stretched out either side of him, he looked like a supplicant to some murderous god. The fur at his wrists was caked with blood, Lynx noticed, and she scoured the floor for the blade that had caused such damage. It was smaller than it should have been. It was then she noticed the word and numbers painted roughly across the tiles behind him. Her name and a set of coordinates. She knew what they were for straightaway and if she'd had any breath left, the realisation would have taken it away with force. After all this time, after all he had done, he was giving her the mother lode. What she had been racing against him to find right from the start. He had got there first, or close enough, maybe he had even seen it for himself, and now... now... Lynx could barely stand the reality of what was in front of her.

She threw her head back and howled.

The sound echoed through the subterranean caves, the only noise to have broken its silence for many years.

Secure Unit, The Mcmillan-Lownds Rehabilitation and
Psychiatric Facility, Classified Location, Present

Lynx woke up screaming. She arched off the bed, pulled back down sharply by the heavy straps around her wrists and ankles. Restraints. For a moment she fought wildly, howling and screeching, kicking and struggling frantically, pulled back onto the bed time and again. A door on the other side of the room opened, leaving a gaping black hole in its wake, and she saw two large men in white uniforms enter, heading straight for her, their faces grim. A smaller lady, clearly a nurse, followed them. Her face was all beatific smile and dimples. In her left hand was the biggest syringe Lynx had ever seen.

'There now, Miss Ruffieux, let's have no more of that.' The nurse gestured to the men to hold her down and Lynx struggled anew. It was futile. They didn't let her get within biting distance and had all the positional advantage. They had her still in seconds, still enough anyway. Lynx wasn't going without a fight.

'Fuck you, lady. You get that thing away from me!' The nurse ignored her and came closer, the syringe looking bigger and more sinister with every step. 'I said get it away!'

'Now, now, Miss Ruffieux, just stay calm and everything will be fine. We're here to help you.' Lynx howled as the tiny woman – maybe the syringe looked so big because she couldn't have stood more than five feet tall in her stockinged feet – plunged the needle deep into her left arm. The nurse dispensed the liquid without missing a beat even as Lynx began struggling again. She was drowsy before the needle had even been removed. Her new friends warped and stretched in front of her eyes, one moment their faces leering straight down at her, the next their heads were tiny buds on human stalks waiting to flower. Darkness vibrated around the edges of her vision, stealing across her line of sight in ever-increasing pulses until...

His face. Like that of an angel. A hairy angel. So handsome, so hers. But not hers. Never hers. Not really. No one was. She was alone in the dark, always had been, always would be.

She remembered fire, the screams of her foster parents. Humans.

She remembered blood, his blood, her blood, the blood of twenty people. Dead people. All around her, since birth. She could taste it, like puddles on the floor, lapping them up, delicious, the tang of iron strong on her tongue.

His touch on her shoulder. Warm hands, hot hands, burning sharply into her flesh, branding her, piercing her. His face suddenly so angry, full of hate. She wanted to close her eyes against him, to look away, anything, but he filled her mind, his anger now hers, filling her, burning her from the inside out. Would it ever end? Hate and guilt, desire and lust, it bubbled up inside her, threatening to scorch through her skin, to spill out, corroding everything in its path, destroying, her heart pounding, her head throbbing, the blood in her veins boiling. She wanted it to end, she begged, she whined, pleasepleaseplease, over and over, but no one came, no one would. She'd always known she was alone. Hot skin, sweat, she could taste it, she was *it. Burning through her synapses, her reactions blurred – did she move forward or back – the light of knowledge just beyond her, confusion slicing across her mind, urging her on even as it held her back, frustration like a turned over cauldron, drowning her, she couldn't breathe, she needed to surface. She kicked out, forcing her way up, the breath in her lungs not enough, surely not enough…*

'Butch!' She cried out his name as her eyes opened, the slash of light making her close them again. But she was breathing, she was conscious. She was real. Where had she been?

'Now, now, Miss Ruffieux…'

'Lynx, my name is Lynx.' She growled the words. She remembered the nurse, remembered her syringe.

'Yes, dear. I'm here to help you. It's always difficult at first, acceptance is hard work, but we'll make sure you're comfortable and get the help you need.' Could the woman be any more patronising? Lynx's head pounded, the grogginess of the drugs making her thoughts slower than usual but she knew where she was this time. She knew this place. She'd been here before.

The Facility.

Fighting down the panic her recollection unleashed, Lynx tried to ease her breathing. She swallowed, buying herself a little time, and thought for a moment. Play along. They would be dosing her with all sorts to keep her quiet, to make sure she was docile, that her claws were firmly kept in their sheathes, unthreatening, compliant. They must have found her in those caves, worked out her subterfuge, and seen the rubbed out message on the wall of the shower. They must have known what it was just as surely as she had and, worse, they knew she knew. That was why she was here.

'Are you going to take your medicine without a fuss this time, Lynx? No more of this *I'm a cat*, nonsense?' That surprised her. It didn't sound like something she'd say, had been trained explicitly not to do so, and neither did she recall saying it, but if she'd been dosed to the eyeballs she could have said anything. 'Honestly, it's not one of the better ones I've heard, dear. We had someone in here the other day claimed to be Buffy the Vampire Slayer. Got into a right old scuffle with Napoleon Bonaparte over a game of checkers.' Her laugh was a high tinkling cackle and Lynx knew she'd be the first to go when she'd worked a way out of the restraints still tying her to the bed.

Her mind raced. The service had been using furries for decades. Hardly anyone knew they really existed; moreover it was likely that no one would even believe they did – that would have caused panic in the wider world – but no one within the service pretended they weren't real. The pieces began to fall into place. So, that's how they were going to play it, was it? She was crazy. Not a lynx, not a furry, just a human. Okay. She could play pretend, could play it better than this nurse and you could take that to the bank. She was nothing more than a bit player in the grander theatre of the service's plan anyway. Just doing her job. They all were in reality. The higher ups moving their pawns around like proverbial chess pieces. Except now this was checkers, like the woman had said, and she was a queen, goddammit, and they would soon know her wrath… okay, that sounded a little crazy, she had to admit. That kind of talk was best kept in her head.

'Would you like something to eat after you've taken your medication, dear?' Yes, thought Lynx, your liver would be a great start.

'Yes,' she replied out loud, nodding at the question to reinforce just how yes her yes was.

'I'm going to trust you to have one hand free. We have a zero tolerance policy here though. One misstep and it's a feeding tube, do you understand?'

Lynx nodded at the question. Oh yes, she understood. There'd be no feeding tube. Her claws were on fire in their sheathes, her canines elongating nicely. Zero tolerance. There'd definitely be no feeding tube.

PINS AND NEEDLES

The path, they said, was very clear,
Not as hard to follow as it appeared,
But Red could not discern the meaning
With the way the sign was leaning.
She squinted hard to see the words
But the letters danced in a lexis herd.
So Red gave up, quite frustrated,
And missed the Wolf who lay prostrated,
Waiting for his chance to come,
To tease the girl and have some fun.
'My dear,' he said, all politesse and charm,
'Are you heading for the cottage, or yonder to the farm?'
Red stepped back, quite affronted,
Not used to being thus confronted.
Regardless, the Wolf bounced to his feet,
Carefully concealing his planned deceit.
He unleashed a smile so completely charming –
Just a dash of charisma, not too disarming –
That Red could not help but stare
At this suitor with such lustrous hair.
Now, she may have been taken aback
When the Wolf appeared just-like-that,
But Red was neither gullible nor fool,
She'd got top marks at Monster School.
Without further thought or deliberation,
She stretched her jaws to dislocation.
Out popped her fangs, dripping with venom –
Red was not your average human.
Her red cloak fell from around her shoulders
As her skin began to pop and smoulder.
Paralysed with terrified confusion,

The Wolf watched the furious extrusion
Of pinkest skin by serpentine flesh,
As muscle, sinew and bone enmeshed.
His frozen stance was most misguided
Because of the opportunity it provided
The snake woman, whose transformation was complete,
And who now looked upon the Wolf as meat.

And so it was, the Wolf got eaten
In one foul swoop, devoured, no need to sweeten.
The snake woman closed her eyes in purest bliss
As she swallowed the Wolf with a mighty HISS!

The moral of this story is:

It's not just wolves that like a jacket
To hide their truly malignant racket.
Snakes come in all sorts of sizes,
And little girls can be disguises.

HOW TO BE
THE PERFECT HOUSEWIFE

Being a good wife is not easy. Being a perfect wife is nearly impossible, but that doesn't mean you shouldn't try. Every husband has dreams of a good wife; by following our helpful tips, you can make his come true.

The tangled aroma of roasting vegetables twisted through the air in a welcoming rush. Kitty let the oven door slam back into place, smiling at the satisfying clunk it made. Kitty was a good wife. Prided herself on it. She certainly tried hard enough to please her husband, had done ever since she'd met him. They were happy. She had made sure of it. He never needed to lift a finger at home; she took care of everything except the Man tasks, but they didn't count. He couldn't fail to be happy with life when he stepped through the door after a long day at work, whether or not he happened to be three hours late, whether or not he'd been drinking whiskey or chasing trollops...

Silly goose. She was standing there wool gathering while she had goodness-knows-what on her hands from emptying the bin. Honestly, what was she thinking? This was no time to be away with the fairies. With a shake of her head, she crossed the kitchen to the sink and dipped her hands into the warm soapy water.

The bubbles were red. Staring down into the sink Kitty wondered at that. It was troublingly hard to think. She felt more tired than she had ever felt in her life. It was like a weight in her soul. It seemed like she'd been on the go non-stop since forever ago and now she was paying the price. She ignored the empty strip of anti-psychotics on the counter beside her. She didn't need them and they weren't for thinking about now.

Shaking the bubbles, red or otherwise, from her hands and the inertia from her shoulders, Kitty grabbed a dishcloth. It was warm from where she'd taken the roasting vegetables out of the oven a few moments before. The hiss and spit from the frying pan reminded her that the steaks were probably well and truly sealed and, after wiping her wet fingers with the warm fabric, she deftly flipped the sizzling meat into the roasting tray.

Always have dinner ready. Plan ahead because having a meal on the table when your husband comes home from a hard day at the office is an essential part of welcoming him home.

Once the tray was back in the oven, Kitty turned her attention to the stock bubbling merrily on the stove. She always liked to have plenty to hand and this batch was going to be a doozy. She poked at the bones with a wooden spoon and did her best to give the thickening gloop a hearty stir, all the time smiling happily. She loved cooking, loved preparing meals for her husband. The way to a man's heart was, as everyone knew, through his stomach. Maybe she should have made haggis from that bitch's... Kitty took a deep breath. It wouldn't do to lose her focus now. She'd come such a long way already.

Keep noise to a minimum. Time it so that the washing machine has finished its cycle, the dishwasher is not rumbling and never allow the vacuum cleaner to be anywhere but in a cupboard when the man of the house is home.

There was still a lot to do. The stain in the hallway would have to be attended to; scarlet rivulets were already making a break for the Persian rug in the living room and that simply would not do. Then there were the walls. Kitty sighed. She hadn't meant to make such a mess, but needs must when the devil drives. It had been so satisfying. Closing her eyes, she remembered another pair, wide with terror, lips moving to make the incessant music of begging, pale skin, trembling hands. It was all a memory now, but it had been a luxury like no other. Better than sex, that was for sure. The swift pinch of a blade point against, into, quivering flesh, the promise of something more, something deeper, more revealing. Kitty opened her eyes. She was losing herself again and there were chores to be done.

Heading for the utility room at the back of the kitchen, she ticked off what she would need in her mind; bucket, mop, scrubbing brush, bleach…

Ensure the children are quiet, that they have clean hands and faces and their hair is combed. Their father does not want to be greeted by filthy unkempt little terrors.

The children. She'd forgotten all about them. Honestly, she'd forget her head if it wasn't screwed on. That's what her Mother used to tell her, over and over, each time punctuated with a hearty thwack of the paddle against the back of her legs. Merciless, but she had learned the lesson well. All the lessons. Each one more cruel, more calculated to demolish than the last. Whining about it was not going to get her chores done any quicker, however, and she had forgotten, hadn't she? Forgotten like the simpleton she was. Well, time to remedy that.

'Children! I'm coming. I hope you've washed your hands and faces.'

Take one last look around to make sure the house is spick-and-span. Gather up any clutter and run a duster over the tables, sideboards, windowsills et cetera. Your husband should feel as though he is returning to a haven, not a war zone.

That was the children attended to. Honestly, those boys

were just like their father. Always running her to the edge of patience, misbehaving with that endearing glint of roguishness in their eyes: irritating, irritating little shits. She had to teach them a lesson, just as her mother had taught her. With any lesson, however, there was often a resultant mess and, darn it all, she was already behind schedule. She was finding it hard to think again; things kept reshuffling in her mind like a dodgy spine on a potholed road. If she didn't start getting it together, didn't regain order over everything, smooth it all out, she was soon going to... The sound of the stock boiling over snapped her out of it. Now she really was in a fix.

Kitty sprinted for the hob, grabbing for the knob and yelped as the hot overspill splashed and spat at her skin. She turned the temperature down and grabbed a tea towel, heaving the large pot onto a dormant burner. Bloody woman. She was still more trouble than she was worth. Well, as long as she was tasty, that's all that mattered now.

Before your man arrives home, take a few minutes to refresh your make up, fix your hair, and change your clothes if need be. Ensure you are nice and relaxed when he comes through the door. Be ready to give him a lift with a smile as you greet him.

It was time for the jacket. She'd worked on it all afternoon when she should have been cleaning. The old Singer was the only thing she'd inherited from her mother - the only thing other than the psychosis and the piquerism - and was still in perfect working order. She took good care of it, just as mother had beaten into her. It still hemmed seams like a dream, creating a beautiful jacket for her out of... That old saying 'silk purse out of a pig's ear' might be deemed appropriate. Kitty chuckled. That woman, - the pigwhorebitch - had learned the hard way. Learned that she, Kitty Darling, was not someone to be messed with, that her family unit was not something anyone else would be allowed to endanger. Not anyone. Least of all some filthy, blowjobbing disease trap...

Kitty drew in a long breath. Her hands were shaking. The

empty pill strips laughed at her from beside the sink, the light twinkling mockingly on the metallic material; mocking *her*. She hated to be mocked. Hated it. Hatedithatedithatedit…

The rage.

A moment of panic flashed through her, but even as she scrabbled to stop it, she felt it bubble over at last.

It shot through her veins, zinging up into her brain like a champion pinball, making it throb. She raked her hands across her face, trying to scrape it out. Red lines scored her skin, but she couldn't stop, not until it was gone. Still it pulsed in her head, her thoughts scattering.

The sound of a key in the front door lock punched through her mania. She'd been anticipating it for hours and now that it had come, she wasn't ready. Goddammit, why did nothing ever work out right? Something always went wrong, something out of her control, something infuri-fucking-at-ing. Fury screeched through her, more potent than ever, those redundant pill packets not mocking her anymore. She felt the terror of the world around her as she stopped making a mess of her face. She felt it tremble at what she was becoming, had become.

As the key turned in the lock, seconds became minutes, became hours. Time elasticised with Kitty as she felt the change finally come over her, punching away the Kitty she'd tried so hard to be, so yearned to be. She'd felt its touch before but never its full force. She'd fought it for so long but every cell, every atom, was infused with red-hot anger, *right-eous* anger. How dare he? How dare he do this to her? How dare he…

'Darling? What on earth happened? Where…'

Although the fury governed her now, she knew what she had to do. There was a kind of calm in the eye of its storm. Kitty stepped from the shadows, the cast iron pan in her hand.

'Welcome home, darling.'

'What the hell…?'

The sound of human skull crunching beneath cast iron echoed around the hallway and the man fell with a splash into the scarlet lake at his feet. Kitty looked down at her shoes and wondered how she was ever going to get the stains out.

Greet him with his favourite drink and make sure that he is comfortable. If he wants to take a nap before dinner, make sure his pillow is plumped and offer to remove his shoes. It is your job to ensure he is relaxed and can unwind unimpeded from his day.

Vodka, rocks. Just how he liked it. Kitty was sure he'd be awake by now. She'd had to help him to bed, of course. Silly man had practically worked himself into a stupor. The bedside lamp cast a soft glow across the supine form of the man on the bed and as she stood in the doorway Kitty sighed at the perfection of his beloved face... except for the blood trickling from the wound just above his hairline. Why did she always have to focus on the details when they weren't important? She'd drive herself mad with them one day. Now was not the time, she needed to stay calm.

'Are you awake, darling?' She kept her voice low, soothing, as she crossed the room to sit on the bed beside him. When he didn't reply, she raised it slightly but made sure not to overdo it, just.

'Kit-Kitty?' His voice was groggy, hoarse. He didn't sound like himself at all. She'd already said it; the poor dear had been working too hard. Well now, wasn't it her job to make sure he relaxed? And wouldn't she do just that, even if it killed him?

'Of course it's Kitty, darling. I've brought your drink.'

'Untie me, Kitty. Please.' The panic in his plea was like a slap in the face. She didn't like it. She didn't like it at all. The heat of the fury prickled at the base of her skull, rolled in the pit of her stomach. No. She wouldn't let it take over again. She had a plan and if you could say one thing about Kitty Darling it was that she stuck to her plans. In the end.

Do not subject him to complaints and problems. He has most likely had a hard day and anything you have to say will probably be inconsequential in comparison. Be considerate and attentive, let him talk to you and not the other way around. However, your husband is not clairvoyant. If you want something from him, ask for it, but make sure you keep your tone positive and never accu-

satory. Whatever you do, never let anger take over.

It was tricky, staying calm, but Kitty had had a lot of practice. Once upon a time, she had constantly been at the mercy of the fury - the cold white rooms, the hypodermics, the placating smiles and 'hush nows' of Dr Tish as he felt her up beneath her gown - but she had learned to keep it in its place. She had.

Deep breaths. The mindfulness book had said to go back into her breathing if she was having trouble focusing - Dr Tish had said the same thing, but for something quite different. She thought it was fair to say she was having some trouble focusing.

Deep breath in, two three four, deep breath out, two three four, and repeat.

Better.

Now. The jacket.

Luckily the other woman - that bitchwhoreskank - was quite a bit bigger than Kitty, so she'd been able to nip and tuck the garment to suit her frame, but it had still been a bugger to get into. Kitty looked at herself in the mirror. She admired her handiwork for a moment, allowing herself just a touch of pride. She'd always been good with her hands. Even when mother had broken every one of her fingers after she'd stolen an apple from the bowl that sat on the kitchen table in the farmhouse they'd lived in - she'd not eaten for days, days, she'd been so young, so hungry, so frightened, always so frightened - they had healed well and only ached when the cold weather came. There she was again, going all goopy at herself. It was time for dinner. She didn't want those steaks overcooking now, did she?

The jacket took a bit of getting used to but, as she made her way back into the kitchen, she was glad she'd made the effort. The look on his face when he saw her was priceless. He clearly hadn't failed to notice it, to realise what it was made from. Her talent as a seamstress was probably one of the reasons he'd married her.

He was sat at the head of the table, just as he should be, and the two boys were pinned to their chairs. It had taken her a bloody age, but pinned they were. Their bowing heads were the only oversight she'd made, making the tableau a little less than she had hoped for, but she had to suck it up for now. Hopefully they would come round before their dinner got cold.

Ensure the cutlery and glassware are sparkling clean. Your napkin always goes in your lap. Never lick your fingers and never ask who you're eating.

The table was set. The tablecloth was gingham. Perfect red and white check. Kitty smoothed the cloth across the table before taking a step back to admire her work. It was perfect, of course. Perfect. How she liked perfect. She felt much better now things were going according to plan again. Calmer. Clearer. Happy.

As Kitty looked around at her family, she wondered if she'd ever felt so at peace before. There might only be four of them, but they were a perfect family. One day maybe they'd have a little girl. She'd always wanted a girl.

'Let's eat.' Picking up her knife and fork, Kitty began digging into the meal in front of her, her left elbow sticking occasionally in the jacket's sleeve. She'd have to take another look at the stitching after dinner. Steak with roasted potatoes, pumpkin, courgette and onions with the delicious gravy she'd made from the stock on the stove. It smelled divine. Closing her eyes, she savoured the meat as she chewed. The meat was succulent and tasty; its juices sliding decadently down her throat. It was cooked to perfection. She had surpassed herself this...

No one else was eating.

'Your food will get cold.' Neither of the children replied, they sat in silence, refusing to pick up their knives and forks. Well, if they didn't eat what she put in front of them they would go without. He was no better. Sitting opposite her, staring at her, the expression on his face one of... no, this was intolerable. She would fix this.

Scraping her chair back, Kitty stood up and walked

around the table. She picked up his knife and fork and cut a large piece of meat for him. Blowing on it gently, she raised it to his mouth. He flinched away, keeping it firmly shut. Kitty pushed it against his - bastard, ingrate - closed lips a second time. And a third. Then stabbed him in the mouth with the fork when he still refused to permit her entry. He yelled in surprise and pain but the fork sticking out of his face muffled the sound. Blood trickled from the wound she'd made and Kitty fought the urge to lick his face. That sort of thing was for the bedroom, not the dining table.

'Now look what you made me do. Eat up or I'll find another way to get it all inside you.' Kitty pulled the fork back out, ignoring his whimpering, and waited. Slowly, he opened his mouth and, smiling, Kitty popped the fork between his lips. 'Chew.' He was clumsy but obedient. She liked that. She liked it a lot, but she couldn't stand there feeding him like a baby - snivelling baby, snot running out of his nose. He might be her husband but she needed (oh how she needed) to eat too. Decision made, she swiftly, with the occasional sticking of her left elbow, cut up his dinner into manageable pieces and used the steak knife to slice through the gaffa tape binding him to his chair on one side. Just one hand. She popped the knife into the pocket of her apron - she didn't want any accidents - and put the fork into the hand she had freed, wrapping his stiff fingers around the handle. Returning to her seat, enjoying the unusual meaty shuck of the jacket's fabric as she sat, she was pleased to see him digging - picking - at his vegetables.

Never overdo it on the wine. A glass or two is acceptable but you should always keep in mind that no man likes a drunk Wendy for a wife. There is also the washing up to consider. You're not going to get that done when you're three sheets to the wind. Remember, first and foremost, a good wife's responsibility is to keep her home spick-and-span.

Maybe working too hard was affecting his appetite - or

maybe he ate before he came home, with his friends or perhaps another woman, maybe he hates your cooking, maybe he knows. Kitty decided to go easy on him. She could be magnanimous; the apple might not fall far from the tree, but it did fall and she was *not* her mother. Picking up his plate, she took it to the sink and began scraping the leftovers into the little tub she kept for…

Sharp pain, intense, sudden, pierced the junction of her neck and shoulder. The sweet spot. Kitty dropped the plate onto the counter, the fork skittering after it in a shower of leftovers. She scrabbled at her back, but he stabbed her again before she could stop him. His reflection in the darkened window - she should have seen him, heard him, stupid stupid - above the sink was grim, determined. The children. She'd forgotten - treacherous little shits - about their plates, their cutlery. Without thinking, she thrust her head backwards, right into his perfect, double-crossing face. The crunch of his nose breaking under her skull fired the fury through her even better than the stab of the fork in her neck. She whirled around, one hand grabbing for the carving knife she'd left on the draining board earlier. She jabbed at him, piercing his chest with a smattering of shallow puncture wounds. He was strong though, despite the head injury, despite the fear - or because of it - and, as her damned left elbow caught again, he punched her hard in the stomach, doubling her over, her hand opening reflexively and dropping the knife. Gasping for breath but not outdone, Kitty bared her teeth and drove them into his thigh, feeling her jaw click hard as she bit down. He screamed so loudly it hurt her ears and then he punched her again, this time in the back. Kitty fell to her knees but she was far from finished. She ground her fingers into the soft flesh at the side of his knee, pinching hard - she was glad she'd cut the bitches hands off now - watching as his leg buckled beneath him. When his face came into view, she head-butted him again, the crimson bloom of his blood splashing across her face. She licked her lips as he fell backwards, the salty taste almost as good as her gravy. Maybe it was for the kitchen, after all.

'Did you enjoy her, you cheating fuck?' She snarled at him, not waiting for an answer. 'Was she tasty? Everything you ever wanted?' He groaned in pain and confusion, on his back - just how the whore liked him - his hands flailing defensively, helplessly. 'I made sure to add a lot of pepper to her tasteless backside. Ha!' Even in his stupor, she could see he heard her, his bloody face clenching helplessly, his eyes wide with shock, as though this one depravity was the final straw, the snap of his sanity. His kids unconscious - dead, Kitty, dead - and pinned to a table, his whore's skin draped over her, they were nothing compared to eating human flesh. 'Delicious, wasn't she?' She laughed then, laughed so hard she thought she might never stop. When he punched her in the face, she stopped. She sat down on her bottom with an 'oof' and stared at him. She'd thought she'd broken him, but there he was, scrabbling to his feet and heading for the front door. Stars danced around her head like a saucepanned cartoon character. She blinked several times. Shaking her head was not an option just yet.

'Bitch!' He'd found her little trick then. Did he think she was stupid? Of course she'd locked the door. Thrown the key away. Banged in some nails. No one was getting out. No one. Clinging to the kitchen cabinet, she hoisted herself unsteadily to her feet. She pulled the cleaver from where it sat on its magnetic strip above the sink and followed him. He was trying for the windows, of course. Standing on one of her beautiful cream sofas with his feet all bloody from the lake on the hallway floor. He'd ruined her plans by arriving home early so she couldn't finish her tidying up and now he was ruining her sofa with his selfish sticky feet. Sticky sticky feet. Oh, he was going to get a lesson, all right, and it was going to be more than sticky.

A shriek tore from her throat as she sprinted at him, cleaver waving in her hand above her head, ready to chop into him wherever she could. He slipped just before she got to him, his sticky - sticky sticky - feet offending her yet again. The cleaver sank into her beautiful cream sofa and she had to pull it out with both hands. He was away from her by then, running for the back door. Kitty was, not for the first time, over his disobedience. Right. Over. It. She chased after him, catching him as he realised that door was locked too. She sank the cleaver into his shoulder with a battle cry that shook the walls. He tried to shake her off, but she let go of the heavy knife and climbed onto his back, clawing at him, sinking her teeth into his flesh wherever she could. He thrashed around, trying to dislodge her, but Kitty was tenacious, Kitty was strong, and Kitty was not giving up. She kept her hold on him despite that tricky left elbow even as he backed into the kitchen wall, wrapped her legs around him and squeezed hard.

'Don't fret, lover,' her breath was coming in short harsh gasps, but she kept talking, 'all this can be explained, sorted out, we can...'

'You killed my fucking wife!' Kitty saw red. How fucking dare he?

'*I'm* your wife, you ungrateful shit!' She snarled the words as she pressed harder with her thighs.

'You made me eat her. That thing... that thing you're... you're wearing her. Oh god! It's touching me!' His voice cracked and he whimpered, the sound making Kitty's patience slip a notch. Slip a few notches, truth be told, but by then it didn't need any help.

How. Dare. He?

'Just because you were fucking her, doesn't make her your wife. I'm your wife. Your only wife, your love. Say it! Say it or I'll make you regret being born, you cheating shit! *Say it!*'

'My wife? No, please. You're not my wife, Kitty.' He sounded out of breath, or was he less sure of himself now, battling to persuade her away from his deceit? 'You're not my wife. I'm sorry. We shouldn't have slept together, I know that.'

'You made me promises, vows, you said you...'

'I shouldn't have done it. I'm sorry, I'm so sorry, so fucking sorry...' His pitiful litany went on and on. He was pathetic. She'd done all this for him and this was all he had? All he could give her at the last?

Red fury filled her with a vengeance. Gritting her teeth, she angled her head so she could look down into his treacherous face.

'You lying bastard, you'd say anything, wouldn't you? I. Am. Your. Wife. Say it!'

'You're our au… our au pair.'

Two blond children, boys, swinging happily on the back garden set. Two smiling faces looking up at her, asking her for ice cream. Twin boys. Twin blond boys. Four glassy eyes as she looked down into their dead faces. Her boys. Her boys. They were hers –

'Please Kitty, please!'

Kitty realised how tightly she was grasping him around the neck, the throat. She was strangling him and he was gasping for air now. This man. This man who denied her. What right had he… *two blond children, eyes like a summer sky; 'Kitty, Kitty, push us some more before Mummy gets home, please, Kitty!'…*

Kitty shut her eyes against the unwelcome memory. She would not be seduced by his words. Would not. She tightened her hold, relishing the feel of his strain for breath, tasting his imminent death on her tongue like a sugar cube.

She enjoyed it too much, it slackened her concentration, and he took advantage - they always do in the end - elbowing her in the stomach and hoisting her with her own petard by smacking the back of his head into her face. He missed the nose but caught her cheek hard. Her grip fell away and as she fell to the floor he stepped back from her, grabbing one of the kitchen chairs and throwing it hard against the kitchen window. The chair bounced off and they both watched - gormless rubberneckers - as it arced back at him. He stepped away before it could hit him, reached for another chair, but the stockpot was already in Kitty's hands. She could be quick, quicker than lightning, quicker than that bitch's knickers hitting the floor. Then the liquid was cascading over him, his whore's (his wife's!) head tumbling out with it, hitting him in the solar plexus like a fist, bowing him forward. He screamed again when he saw what had done it, but this time there was something broken, something feral about the sound. He stood there screaming, eyes wide and staring at the skinned head as it rolled aimlessly on the floor, screaming and

screaming and screaming. Kitty would have laughed but...
she was so tired now... she needed to finish this. It had all
gone so horribly wrong, despite her careful planning, despite
her attention to detail. How she wished it had turned out
differently. How she wished... but if wishes were horses, as
her mother used to say, beggars would ride. In truth, it was
simple. She needed to decide. Keep him or kill him?

It was no decision at all, not really.

Carefully, Kitty placed the wig she had made on her head,
pulling it firmly - that bitch's scalp was big and she'd had
to pad it right out - down over her own hair, fiddled with
it until it sat just right and then checked her make up.
The red scratches and burgeoning bruises on her face were
hidden beneath a thick layer of foundation. She decided she
looked a bit like Marilyn Monroe. She'd always wanted to go
blonde and now she'd had the balls to do it. She smiled at
her reflection. After a moment of rightly earned admiration,
she turned, grabbing the holdall from the sofa (ignoring the
sticky sticky stains) and the car keys.

The body of her dead husband - employer, lover - had
made her cry at first, but she was over that now. She'd mistaken him for the love of her life, for her destiny. He hadn't
been, he had been a wicked lying cheat instead. So she had
killed him and he had deserved it, but now what? Her life was
nothing without Him, without The One. Kitty knew what
she had to do. It would complete the circle and she would
be with her family again, in another place - deepest darkest
Hell, you snivelling bitch - and they would be happy again.
She just had to find them. That was her purpose, her mission.
Her family were out there. She knew it. She just had to take
it back from whichever bitch had stolen it from her.

A perfect wife knows her place. Perfectly.

THE SWEETNESS OF YOUR SKIN

Every night the dream is the same.

Of Cherryade and bubble gum, of sugar and spice and all things nice, of the crackle of kindling as worlds that never were and never could be end, and she wakes with the taste of salted skin on her tongue.

Bewitched.

She knew the word before, had heard it in children's tales, an old show on the television, but now it is hers, she owns it, holds onto it as an explanation because every night the dream is the same.

The woman comes, cinnamon skinned, flame haired, dancing in the fire that has always burned inside her. She drowns in her, is tortured by her heat, and yet in her dreaming state she is more alive than she has ever been. She feels something for the first time in so long that when she wakes she tries to hold onto the dream, closing her eyes tight and breathing deeply so she can slip back into the woman's embrace. It works but only for a moment and then the warmth is just a memory again. And she yearns for night to come so she may sleep once more. And dream.

October slowly turns its face to November, autumn settling with a shudder. Her days are as monotonous as the heavy grey skies. Each morning she wakes, the world unwelcome, unwelcoming. She rises, slips into her uniform of cheap polyester and itchy nylon, her battered shoes held together with felt tip-penned scuffs and cheap glue. She cannot afford another pair. She must make do. Her whole life is about making do.

The hotel is barely a one star, the money terrible, the work backbreaking, but since the dream has come she doesn't care as she once did. She doesn't feel the wrench in her back as she lifts the bags of soiled linen, doesn't notice the tear of another fingernail, the burn of bleach on her skin, or even the lascivious advances of her clichéd sweaty boss. She bats it all away with the power of the other woman's touch, focussed only on becoming tired enough to sleep so that she may dream.

And every night she does. And every night the dream is the same.

As the nights draw in, the dreams become stronger. More and more often she wakes abruptly, thrust into the cold night and crying out perhaps in passion or maybe terror, she does not know. Her sheets are damp with sweat and she begins to feel unrested, less satisfied. The ache for more grows. The veil is edging closer to its thinnest and as the distance between them diminishes she needs more and she can feel that her cinnamon dancer needs more too. Every ounce of her desire is matched and she can no longer fool herself into thinking it is just a dream – she never really did – she knows this is something more, something she overheard her grandmother speak of in a hushed voice to her mother when they thought she was asleep in their tiny two-room house, destroyed when she was ten years old, turned into the rubble of rich men's wars even as it turned her into an orphan. Displaced. Dislodged. Dislocated. It was the only place she has ever thought of as home.

Until the dream. Until the woman.

One night she wakes, sweat slicked and breathless and the woman is there, standing at the end of her bed, waiting. She is barely more than a flicker and at first she thinks she is imagining her, that the vision is an overhang of her dream. It wouldn't be the first time. She blinks and rubs away the sleep from her eyes and the woman is still there. She reaches out to touch her, the movement automatic, innate, as natural as taking her next breath... and the woman is gone.

The day that follows feels a thousand years long. She does not have the energy to haul the sacks or to fend off her boss, and finally in the late afternoon he catches her unawares, trapping her in a broom cupboard, the fetid stench of his lust choking her. She knows he will not let her go without some sort of price – the debt, somehow, is always hers to pay – and although she would rather kill him than pay it, she knows she cannot, she must not. Who would believe her? She does not even belong here. She has been told as much so many times – *foreigner, scrounger, scum*. Her boss steps closer and raises a hand to her chest, no romantic this one, and she draws in a breath, ready to close her eyes and wait for whatever will come, only hoping it will be over quickly.

The smell of cinnamon pulses through the air. It is so strong they both pause, staring at each other in silent puzzlement for a moment. Behind him, she catches the flicker of flame red hair and then suddenly he is clutching at his chest, his skin greyer than her washed-out blouse, gasping and begging for her help. She half catches him and they fall to the floor together.

The men from the ambulance say she saved his life. She performed the manoeuvres she was taught by the Auxiliary Unit but there was no real intent in it. Whether he lived or died was no matter to her. There are always other men, worse men, and she supposes she prefers the devil she knows. He thanked her as they carted him off to the hospital. Maybe it will work in her favour. Maybe it was supposed to. All she can think about is the scent of cinnamon.

That night, she gets ready for bed carefully. No quick strip-wash with her threadbare flannel tonight though. Instead, she dares the cold of the shower and indulges in a little of the body wash and then, once she is dry and trying not to shiver, the cream she pilfered from the hotel stores. She does not like to take things, she knows what people would say, what they do say, but these had already been opened and she cannot feel too badly about it, not as she rubs the cream into her skin, not as she breathes in the sweet scent of it. Her grandmother always told her she was special because she was a sweet delight sent from God, a tasty morsel everyone wanted for their own. A child of the sweet vale. She warned her too of others who would steal her away to taste her for themselves, to exchange their bitterness for her sweetness, more addictive than any opiate, if she was not always on her guard. Old Mothers' stories from a land long gone. She does not find the thought of the cinnamon woman tasting her skin something to be afraid of. Rather, she finds it makes her heart beat faster, stirring places long forgotten, too long untouched even by her. She cannot remember the last time she felt glad to be alive.

The sound of fireworks make her jump, but they light up her tiny room with reds and yellows and oranges that remind her of her dreams, of her cinnamon woman. The smell of burning has been on the air for days now. It is the time of year when this country, one she had once thought of as a promised land, somewhere for dreams and hopes to thrive, to be safe, celebrates a long dead martyr with fire and flame just like any other. It is another disappointment in a long line of them, but now, finally, she has something to hold onto, something to live for.

Folding back the sheet, she slips into bed, fidgeting until she finds the sweet spot, the not-so lumpy patch between the ossified springs of the long dead mattress. She is almost too excited to sleep, but the dream will have its way, and soon her eyes are closing and her mind is drifting across the ether to the woman. Her woman.

Every night the dream is the same. Every night the woman is there to meet her and tonight, finally, she knows it is more. The body that appears before her exists both in the dream and in reality. She dreams the touch of her fingers against the woman's skin even as she feels the brush of her lips against her throat. Oh, gods and goddesses and all things holy, she thinks, this is what I was made for. Sparkling light streams around them, reds and yellows and oranges, bursting as they embrace, discovering each other, learning each other's shape, the soft and the warm, the wonderful and the familiar. It is more pleasure than she has ever known and it makes her whole.

'I would not let him have you. You are mine.' The words are silk against her skin and as they whisper across it, meant to seduce, she goes cold.

Suddenly, the dream is not the same.

The woman's grip becomes harder, her mouth more demanding. Her skin begins to pucker unbearably, as though it is being pulled away from the muscles beneath. She thinks she hears a rip, a tear, and the pain is excruciating. Understanding dawns. She is being stripped, consumed. Her sweetness in return for the cinnamon woman's bitterness.

'Mine, all mine. You will nourish me, sweet one. That is your destiny. You will serve me well, my sweet love.' The voice, now it is finally speaking to her, makes her ears ring. This is not the voice of a lover and it is not the voice she thought she would hear. The tone of possessiveness is too familiar. There is no wonder here. This is something she knows too well and it jars her back to her senses.

She is not a commodity. She belongs to no one but herself; no man, no woman, and certainly no apparition will ever hold her soul. She has fought to stay alive; she has earned the right to live for herself. She has won the right to wish impossible things.

Her limbs are dream-heavy with desire, but they obey her when she summons them to action. Bringing her arms up sharply, she pushes the cinnamon woman away from her, the strength she finds surprising them both. The cinnamon woman reaches for her again, confusion clouding the once bewitching features, her consternation clear and, at last, she sees the true face of the woman-thing. It is all hard lines and sharp angles, shaped not by love or even desire, but by anger. It is the face of a demon, of corruption. Greed. Why had she not seen it before? She should have known, should have known it was too good to be true, that even her dreams would be used against her one day. Fury fills her, shaking foundations laid long ago amidst fire and loss, and as her anger focuses, gathering at the very core of her being, light punches forth from her chest, bursting from her eyes, her mouth, every pore streaming with scorching, endless light that is as pink as bubble gum, that is as sweet as cherryade. It sears the woman-thing's flesh, hissing as it hits meat, seizing hold of its power by the throat, turning the tables and taking it for its own, using it against it, sending it wheeling backwards, hands clawing at the air. Its skin blackens to a crisp, sizzling like well-grilled steak, crackling like the fallen leaves beneath her shoes on the walk to work, and the whites of its eyes burn away to reveal the red demon depths beneath.

The woman-thing bares its fangs, hissing at this unexpected twist, but it is too late. There has been a miscalculation, an underestimation. Only now does it see – this one is not simply a child born of the sweet vale, to take such a one too lightly is to bring misfortune, it is true, but this one has been thrust from that place into a world of cruelty and despair. She has more iron within her than sweetness. And the iron burns.

The woman-thing learns this lesson. Learns it as it blisters away into the dream ether, learns it even as its dream flesh melts. Learns it as all those who seek to consume the sweetness of the world so that it might temper the bitterness of their souls must surely one day learn it.

When she wakes, the night around her is cold, her heart beats faster than ever, her skin is flushed and hot to the touch, but this time she does not scream.

Finally, she understands the sweetness of her skin. She savours the power within her, accepting it as it runs through her veins, feeling its pulse deep down in her very marrow.

Those wishes no longer seem so impossible and, for the first time in so long, she smiles.

The end is all that is ever true.

PROFESSOR VENEDICTOS VON HOLINSHED VERSUS THE SORORAL LEAGUE OF BAZOOKA-BIKINI-WIELDING DEMONIC DIVAS FROM OUTER SPACE (DENOUEMENT)

Screenplay by C.A. YATES

INT. – A LABORATORY – NIGHT

The laboratory is dark except for flashes of lightning that flare through the high windows. The CAMERA pans to the right, the lightning haphazardly illuminating the workspace, and we see a light from a clearly different source gradually growing to the right of screen. Strange machines adorned with great dials and levers, flashing buttons, screens covered with scrolling digital numbers and paper readouts spilling from dumb slots are haltingly revealed. The sounds of thunder, whirring, beeping, and someone hammering metal while cursing fill the air. The camera cuts to empty space and a hammer comes abruptly into view as though lifted into the air with vicious intent. It descends, and the camera pulls back to reveal PROFESSOR VENEDICTOS VON HOLINSHED in a white lab coat hunched over a worktable, surrounded by shelves full of scientific equipment, from semi-built mechanical body parts to bottles of poisons (marked with a skull and cross bones, of course) to an eclectic plethora of tools. He pounds the hammer down onto what looks to be a rather complicated hunk of metal.

VENEDICTOS

These robot legs will be my salvation, the final piece of my ultimate weapon. I will conquer those Bikini-Wielding bitches into next week as I bound across mountains and leap wide chasms. I will deflect their alien tit-guns with the shields I have installed in the left callipygian panel and fire my own sallies in retaliation with my patented Gonad Gatling Gun. I will pound them into oblivion where they belong and never again will I be...

The door to the laboratory is thrown open, hitting the wall with a crash. ENTER three women – BOSOM DON BLOSSOM, FAT TATTIES, and GLADYS TANGA. All three are clad in shiny thigh-high boots and rubber/metal bikinis, each woman in a different bright colour. Gladys is tall, blonde and stacked like a playboy model. Fat Tatties is a curvaceous redhead, while Bosom is raven haired and built like a bodybuilder. BOSOM DON BLOSSOM steps forwards, hands on hips, her bikini clearly locked, loaded, and aimed at Venedictos.

BOSOM

Halt your nefarious shenanigans, puny maggot. Lay down your hammer and kneel before us at last. You are no match for our mighty Bazooka Bikinis!

VENEDICTOS

(He waves his hammer at her, his face twisted with fury)
By Hell's horses! I will never submit to female fiends from the depths of space!

BOSOM

(She throws her head back and laughs)

Ha! Your feeble weapons are no match for us! We know all about your ridiculously grandiose plans and that your robotic legwear is not yet complete. You have overstretched your genius, Von Holinshed. You have nothing left to fight us with. We have bested you once again and this time you will suffer the consequences of your defiance, stubborn fool. Too many times have we had you in our grasp only for you, greasy little toad that you are, to slip through our fingers at the last. The power of our improbable bustiers will dispense our glorious alien wrath!

VENEDICTOS

Ha! Harpy of Doom, how little you know!

Venedictos tears off his lab coat to reveal a mechanised torso. Metallic nipple-doors move aside, with a whirring sound, to uncover tubes that are actually the barrels of some kind of gun. The barrels push out from his chest and point at Fat Tatties and Gladys. Bosom motions for the women to stand their ground.

VENEDICTOS

You think I would trust that turn-spittle Scalpel Mickey Bang Bang with the full details of my cunning and evil plan? (Throws back his head and laughs) He is a worm and even now chokes upon the poisoned cheese bap I left for him in the guise of a peace offering.

Cut to the image of a short, greasy haired man wearing a doctor's head mirror and a white coat, clutching at his throat, his face turning purple, froth bubbling from his mouth, falling to his knees, the remnants of a cheese bap spilling to the floor as the hand clutching it spasms in obvious agony. The camera cuts back to the present action.

BOSOM

Herr Bang Bang was only one of our many sources of information, Von Holinshed. Do you think he was your only enemy? The only person you have crossed in your reign of impotent anarchy?

VENEDICTOS

Impotent? Impotent! (He splutters for a moment) How dare you? You, who hail from a barbarous galaxy far from our civilised own, with your diabolical bikinis and desire only for dominion by force! You have no idea by what means I have assured my infamy, with what finesse I have dealt with my enemies and now, at long last, after all my cunning and guile have been tested to their very limits, I will overthrow your race of evil alien would-be overlords. You have nothing more on your side than teat weapons!

FAT TATTIES

(Her speech is stilted as though she is only just coming to grips with the alien language of English)
You wrote that book.

GLADYS

The one with your ten most ingenious (the three women look at each other and snigger) plans...

and how they failed. Spectacularly.

VENEDICTOS

How dare you, you mechanically over-endowed hags! I am working against the system, always against the system. First the idiot governments, the spies and the teenaged superheroes, and now you hyperspace harlots. It was a treatise, a demonstration of my potential, a guide for those treading the same thankless path of evil greatness as I. For from failure comes success and only from our errors will we discover...

BOSOM

(sounding very bored)
As ever, nothing but empty hyperbole and blustering rhetoric, Von Holinshed. Stand down, Professor, stand down before we bring you to your knees.

VENEDICTOS

(Venedictos looks at Bosom for a moment as though he would like to smite her with just his eyes. Then he smiles, slowly) These nipple guns are high velocity, precision poisoned dart dispensers and their venom will have your companions frothing at the mouth, clutching their agonisingly spasming guts within moments. You think I have not covered my bases, that I have left one stone unturned, one corner uninspected? More fool you, you tit-wielding tramp! I am Professor Venedictos Von Holinshed and I will NEVER be defeated by degenerate divas from outer space. You have met your match at last, you have shot your last teat blast and you have defeated your own...

The Camera cuts to Bosom and her colleagues as their bikinis fire at the Professor. It switches back to Venedictos as he is hit by their blasts, directly in his unprotected scrotum, and is thrown backwards across his unfinished robotic legs. Smoke fills the room and, as it clears, Bosom, Fat Tatties and Gladys cross the room to the incapacitated Venedictos. Gladys takes a look at his robot torso for a moment, before flicking a switch on it. The barrels retract and a sucking noise emanates from within the torso, getting louder with every passing moment. Venedictos's eyes bulge and he begins to froth at the mouth, clutching at his stomach in evident agony.

FAT TATTIES

(shaking her head)
Men. Always so disappointing. This one. Such cliché.

GLADYS

His only line of defence to his inner sanctum was a thick wooden door and a Yale lock. Yale! We had to Kegel that on the Cosmic-TideNet, it's so outdated. Not so much as a deadbolt (They all laugh as though deadbolts are a thing of comic genius). Then, there's the gloating. Pausing in his moment of triumph, rubbing our noses in it when we're pointing weapons right at him? And, as though that wasn't stupid enough, he puts a reverse switch for those poison darts things right on the front of his robot chest. Labelled too. What an idiot.

BOSOM

(shakes her head sadly)
Hoisted by your own ballbaggery, Von Holinshed, by your own ballbaggery, I say. Still, our work here is done. Let us...

Fat Tatties screams as she is hit by a laser beam. The camera flashes from her face to Venedictos who is holding something hard and silver in his hand. A phallic-looking weapon. Gladys moves to assist her fallen comrade as Bosom steps in front of both women.

VENEDICTOS

(His face is twisted in triumph) No stone unturned, I said! No. Stone. Unturned (he laughs maniacally). Did you think I wouldn't already have devised an antidote? A failsafe? Foolish uddersome wench! All it did was buy me enough time to locate my hand held death ray, which is fully operational at last!

Rays flash from Bosom's bikini guns, zapping Venedictos until he is nothing but a smouldering pile of ashes.

BOSOM

So are mine, bitch. (She wipes the sweat from her forehead and her chest, then tinkers with her still-smoking bikini)

GLADYS

They never learn, do they?

The unharmed divas tend to Fat Tatties and the camera pans over to where the pile of embers, all that remains of PROFESSOR VENEDICTOS VON HOLINSHED, still glows.

FADE OUT.

THE END

KIKI LE SHADE

The parking lot of a rundown motel, seven miles outside a nowhere town in the arse end of No-One-Cares. It was a setting. No more, no less. All the spaces were empty except for one housing an old Ford that had seen better days. Everything there had seen better days – at least you'd hope so – including the haggard looking drag queen with a cigarette bouncing back and forth between her browning fingers and that lipstick slash of a mouth, cheap black wig clinging tenaciously to her pate. Sitting on an old white plastic chair, one of those that'll bite you in the arse given half a chance, with one leg crossed over the other, her laddered tights revealing the ill-considered tattoo of a Peacock above her right ankle. She'd thought it beautiful at the time. Like so much since then, she found it ugly now.

Kiki Le Shade was not what she had been. Who was? She often wondered if any of the others had ended up in a shit heap as boringly dreadful as hers. In her heart of hearts, she wished them all dead. Every last fucking one of them. Nothing but liars, cheats, and thieves, and she'd washed her hands of them long ago but still, sometimes, she wondered where they were, what they were doing, what nasty things they'd done, what nastier things might hopefully have been done to them. It probably wasn't healthy, but she had sod all else to do. The sound of a car engine broke her vicious reverie and the drag queen sighed. It could mean only one thing; *company*. Apparently, it was that time again. She drew another cigarette from the pack in her lap, lit it from the one dying in her hand and took a deep drag from the fresh tab. She liked the idea of her lungs clogging slowly, every puff a blow against doing the right thing. It made her feel alive.

The young man pulled his cheap rental into the lot, parked it next to the Ford and killed the engine. He sat behind the wheel for a moment, as though gathering his thoughts. Kiki waited. Eventually, he emerged from the car, slowly unfolding a long, thin frame – gangly – his head smothered in a ratty grey beanie and a face overpowered by thick black spectacles. Great. A geek. He looked around him for a moment as though there were a million things to attract his attention in that godless place before seeming to realise, suddenly, that Miss Kiki Le Shade was sitting right there, in the middle of a parking bay in the middle of the parking lot, practically in front of him.

Kiki saw it all race across his face, despite those awful glasses. She waited. She always waited.

'Miss Kiki?' It had been a long time since anyone had called her that. His words were little more than a whisper. She gave him a moment. 'Kiki Le Shade? It's really you?'

Kiki forced a brittle smile to her lips and gave him a little flourish with the hand holding the smouldering cigarette.

'I'm… I'm your… I'm such a big fan.' He took a few steps closer, stopped, took a deep breath and then came a little nearer.

'There's no need to be shy, darling. I'll only bite if you ask me nice.' Was that her voice? She hadn't spoken out loud in a while and she wondered if her eyes had widened as much as his at the harsh sound of it. Anyone who had ever heard her sing would have been surprised too. On consideration, Kiki wasn't so shocked. That's what happened when you smoked three packs of cigarettes a day and gargled with bourbon for a pick me up.

'I've wanted to meet you for so long… I mean I admire your work, Miss Le Shade. I've studied you over and over.' Was it her imagination, or were those compliments loaded with something else, something less than flattering? She couldn't quite pick it up; her sense of smell had been the victim of too much Charlie a long time ago now, but she was no fool.

'Well, there's no accounting for taste, chickadee.' She watched him. His glasses worked well to obscure his eyes but he was working hard not to make eye contact with her anyway.

'Oh no… you were the best?' Kiki wondered if that was a question. His intonation suggested it was, but as he hurried on with his no doubt rehearsed sycophancy, she decided she would indulge him. Why not? She didn't have anything else to do. 'The thought of you kept me going through some of the worst times in my life, but I'm never going to be like you. I'm definitely never going to be like you.'

If Kiki hadn't just taken a big drag on her cigarette, she might have wasted a belly laugh on that – or choked on it. Be like her? Look at her! She was a banged up remnant, little more than a cut off... or was he taking the piss? She had a suspicion he was. Either those were rose-tinted glasses the boy was wearing or he had a ball ache of bile stored up inside him. Why though? Kiki wasn't sure she cared. She just wanted this over with.

'So, existential crisis is it? I've seen a few of those and they either kill you or make you stronger, no T no shade, honey.' She chuckled, smoke billowing out of her nose in long white streaks. The boy looked down at his scuffed hi tops – hi tops, for fuck's sake! What self-respecting queen wore broke-arse, no name hi-tops? No wonder he didn't think he'd ever be like her – she'd been a star! A STAR! This kid screamed Emo nerd reject and the beaten down hunch he'd adopted made her furious suddenly. He screamed submissive, rolling over for the Grande Dame at the slightest challenge. 'What do you want me to do about it, kid? Huh? Look around you; this place ain't nothing but a gateway to the slop bucket of the Underworld. Does it look like the place to find an answer? Any answers? Stop wasting my time if you don't even got the balls to ask the questions.'

'I don't know where to start, how to do this.' Kiki took another drag on her cigarette, the fury rushing out of her as suddenly as it had come at the boy's hopeless tone. There was no point in her anger, not much point in anything. Least she could do was help him out. It would get things moving along. She might not believe in hurrying these days, her old bones didn't like to be rushed, but there was already enough stagnation and hopelessness around to start a war. This no clue kid didn't need to add to it.

'Well, I suppose you want to hear it, my story I mean.' The boy nodded, although more reluctantly than Kiki would have liked. She'd been a star once, bright and vibrant, streaking across the firmament of club land and beyond like a meteoric fireball. There had been theatres and television, the chat show and the game show, the sitcom and the telethons. It had been glorious, her headiest days. Yet, here, now, she wasn't sure if she even missed them. How had it all come to this? That's what they came to ask. Once it had been hundreds, then it had steadily reduced to a steady trickle, but now it was just the odd one or two, now and then, and they all wanted to know the same damned thing, still. They all wanted to know how this had happened to Kiki Le Shade. How the once oh so mighty had fallen and what they could learn from it, from her. She hated every single tedious one of them. She wasn't a learning curve. She wished she could just slap each one back to whatever turd poke town they came from. Saving them from themselves, that's what she'd be doing – and maybe she would save her soul in the process.

Ha! Now that *was* funny. Her soul. She still had the gags.

The least she could do was make it easy for him. In the end, she always took a modicum of pity on them, couldn't seem to help herself. It didn't cost her anything and she was getting too old for this bantering shit anyway. 'Well, draw up a chair,' she gestured to an old wooden box laying in the gutter, 'and I'll begin.'

Kurt watched as his father told him the glorious story of his life. It was heavily edited, the bits concerning him taken right out. He wondered if Kiki even remembered he had a son. Oh, it was a rollercoaster all right, a veritable saga of extravaganza eleganza, but it was reconstituted bullshit. No truth, not as far as he was concerned. He didn't even mention a son. No culpability, no regret, just one Kiki glory tale after another. It made him sick to the stomach, but he was long past sad.

He should have known Kiki would be a coward.

It was the main thing he'd inherited from him. That and his appetite.

'And that's how I ended up in this godforsaken fleapit. At least, I think it is. I'm still to this day punch drunk from the fall, I guess.' He laughed that deep croaking sound again. Kurt stared at him. 'I know, I know, appalling, I know, but them's the breaks, kid. Life's a callous bitch and it will fuck you without a please, thank you, or how'd you do. The mighty fall, the small-minded rejoice, another rises, and the circle begins again.'

Kurt stared at his father's face, at the smeared lipstick and the thick layer of foundation, at the powder and the scrawled on eyeliner. One false eyelash was coming away from the edge of his right eye and it made him want to howl in frustration. What had he been looking for anyway? An apology? A reason? A miracle? He was an idiot. Hadn't he been beaten, kicked, punched long and hard enough to know how true that was? In those early days it had been tough, but he'd learned.

Oh, how he had learned.

Now, watching this broken down has-been relive his halcyon, and not so halcyon, days, he was angry. He'd had enough.

'Kiki, do you remember Elspeth?'

His father's head shot straight up and for the first time since Kurt had arrived in the parking lot, he saw fire in the older man's eyes. His anger strengthened when he saw that fire doused by suspicion and then evasion.

'No.' A simple answer. The wrong answer.

'You don't remember my mother?'

The reaction was swift.

Kiki stood up so fast the plastic chair flew backwards with a hollow crash. The ash from her half smoked cigarette flew into Kurt's face, a sudden breeze coming from who knew where. The crimson lips curled backwards into a snarl, the wig almost dislodged.

'You shouldn't have come here. You were told.' Oh yes, he'd been told. Kurt had one thing from his father, one thing, and that was the note telling him never to come find him, to never ask for answers to the questions he would inevitably have, that anyone would.

'Funnily enough, dear old Dad, I don't give a rat's arse what you told me. I'm your son.'

'Ha! You say that like it's a rare thing. There are probably hundreds of you, you stupid boy. I left you that letter to try to protect you, to keep you away. Elspeth was different. I made promises, fought so hard... but it ended the same way it always does. I was doing you a favour. I've tried so many times but balls or birds get the better of you boys every time. Do you know what you are? What I am?'

Did Kurt know? Did he really know?

Seven years old and pinned to the floor by a boy twice his size in an unfair fight for his small scratch of lunch money. His glasses in the boy's hand, the shocked expression on the kid's face. The boy stared down at him, looking closer and closer until... the taste of blood was the first thing Kurt remembered after that, spitting the boy's nose out of his mouth the second. The urge to chew it and swallow it had pounded through him. He was so hungry. He should, he must, had to, chow down on it, savour the taste, slap his gums and dream of more. His stomach gurgled in anticipation but the screams coming from behind him, the woman with the dark hole of a mouth running towards him, her eyes bulging, had made him spit it out. The punishment he'd received, on top of the beating the now noseless kid had already dished out, had persuaded Kurt that his appetite needed to be kept private, that he needed to find a better way to ease the cravings so it never happened again.

He'd been surprised when, a few weeks later, a teacher at his new school had allowed him to look after the science class gerbil. He didn't think it would last long. He'd been right.

There'd been other incidents, of course. He'd killed a girlfriend during sex once, when the hunger had got the better of him. She'd come to his place after swimming practice. The taste of chlorine had made him heave the blood he'd drunk back out onto the floorboards. He'd cleared out of there pretty quick after that, leaving her mangled mess as far behind him as he could and, since then, had avoided sex at all costs, despite his urges (his hot desperate urges). The little boy in the back yard of a crackhead neighbour's house three years later had been the worst. He'd started crying quietly before Kurt had even picked him up, as though he'd known his fate and been resigned to it. That had spooked him and the taste of the boy's tears had haunted him so badly that he'd not touched another person for nearly a year afterwards.

While he couldn't remember them all, he remembered their tastes. Every one. Never greedy, he'd only been careless when the hunger had escaped his control and led him by the gut and teeth. All things considered, he thought he'd done fairly well considering he'd had no guidance, no one to explain to him why he was like he was – *what* he was. He'd generally been met with censure and hostility from others, had always been aware of their instinctive fear towards him. Yet he could charm the birds out of the trees when he had a mind to. It had got him out of some tight scrapes. He knew where he got that from, had known it the first time he'd seen his father on television. Miss Kiki Le Shade, everyone's favourite auntie Drag. He knew why the older man had taken that route, plastering his face with thick make up, covering his pate with wigs, dizzying onlookers with sequins and glitter. A mask. To hide what he truly was, but hiding it in plain sight. Clever. Kurt knew all about hiding. Despite himself, he'd almost wished he could be like him – effervescent, loved – but the modicum of charm he possessed and the flamboyant joie de vivre Kiki Le Shade radiated were two very different things.

Kurt hadn't expected the boy. The bar was busy and he'd been working flat out all evening, thanklessly dodging the big city boys and their high-flying skirts. He liked to keep a low profile; he didn't actively avoid people, that always seemed to be an invitation for intervention, but he'd learned to give just enough of himself to keep folk off his back. Ask me no questions, sir, and I will tell you no lies.

Vanilla and sweet cinnamon, he had smelled him before he'd seen him. His loins had tightened and his stomach rumbled. Turning, his tray full to groaning, the red hair had caught his eye first. Fire with ice cold white beneath it, his eyes the frostiest things he'd ever seen. Eyes like his. He was staring back at him and suddenly he felt all fingers and thumbs, blushing at having been caught, having been seen. Really seen. The boy scrunched his nose at him and smiled. He knew what he was. He could taste the recognition in the air.

It frightened him but Kurt wanted him. Wanted him like nothing on earth. He'd taught himself not to but there he was, all scarlet temptation and lush seduction. He hadn't needed to say a word; he was his already, just from that one look. Ready to dash himself on the rocks before he'd even been asked to make a sacrifice.

The crowd had taken him away, blocked his view. Realising he'd been straining to find him again, Kurt checked about him to see if he'd attracted attention. Of course he hadn't. Why would he? He was just a busboy, a nobody, nothing. He took his load back to the kitchen. When he went back out into the bar, the boy's scent had weakened. He knew he'd gone. Disappointment was like day old ashes in his mouth. He had been as close to perfection as he'd ever get, he knew that, and now it was gone. Still, at least he'd had a glimpse. That would be enough to fill his dreams for a while. It was more than he had ever dared hope for.

Finishing work that night, he'd pulled up his collar (out of habit rather than necessity), hefted his duffle bag onto his shoulder, and headed out onto the streets via the back door. He got two steps. Stopped. Vanilla and sweet cinnamon. Turning, he'd met those icy white eyes, glowing in the dark.

'Take your mask off, sweet thing.' His voice was cold honey.

'I'm not wearing a mask.'

'We all wear masks, even the humans. Take the glasses off and come to me. I know you. I see what you are.' The boy slipped out of his coat, his naked body untouched by the cold of the night. Kurt hadn't been with anyone for such a long time, and never with one of his own kind, whatever that was. His cock had been rock hard behind his fly – if he was honest, it had been that way ever since he'd picked up his scent in the bar earlier. He went to him and, if he'd known what one was, it would have been like coming home.

He said his name was Mimsy, although he shortened it to Mim. 'Like the borogoves,' he'd said. Kurt didn't get the joke, but he laughed anyway. He was intoxicated. He could think of nothing but him, but the boy was restless, he wanted more. Mim seemed to want something from him, expect something – but he could never work out what it was. He didn't know how to ask him. What did he know about relationships? About people? He tried everything to keep him happy, exhausting himself as he did everything to keep him charmed, but Mim saw through it, saw through him and, as the weeks then months passed, he could smell the disappointment on him, stronger every day. He wasn't the only one. He felt increasingly impotent, powerless over his own life, just as he always had. Mim hadn't told him much about their kind and Kurt had come to the conclusion he knew almost as little as he did. Despite all that, he still wanted to please him, even after they could barely stand to look at each other. So when he'd seen an old re-run of one of his father's shows on the television, he'd pointed him out to him, revealed the truth. Excitement had practically steamed out of Mim like one of those old school trains. It had been instant and it had frightened him like nothing else. He'd glowed with it and the world had tilted.

'Kiki Le Shade is your fucking father?' Kurt nodded, steeling himself for a fan attack; it had happened once or twice but not for a long time. He rarely let people into his business. 'Jesus, Kurt, why didn't you say? Do you know what this means?' He hadn't known, couldn't have known. Mimsy clapped his hands and jumped up from the sofa. 'It means everything! E-V-E-R-Y-T-H-I-N-G!'

That was when he had finally revealed what he knew of their kind. It wasn't much but he wolfed every scrap down, so hungry was he for knowledge and so eager to please his boy – that more than anything. Talk of killing his father and reviving the clan was heady stuff. Empowerment, leadership, family, they were all buzzwords of a world in which he'd never had a part. As Mimsy spoke, Kurt watched the flush of his cheeks and the rapid rise and fall of his chest as he whipped himself into a frenzy. The tightening in his groin had grown with each word that crossed those cherry lips. It was their way, he'd said. He had to prove himself against his father and then the others would come. They would come. There hadn't been a clan gathering for a hundred years. He was sure they would come. His words had a desperate edge to them that Kurt found unsettling. He wasn't sure, after all this time, that he wanted any part of a clan, but he had been pretty keen on the way Mim had gone down on him after that. He didn't want anything to do with his father, but how much of a problem would it be to do away with a washed up old fairy living, if the rumours were true, in the middle of Nowheresville? With Mimsy's lips around his cock, he'd decided it wouldn't be too hard at all.

It had just happened. He hadn't expected it, wanted it, but it had happened anyway. He'd looked down at the mess of body in his arms and wept. Mimsy's cold white eyes were even colder in death, their blankness an accusation. The hunger had struck him the moment he'd thrust himself inside him, his eager warmth too much for him on top of all that talk of power and strength, his control weakened by his relief at Mim's reawakened desire for him. His lover's pale skin was peppered with finger marks, *his* finger marks, bruises marking his love, betraying his crime. The ones around his neck were worst; where the teeth marks didn't break them up at least. Anger welled up inside him, spilling out, radiating from his skin, his sinew, turning him into a walking bomb. He wanted to scream, to rage at the unfairness of it all and to tear the world to pieces but, just as he thought his blood would boil with fury, he found clarity instead; a purpose. He would do it for Mim. He would make his final wish come true. He would see his father. He would make his mark on their world. He would do it for his one true love, felt as though the lifeless body in his arms was crying out for him to do it. He felt it in his bones, tasted it in the congealing blood as he fed on Mim's dying flesh. It wasn't his fault, not his fault, not his. It was Kiki's fault, fucking Kiki Le Shade who had killed his mother, abandoned him, and left him to fend for himself. All those bodies in the past, the one in his arms now? They were all his doing. Clan or no clan, Kurt would make sure the bastard paid if it was the last thing he did.

'I knew you'd come one day. They always do, but I hoped you'd be different. Smarter. Maybe that's why I'm still waiting.' Casually, although she knew the boy who thought he was a man would see her hands shaking, she bent over and picked up the cigarette packet that had fallen to the floor, pulled out another, and lit it from the butt of the current one. She flicked that to the kerb, took a big puff on the new one, and expelled the smoke like a gaudy old dragon. It felt like such a long time since the last one had come, an age. She wondered if she was in shape for this, but as she rolled her neck a couple of times, she felt it there, just beneath the surface, always ready, always waiting. It surprised her, the strength spiralling down her neck like so much heat. Her hunger was rising and it felt good. Certain. Little in life was that.

'Do you want to see my face, Father?' His voice was all defiance, all anger and hand jacked ego. Good. She liked them cocky, even if they were pretending. This one was. So much tastier when they were scared and righteous, she thought, licking her lips at the prospect.

She grinned then, ripping her wig from her head and freeing the scaly crusts of her pate to sparkle in the yellowing light of the sickly streetlamp. Let the boy see what it was he'd really come asking for.

'You boys, you always think arrogance and spunk make a man, but you've no idea. Not one bit. This isn't a mask because I don't need to hide. This is the real me. I was born into a world of clans and teeth and death but I ran from it. I knew who I truly was and I ran so hard and so fast from what they tried to make me. Who's been filling your head with stories? Some little tart with an eye on my kingdom? Ha! Foolish, always so fucking foolish. I don't have a kingdom, not one like they wish I had. I only have my heart and my backbone. That's all I need. Can you say the same, boy? Can you say the same?'

The boy flew at him then, the screech that ripped the air full of hate and frustration. Didn't he know it only fuelled her, made her stronger? Fury pumped their kind's blood, whetted their appetite, nourished them. Kiki bared her teeth, saliva dripping from elongating canines; she was ready. She was always ready.

There was little left of the boy's body. In some ways it was sad. Why couldn't they ever be happy with being what they were these days? Why did they always have to have their eye on the main chance? It felt like she had always been alone, even when she'd been famous and everyone had loved her. She had known it couldn't last and, if she was honest, she had been happy when she'd blown all her money and ended up back in the motel where her mother had birthed her. She'd died when Kiki had been six years old, died of the fever that wiped out half of their people in the eighties. Her father had been long dead before that, a sacrifice to her mother's Alpha appetite. She'd been alone too; didn't they get that? No one had told her jack either. No one had been there to wipe her arse, pick her up when she fell, tell her why she craved the taste of blood so damned much, or why her teeth lengthened and her muscles spasmed at the faintest smell of it. No one had explained to her why she could never get enough sex, why she'd do it with anyone, anytime. She'd known nothing about being an Alpha and yet they all expected her to have the answers.

Well, fuck them, fuck her, and fuck it all.

She wiped her mouth and sat back down on her plastic chair. She lit another cigarette, made a vague effort to straighten her wig, and began the wait again.

THE CITY IS OF NIGHT, BUT NOT OF SLEEP

As the two suns sank slowly below the horizon, the light in the city did not change. Kiet watched them go.

She laughed.

It was never dark in the city, she knew that much. When the suns went down, its inexplicable lighting system – oh, how *he* had tried to figure out how it worked, over and over, ad infinitum – kicked in and every corner was lit up.

Darkness.

Close your eyes, remember.

She couldn't remember. Couldn't remember the last time she had slept, couldn't remember what darkness was like. She could only laugh, laugh until she started to cry and her stomach cramped sharply. How she wanted to remember, was desperate for the memory.

It was all so pathetic.

The last act of a dying race.

They had come so far and this is what they had found.

Light. That was what they had sought, the light of hope to be precise. The Fathers had sent searchers out into the dark ocean of night in a futile attempt to find something, someone, anything. Well, they had certainly found light; yards, hours, tonnes, miles of the stuff. It was everywhere, never-ending, always light.

Always. Light.

'What are you doing?' *His* voice. How she hated the sound of it. She hadn't heard him creep up on her again, even though the city was empty, silent, so taken had she been with the search for a morsel of sensory memory that wasn't suffused with light. Kiet turned, no longer bothering to hide the sneer that came to her face whenever he was near.

'What do you care?'

'There are things to do.'

That only made her start laughing again. She laughed as the

94

flat of his hand made stinging contact with her cheek, laughed even as he followed it with a more solid sounding fist.

Sand.

Kiet dreamed of sand and of darkness.

It whispered to her, soothed her as it sang to her of a place beyond, a land where she would be free of this pain…

Pain… searing pain ripped through her dream, bringing her back to her senses, what was left of them.

She hadn't been asleep. She was on the floor. Again.

Kiet groaned.

She hauled herself up, gripping the sides of a shelving unit with shaking hands. Her throbbing ribs made breathing all but impossible, but she refused to give in to the pain. She fed on it instead, fuelling herself with an emotion she had rarely felt before they had stumbled upon the city. Anger. Hot, boiling fury at her impotence, at being trapped here, at being trapped here with *him*. She could take the punches, the kicks, the insults, but the idea of being here with him for the rest of her life while outside was… no. No. No.

The ship might be a write off, the sand had claimed it days ago, but she didn't have to stay here with him, she could…

Leave the city, go outside. Into the sand.

Close your eyes and remember the darkness beyond the sand.

Kiet shook her head. Her hair was longer than it had ever been and it tickled her cheeks as it brushed across them. She smiled.

The sand would save her.

From him. From the city.

The city was a house of lies. It offered hope, but it contained none. Its bright corners and lack of shadows made it appear like a beacon –they'd checked and re-checked the instruments as it had become steadily stronger, never really believing they would find anything – but it was a tomb. She'd known it for what it was the minute they had stepped off the escape pod. They'd been forced to evacuate the Fathership when the instruments had suddenly stopped functioning after entry into the planet's atmosphere. The ship had power but they'd been unable to access it. Brix had tried everything

– *so* he *said* – but the ship, the pinnacle of their race's engineering, had been shut down just like that. They had become impotent in a matter of moments, unable even to help the rest of the crew who had been trapped in their hibernation berths. The escape pod had been their only way off the ship. They had watched from the bright city as the craft had finally lost altitude and crashed into the deserts beyond. One week ago. One long, mostly sleepless week. No time at all, but now she wished she'd stayed on board and shared their fate. Out there in the darkness. Where she belongs.

It wants her. Needs her. It will protect her; she feels the truth of it inside her, in those same veins that are hot with anger towards *him*, the one that keeps her here.

Her husband. Brix.

That bastard.

The cant that gave life to the Fathers of the Patriarchy's familiar hypocrisy rang in her head, reminding her it was her duty to submit to her husband in all things. It throbbed around in there, buzzing at her, trying to pull her back but she was a lost cause, however much they might have wished it otherwise. She had swallowed their dogma for too long, had been cowed by it like all the others, but now she laughed because they were probably all dead. Dead and gone. When she walked out into the sand and met the darkness, she would curse the Fathers Twelve and sing only of the Mother True. The poor betrayed Mother whose only crime was to love her child. Kiet had hated the stories vilifying her, the ones celebrating instead the Father Fierce who had taken his son and taught him to be a cold calculating warrior with his brothers, never to see his mother again. A mother's love crushed, a reminder that a woman's function was to produce children, not to nurture them. Her people were not supposed to believe in love. Her mother had been different. She was probably dead now too.

The sand will love you. The voice again.

Don't let him keep you in here. The darkness will embrace you, love you.

She knew it was true.

The heavy piping was difficult to lift, but as it crashed into the back of Brix's skull, Kiet knew she had chosen well. There was no getting up from that. He wasn't dead – yet – she could still see the shallow rise and fall of his breathing, but he wasn't about to wake up either. The dent in his head would have been sickening had it not signalled an act of liberation. Her liberation. The grunt he'd made on impact was like a symphony to her ears, the ringing of the metal hitting the floor as she dropped the pipe an exultant anthem. She grinned, Cheshire cat glee. She had her ticket to the place beyond the sand.

Once outside, it was easy, right. With no one to stop her, Kiet laughed as she ploughed through the sand dunes, fuelled by the truest happiness she had ever known. As she walked, euphoric, she felt the wind beat against her skin and then the sand, whipping her, ripping into her. She felt no pain as it pummelled her, deconstructing her, the stuff that bound her caressed into the sweetest oblivion. It communed with her then, the sand, binding itself with the very essence of her, making her its own, making them one.

There was no one to hear as once-Kiet cried out with bliss at the final moment, the echo bouncing across the deserts, meeting the two suns as they rose.

As Brix came round, his head foggy, he heard it. Someone was whispering. The crazy bitch was probably waiting to finish the job. He knew she'd had some vaguely radical ideas, but she'd never been anything other than submissive back home. Once they had come across the beacon, however, she had become unreachable, obsessed with, of all things, sand, of feeling it once more between her toes, scratching against her skin. Over and over she would whisper about it when she thought he couldn't hear, a litany of madness that hadn't worried him. He didn't need her to be sane, he needed her to be fertile. The whispering had eventually driven him to distraction and he'd been forced to correct her. It was the way of their people, but he'd barely had to touch her like that at home. When he'd found the life support of their sleeping crew had malfunctioned, killing them all, he'd never once suspected Kiet, but since being in the city he had begun to wonder. More than wonder. Suspect. The beacon had changed something in her, and it wasn't something good.

Murderous bitch.

Brix tried to shake his head but the pain was immense. He almost blacked out but – *stay awake, find her* – managed to hang on to consciousness. He needed to find her. He needed to put an end to this somehow – *kill her!* – He needed to find the wreckage of the Fathership, to find the truth.

She did it! She did it on purpose, killed the last of you, and she would have murdered you too.

The voice in his head was more than just the effect of the blow he'd received. He had thought it was a dream at first, days ago, but he'd not been able to sleep long enough to dream. It was louder now than ever and he knew what it was. The voice of the sand. Just like Kiet had said.

Touching the back of his head gingerly, he felt the sticky blood still warm against his fingertips. When he saw the scarlet smeared on his fingers, he felt something inside him slip, something dark. Fathers, he was going to kill that bitch of his when he found her.

Bitch! Yes. Come!

God, it was so loud now, thumping in his ears, over and over, like a death knell. Kiet's death knell.

She's here, waiting.

Oh was she? Well, it was time to show her how the Fifth Law of the Fathers should be enforced.

Hurry.

He staggered to his feet, his eyes still blurry, and stumbled along the corridor in the direction of the doors they had entered the city by on that first day. At last, he stepped outside and into the sand.

The city had sat in the middle of the desert for more than a thousand years. Empty, but never alone, it waited. It served the sand and the darkness beyond. It fed it with violence, morsels of anger and fury. Despite the light, it was of night but not of sleep.

EMMELINA IN LOVE

Emmelina sat cross-legged on the box, her face scrunched in concentration as she knitted. It was going to be a scarf, probably not a good one, but it was meant for her soon-to-be lover and it's the thought that counts. She jumped a little in between stitches as the thumping from the box continued. It wasn't a huge box, that was the point, but, while every defiant strike of its innards was a disturbance, Emmelina continued to knit. She was dogged like that.

Soon enough the banging petered out. The shouting turned into mournful begging, then descended into a soft litany of quiet pleas, and still she knitted.

'Please, Emmy, let me out. Please.' His voice was tired, breaking in places like the inevitable holes that already punctuated her burgeoning scarf.

Emmelina kept right on knitting.

The cursing was a bit unnecessary, she thought, but she understood his sudden burst of energy. One last hurrah. It must be hard, she couldn't imagine doing it herself, but sacrifices are never easy and she would not diminish his by giving up too soon.

Click clack went her knitting needles.

When Emmelina couldn't remember when she'd last heard or felt anything, she decided it was time. Cautiously – she wasn't an idiot – she put down her knitting and slid off the box. She bent and pressed her ear to the wood, listening for any signs of life. When she was satisfied there were none, she opened the box.

Emmelina smiled.

A KICK IN THE HEAD

The knife was hot and sticky in her palm but no matter how much it made her want to heave – and thinking about what was dripping from it wasn't going to help with that – Maxxie Vickers refused to drop it. Even as the car screeched to a stop in front of her, and she could have sworn her heart stopped with it, she held on. That once vital organ became a static lump in her chest and it felt as though it wanted to choke her but she held her ground. If she was finished then these motherlickers were going down with her. All she'd wanted to do was earn a little extra money to pay for new veneers and now here she was, dead body at her feet, blood splattered all over her favourite dress and a carful of cropped haired trouble heading in her direction. Life was holy Kar's soiled bitch.

Mr Mo had offered her the job that morning. He always asked and she always turned him down, but since Lover Boy had sticky-fingered her rent money last month and spent the lot on junk, her resistance had all but disappeared and she figured she might as well do it. She didn't have much else to lose. The irony of that was not lost as she waited for the goons to get out of the car. Mr Mo ran his operation from the back of the club she danced in. She'd been taking extra shifts cleaning in the mornings to help pay for her new teeth but she knew she was never going to make enough to cover the rent too. It wasn't vanity that was driving her; it was the hole where several of her bottom teeth should have been. Lanky Lottie Stilts, the circus act freak show that went on after her every night, who somehow made enough in tips to rent a penthouse overlooking the river and a boob job every couple years, had whacked her in the face with one of her extra legs two weeks ago and Maxxie had been spitting blood for days. Swung the right way, those legs were a lethal fucking weapon. She'd tried to get her to cough up for the dental treatment she needed, but Lottie was blowing Big Curly three times a week and, as it was his club, what he said went. So Maxxie had been reduced to cleaning up puke and mopping out the toilets in a dive that was barely palatable front of house. The departure lounge, as Big Curly called it (and didn't he laugh like an A-class jackass every time he said it), was a lower circle of hell. So when Mr Mo had made his offer that morning as per, she'd accepted. It wouldn't do any harm to step over the line just a little, she'd thought, just this once.

Just this once.

Were there three other words that could get you into trouble faster than you could spit? Right now, Maxxie didn't think so. At this point, amnesia would be a Kar-send. She wanted to forget all about the package. She wished she'd never had anything to do with any of it but, like they said, if wishes were horses…

'Maxxie, you're a good girl, you're making an old man very happy.'

'Yeah, you said that already, Mr Mo. Now spill, what've you got for me.'

'So young, so impatient.' Mr Mo laughed. 'Well, it's easy peas. You got to make sure the package makes the train.'

'Is that some sort of code?' Mr Mo laughed again at that. His mouth was ridiculously large considering how small his head was. It was made even more incongruous by virtue of every tooth in it being gold. Rather than putting her off, it made Maxxie want part of the action everyone else seemed to be making good on. She needed new teeth too.

'No, little Maxxie flower, it's as simple as it sounds. I have a package – now that is code, in this case it means a personage – and that package needs to catch a train out of this shit hole at quarter to three this afternoon. Central Station. Platform five. Some folks will be waiting to take it off your hands. Up to it?'

'Sounds easy enough. Sure, why not?'

'Excellent.' Mr Mo whistled and nearly seven foot of meathead came barrelling through the door to his office. 'Get the boy, Gerard, and try not to break anything this time.'

The urchin Gerard the Lug brought in, although dragged

might be a better word, was way younger than Maxxie had expected. Kid couldn't have been more than eight or nine years old and he was cradling a plastered arm. Gerard had obviously been clumsy. She looked at him for a moment, then back at Mr Mo.

'This the package?'

'Certainly is.'

'He's just a kid.'

'He's a package. Can you handle it or not, Maxxie my love? Don't waste Mr Mo's time, sweet baby.'

The kid just stood there staring straight ahead. Something about him gave Maxxie the creeps but, at the same time, was oddly familiar. She looked at him for a minute. He didn't blink, not even once. Finally, thinking about those veneers, eyes on the prize, Maxxie shrugged and smiled at Mr Mo.

'Okay, I'll do it. He's not my kid.'

'Excellent. Boy? Boy!' The kid finally blinked and turned his head in Mr Mo's direction. 'You go with Maxxie here. She takes you to lunch then gets you to the train station. Do as she says and your old bitch won't have to pull your teeth out of your arse. We good?'

The kid nodded. Maxxie wondered who the kid's bitch could possibly be. He didn't look at all likely to have *bitches.*

Mr Mo went to his desk, pulled open a drawer and took out a wedge of cash. He handed it to Maxxie, who thought she might pass out from the sheer amount of dough he was giving her.

'Take what you need to feed the kid, get him to the station and buy his ticket. Keep the rest.'

'That's a lot of money, I can't …'

'It might not look much but this package is important. Some real ugly people are waiting for delivery and I can't have it fucked up. I give you plenty of money, you get the job done without so much as a flinch, right? That's the way I like it. Now go. And don't forget the package.'

'Okay, no problem.' Maxxie headed for the door, grabbing the boy's good arm as she went. He complied without hesitation. Somehow that bothered her more than if he'd put up a struggle.

'And Maxxie?'

She turned to look at Mr Mo once more. 'Yes?'

'You fuck this up and I'm going to enjoy beating more than just what's left of your teeth out of you. We good?' Maxxie swallowed hard, and then forced a bright smile to her lips.

'Of course, Mr Mo. Don't worry about a thing.'

Ha! Don't worry about a thing? She was currently drowning in some deeply vexing shit. Maxxie watched the buzzcuts get out of the car. There were only two of them. Mr Mo obviously didn't think she was going to put up much of a fight. She suddenly remembered clearly when Winnie Fango, the fish-faced fan dancer with a bad attitude and three eyes, had tried to steal a couple of bottles of hooch from Mr Mo's hooky stash. He'd put six thugs on her, to 'set an example'. He'd kept one of her flippers and was reportedly planning to get it stuffed. Mr Mo liked a souvenir almost as much as his heavies liked to shoot the shit.

As she watched the goons approach, Maxxie flexed her grip on the slick knife. It was slippery but she couldn't hold it too tightly, she needed to be able to slice from any direction and stiff knuckles would slow her down. She loosened her stance, ready to roll should the need arise. She hadn't grown up on the wrong side of the Harbour tracks for nothing. Her mother, Kar and his Siblings rest her lecherous drunken soul, had made sure she could take care of herself on the streets of the city. After all, she'd only been a little older than the boy when she'd first been sent out to work them. She had learned her lessons well. If only old Mother Vickers had taught her what to do when deals with someone like Mr Mo went tits up; she could have done with some sage advice to draw on right about then.

'Evening Maxxie. Mr Mo sends his regards.' Gerard the Lug, breaker of little boys' arms, was grinning like the Empress had just sent him a telegram. Quel homme.

'Hey Gerry. I'd say it's nice to see you, but it's not.'

'Yeah, whatever. Don't matter how smart your mouth is,

you been really stupid. Time to pay the piper, the boss says, but first hand over the boy.'

Sitting in a corner booth at the Mighty Gerund Laundrette and Diner on the corner of Trotter and Campus, Maxxie watched the boy eat. He clearly wasn't normal, not even for that messed up town. She didn't know if it was nature or nurture but either way he sure could eat. Kid had barely come up for breath as he'd ploughed through a triple helping of Sea Egg omelette and toast. He was sweating by the time he finished – which was exactly three minutes after it had been set down in front of him. If she hadn't seen it for herself, she'd never have believed it.

'Where you from, kid?' The boy just sat and stared at his now empty plate. 'Not a big talker, huh? Well, me either usually but seems like you got my jaw all loose. Do you want anything else?' The nod was unexpected. The kid must have hollow legs. 'Same again?' He shook his head this time, grabbed the menu and pointed at another dish. He held up three fingers again, put the menu down and settled back into the cracked plastic upholstery. Maxxie sighed, waved for the waitress, who took her own sweet time to grace them with her presence, and made the order. The waitress raised her eyes onto her forehead in surprise. Maxxie shrugged, the waitress answered with one of her own, her eyes settling back into their sockets, and she went off to holler at the short order cook. The kid just sat there, still staring at the empty plate the waitress hadn't bothered to pick up.

Maxxie tried to focus on the money and not let the weird kid bother her. When the waitress delivered the next heap of food, the kid just dived right in, barely letting the plate hit the table and it was gone in not much more than the blink of an eye. When Maxxie asked him if he wanted anymore, she was joking.

'What, really?' She stared at the boy, watched him nod again, and wondered what the fuck was sitting in front of her. Growing lad he may be, but the kid was eating like a stoned pro-wrestler and he was barely five feet tall. He was scrawny too, his clothes were threadbare in places and she doubted if his hair had seen a comb recently. Maxxie sighed. Poor kid. His life was hardly going to get any better. She wasn't stupid enough to believe she'd be handing him over to his guardian angels at the station. Still, she needed those veneers and if that was what it took to get them then that was what she'd do. Besides, nobody had ever felt sorry for her. No one in Fable City was innocent. No one.

'If you eat anymore, kid, you'll explode.'

'Won't.' Maxxie was so surprised she jumped.

'Jeepers, kid, give me a heart attack why don't you?'

'Won't explode. Need food. Make strong.' So he could speak, but he was hardly Hozzamun Harshtongue, Wit of the Seven Cities. Maxxie looked at him for a long moment.

'Do you really want more?' He nodded. 'Okay then.' She signalled for the waitress who came over with their bill. When Maxxie ordered yet more food the other woman looked at her like she was crazy.

'If the kid pukes on the floor, it's gonna cost ya.'

'Yeah, yeah, whatever, just fetch the kid his eats.'

Three platefuls later and the boy was flushed but smiling.

'You done?' Maxxie almost giggled when he grinned at her and nodded. Giggled. Maxxie Vickers did not giggle. Was she letting him get to her? She focussed on her teeth. She needed those teeth and this kid was going to pay for them. 'Right then, get your stuff. We need to get gone.'

The walk to the station was easy. It was what happened once they got inside that turned the day to cock. The kid was fine, following Maxxie without a word. She didn't even feel like she needed to hold onto him and it irritated her that he was so fucking compliant. This wasn't a city that bred trust in its young and she found herself worrying about his future. She was fairly bristling with it as they headed towards the ticket booth and, just before they had reached the back of the queue, it happened.

The Kick.

Her cycle had always been regular; she wasn't prone like

her mother was to it, coming on with any and all strong emotions. She'd had episodes no more than three times a year for as long as she could remember and then only when the Moon was on the wane. Yet as they walked across the marble floor, her high heels clicking, his battered sneakers scuffing, Maxxie felt the familiar thrill lick up her spine like a sizzling hot fudge sundae. Thick, sensual, forbidden.

She tried to shake it off, but the feeling intensified, tendrils of want and fury unfurling from her core, pulsing through her muscles, aching in her throat. Her mouth watered.

She needed to feed.

It was on her full throttle now. It always happened like that, a swift surge that propelled her into a world of sensation common sense had nothing to do with. It was all about instinct, want, hunger. Her innate desire to feed was the driving force now and she knew which side of her would win.

The side she wanted to win.

The side that took and never apologised.

The side that made her powerful, that made her feel as though, finally, she was the one in control. If she'd been able to see through the blood lust, she might have mused on the irony of that.

The kid was handing the money over for his ticket by the time the sweats started. Maxxie could feel the soft run of her bones as they shifted, yielded, unctuous as they metastasised. It was heaven and it was always the glorious same. She exulted in the change, revelling in the way it elevated her, swept her away from the crassness of mediocrity and into the realms of deity. By rights she should have been a goddess to the puny ordinaries all around her, they should have knelt in her presence, but more than anything they should have paid tribute so she could *feed*.

The kid swung away from the booth and stared up at Maxxie, a frown marring his almost anonymous features. He swallowed and took a step back, but Maxxie grabbed him, pulling him along behind her as she headed for platform five. Common sense was long gone, but the feeling of anger at his helplessness was stirring something inside her, something protective? No. She couldn't name it, she didn't want to, but as she swept along the platform and clocked the delectable gentlemen waiting for their shiny package, she felt a rage so deep, so effervescent, that she had no choice but to unleash it.

All things considered, the first of the three men was lucky. His severed head was bouncing along the train tracks before he even knew there was any danger. Maxxie licked her arm clean of the blood with her swollen tongue and stared at the other two, daring them to step up, to take her on. The one on the left had barely got his hand to his inside pocket, looking for whatever weapon he had concealed there, before Maxxie was on him. She ripped off his head in one go too and gulped at the jet of blood that shot from the severed neck. It was hot and warm on her face, in her mouth, and she swallowed greedily, filling her stomach with visceral goodness. By the time she had finished gorging herself, her predicament forgotten in the ecstasy of feeding, the remaining goon was gone. People were looking. Not even in this City did mid-afternoon murderous rampages in a public place go unnoticed. The boy was standing behind her, mouth agape. She couldn't blame him. He seemed to have grown in the past few minutes; his cheeks had a healthy glow and was his hair going green? Maxxie shook her head. Post feeding, her senses were on overdrive. She was imagining it.

'Come on, kid, we've got to split.' Thankfully her wings were fully powered now, and as she grabbed the boy's hand, she felt them peel away from her back, tearing her clothes, stretching, testing until finally, hummingbird strong, they propelled them both straight up into the air. This was her natural state, Maxxie thought, as they climbed into the sky, leaving the filth of the City far below them. She was strong, powerful, glorious, just as nature had intended her to be. If only it were permanent, then they could have busted that shitty joint. She could have delivered the boy safely home and gone off to make her fortune some place good, some place clean. Somewhere she wasn't just another cog in the wheel. Somewhere she could be rightfully adored.

Nearly overcome with the euphoria of her fantasies, Maxxie suddenly remembered the boy she was clutching in her arms. She had urgent matters to attend to. Using her heightened sight to scout the land below them, she forced herself back to reality. They needed a safe spot to land

The harbour.

The day was beginning to fade and there were plenty of places to hide down there. They could lay low until she figured out what to do. She knew things were royally fucked up but she was confident she could come up with a plan. This was why she loved the Kick. Even while her common sense told her she should just fly hell for leather out of there, the Kick told her she could handle whatever shit came her way. The feeble creatures below were no match for her, no match for ...

'That was my husband, you bitch.' Maxxie nearly dropped the boy when he spoke; she'd been wrapped up in getting them to safety and it wasn't like he'd been a chatterbox up until then.

'What?'

'You ate my fucking husband.'

'Your what?' She'd heard him all right, but what he said didn't make any sense. Only then did she realise how heavy he'd become. He must have tripled in size since they'd left the train station. Something was sure as shit not right.

'What doesn't make sense, Vickers? You. Ate. My. Husband. Get it now?'

'Damn it.' Maxxie swooped down towards the water, skimming the boy's legs across its surface before pulling up slightly once she'd managed to gauge his weight correctly. She pushed on a little further before setting them down behind a large container. Once her wings had settled back into place, she cautiously checked the boy over, noting with some astonishment just how swollen his belly had become.

'Now, what the fuck are you talking about and what's happening to your guts, kid? You look like you swallowed a blimp!'

'My husband was one of those guys waiting at the station.'

'What are you, nine years old? Mr Mo said ...'

'Mr Mo is a rat bastard.' Maxxie flinched in surprise. Seemed like the kid was finally letting loose. 'He likes to talk big and make out like he's a player, but he's a two-bit hoodlum who needs taking down a peg.' Maxxie was too concerned with the colour the kid's face was turning to pay much attention to what he was saying. Deep red blotches had bloomed across his cheeks and were spreading down his neck at an alarming rate. His temples were pulsing, his forehead beading with sweat and for the first time Maxxie was genuinely scared. Something was way more than wrong with the boy and she didn't like it, not one little bit.

'Holy fuck, kid, what's going on with you? You look like you're about to burst all …'

Tempting fate. Her mother had always warned her against it and she should have known better but, as the kid's head exploded, all Maxxie Vickers could think was 'shit.'

Splattered by head meat, she tried to back away, but the rending noise that punched through the air rooted her to the spot. Her mind refused to take it all in, and she'd seen some shit in her time. The kid's meat-suit split down the middle and fell to the ground, the slap of flesh and organ on the concrete floor like the sound of a hundred overripe beef tomatoes falling out of the hole in some giant's shopping bag. Maxxie gagged. If the sight hadn't got to her, the stench would have done. Doubling over, she heaved, bringing up most of the blood she'd drunk at the station. Straightening up as quickly as she could, not wanting to be more vulnerable than she had to be in a situation where she clearly had no clue what on Kar's green lands was going on, she looked to where the boy had been standing moments before. Unfolding herself from the middle of what now looked like a mad butcher's bad acid trip was a woman. A woman with sleek flippers instead of arms. It took Maxxie a couple of heartbeats, but only a couple.

'Winnie?' Winnie Fango. As she lived and breathed she could not have been more surprised if she'd tried. She hadn't been imagining the green tinge in the kid's hair after all.

'Darn pissing tootin' it's Winnie. In all that's holy, Maxxie, what the fuck is wrong with you? All you had to do was get me to the station and on that train. Mr Mo would have been none the wiser. But no, Maxxie Vickers, tart without trace of a heart, let alone an ever-loving brain, has to come along and mess the whole damned thing up.'

'Why didn't you say anything?'

'I was incubating, bitch. Honest to gods, you're thicker than molasses. The kid was a cover, not to mention a place to lick my wounds. Regeneration, y'know? It ain't just for starfish.' Winnie ran a flipper through her bright green, tightly curled hair, her eyes glistening with unshed tears, her face tight with anger. Maxxie could understand that. She could understand fuck all else, but she could understand that. 'Did you really think I'd let that greasespit Mr Mo get away with what he did to me? No fucking way. My husband and me came up with a plan to shake him down. A couple of sessions with the Meat Mages on Gardner Street and we were set. Body suit, regeneration module, call it what the fuck you like, it worked and Mr Mo thought he'd just happened to stumble across the kid the Wanger Bangers have been looking for, the one with the weird quirk or whatever. Weird is hardly unusual around here, but them Wangers have got their thing, y'know? Anyway, he figured he could trade him in for some good will. Kar knows he needs it. It all had to be kept on the down low because no one wants to let on whose in bed with who, that's no good for business, and it suited us just tickety boo. We changed the place of the meet, touch of sleight of hand here, a couple of false moves to the Wangers there, just enough to make them think Mo had traded the boy to a higher bidder, and their wrath was sure to follow; it was a perfect set up. And then, wouldn't you know it? Maxxie Vickers stomps her cheap arse in and shoots it all to hell.'

Maxxie stared at her old friend. The last she'd seen of her had been a disembodied flipper in the dumpster out back of Big Curly's place. She wasn't even sure if she was really seeing her, if this wasn't some messed up hallucination left over from the Kick. Even as she thought it, Maxxie realised how much of her strength had already gone. She was barely even tingling anymore.

'You bit his head off. Clean off. I knew there was something wrong with you, but I didn't know it was that, that you're one of *them*. Now normally, I wouldn't mess with your kind, but you bit my husband's head off and that can't stand.'

Winnie hopped gingerly out of the remains of the kid and took a step towards Maxxie, the anger on her face darkening. Her top lip curled back under the two air holes that sat just over her mouth, exposing far too many razor sharp teeth. She intended to do Maxxie harm, that much was obvious. 'I'm thinking there's some recompense coming my way and I can see you're depleted right about now. Been a busy day, hey? So, how about we say an eye for an eye?'

Hot fudge.

It sizzled along Maxxie's cerebral cortex like an old friend.

The Kick wasn't done yet.

Without thinking, she let herself react. The knife she kept in her boot was ready, as always. Lightning fast, she pulled it out and swung it up and into Fango's throat. As she pulled it out again, Winnie's eyes bulged, her mouth opening and closing spasmodically. She gargled for a few moments, blood spurting from the wound. Maxxie was destined to end this day covered in blood one way or another, she reasoned, so she stood her ground, not wanting to slip or be caught out. She licked her blood soaked chin and grinned. This might still be fun. Suddenly Winnie reached for her, sharp edged flippers snatching at the air in front of Maxxie's face, and then just as suddenly she gave up, her lifeblood easing down to a trickle as one minute she was standing, the next she was slapping down into the torn meat suit on the ground. Dead.

That's when Maxxie heard the car.

She should have known there wasn't any getting out of it. Mr Mo would have heard what had happened at the station and sent his goons out after her. He might know nothing about Winnie Fango's plan, but he knew he'd sent Maxxie on a job and that she'd fucked it up royally. He was going to get his pound of flesh.

The knife felt hot and sticky in her palm but Maxxie refused to drop it. It was all she had left now. The Kick was gone again, leaving her like a washed up addict hankering for the next fix even as she swore she'd never shoot up again. Don't worry about a thing, Mr Mo, she'd said. She almost laughed as the two buzzcuts got out of the car. She flexed her grip on the slick knife. She was ready.

'Evening Maxxie. Mr Mo sends his regards.' Gerard the Lug had a shit-eating grin plastered across his ugly face. He was clearly going to enjoy ending her days. Well, he wasn't going to get away scot-free, that was for sure.

'Hey Gerry. I'd say it's nice to see you, but it's not.'

'Yeah, whatever. Don't matter how smart your mouth is, you been really stupid. Time to pay the piper, the boss says, but first hand over the boy.'

Maxxie did laugh then. She couldn't help herself. She laughed so hard she thought something deep down inside might burst. Her chest ached and her jaw cracked. One of her teeth fell out. Wouldn't you just know it? Maxxie laughed harder.

And then it happened.

The tingle that had all but gone flared back to life, crackling through her veins like wildfire. She was suddenly burning up from the inside out; the change coming on more quickly than it had ever done before. Mind you, she'd never stood waiting to die before. Old Mother Vickers hadn't let her girl out into the world without some know-how though and she was going to get out of this. She could taste it. The power flowed through her, from her – the bright light spilling from her eyes, her mouth, punching through her skin in a million places. The buzzcuts took a couple of steps back, clearly frightened and they had good reason. The air around her pulsed with it as Maxxie tilted her head back and roared – exploding in a ball of fire and bright white light, scourging the ground, searing anything she touched. The buzzcuts were obliterated instantly. The flare could be seen all over the city; the power of it shook buildings and stirred the water into a boiling frenzy. It knocked down power cables and stopped trains right in their tracks. No one failed to hear it.

No one but Maxxie.

A CACKLING FART

The sharp, shameless staccato of a cane marked the tall man's progress along the suburban road. He swung it gleefully, tip-tapping his cares against the pavement and into the night air. Truth be told, however, he had not a one in the world. Professor Alphonso Vulpinari was a success. He was a scholar, an author, an expert, a man about town with every luxury and opportunity at his fingertips. His long red hair might well have been considered démodé on another man but it served only to lend a somewhat wolfish edge to his seemingly effortless elegance. People found him more attractive than his spare features and sharp eyes should perhaps have allowed. Maybe it was his silver tongue, the silky words he used so easily to manipulate anyone into doing anything he wanted, or maybe it was the laconic confidence with which he deflated any and all detractors. Maybe he was just one of those *special* people. Whatever it was, Alphonso took it in his stride. He took what he wanted and revelled in it. He was what he was – and those others didn't know the half of it. They never would. The cursèd fools.

On this balmy evening, he was feeling particularly chipper. As he ate up the pavement with his loping gait, ignoring the terraced houses that flanked the street, making his way home from a lecture he'd delivered to a distinguished audience of his peers – *peers*? Alphonso sniffed, he didn't have peers! – he relished the sense of accomplishment and peace he had found – no, not found; cultivated. He had achieved it all by his own hand and this was his time. He had sacrificed much for it, had turned his back on his old life and love, had fought and clawed his way to the top and he was thoroughly enjoying every moment of it, just as he had longed for and intended. He had let nothing and nobody stand in his way. With a skip in his step suddenly, he began to whistle. Good lord, he felt marvellous …

… Wait …
What …
Was …
That …
Smell?

Thunderstruck, Alphonso stopped mid-stride. He blinked several times and then inhaled deeply, his eyes closing as pleasure suffused him. The smell was so sweet, beyond delicious and so teasingly, temptingly familiar. He stood in the middle of the pavement with his mouth open, salivating.

Good lord, but he was slower than molasses – he knew exactly what it was – but how could it be? He wrestled with his common sense for a moment, denying the very obvious proof of his senses. Could it really be? Great heavens, of course it was! It was irrefutably, categorically, could incontestably be nothing but a Cackling Fart fresh from the arse of a chook. He hadn't smelled anything so perfect in far too long. He couldn't even remember when last he'd been fortunate enough to smell anything as organically exquisite as a freshly laid egg – one laid without so much as a snifter of the pitiless constraints imposed by modern industry. People didn't tend to keep chickens in the city like they did back home in the country and he didn't go back to the country unless absolutely necessary these days – in fact he hadn't been back for years. His time was far too valuable to waste on Hick Town, Squalor County.

'A Cackling Fart, a Hen Fruit, call it what you will, my boy, but the fact remains that a freshly laid chicken's egg is the finest victual you will ever have the pleasure of consuming.' Alphonso remembered his father's words well and he knew the truth of them for himself. There was nothing a right-minded fox liked more than a hen's egg straight from the straw. If the hen got in the way, well that was just part of the dining experience, wasn't it. Delicious memories suffused him. His primal instincts were usually kept firmly in check – an academic of his standing simply didn't whip off his trousers and mark his territory when someone tried to borrow a library book he'd been eyeing, for example – but right at that moment he would have done anything to find that damnable egg.

His nostrils flared, tracing the scent, mapping his route to the prize. It was all pure reflex; his senses were as sharp as they'd ever been. While he had maintained rigid self-control in many aspects of his life, he'd found it necessary to rely on his instincts in certain more *specialised* areas of his life. His pursuit of success had been hard fought and he had not always fought fair. His conquest of women – and he considered himself every bit as much of an expert on women as he did on literature – had at times warranted the employment of his superior hunting skills to secure, for want of a better word, his prey. They'd always succumbed, no matter how much they'd protested.

Now, with that scent filling his nostrils, his vulpine senses on overload, Alphonso wanted that egg more than anything in the world! He wanted it badly enough to skip out on his clandestine dinner with a young but foolishly eager to please PhD student, rip off his trousers and get going after it.

No.

He wasn't some urchin cub scrounging for scraps. He was an esteemed Professor of Literature at a prestigious institution, he had been published in journals the hoi polloi didn't even know existed, had written books and articles on so many subjects even he could barely keep up. No, he had earned his chops and he wasn't about to throw it all away for the sake of one silly little …

Egg.

So fresh.

So pure.

He sighed, his eyelids fluttering closed. And sniffed again.

Maybe it would have been different had it been just any egg, but this was very clearly no ordinary egg. The succulent ovarian fragrance wafted across his nostril hairs once again, stronger this time, setting his ears to twitching and his tail to flicking impatiently against the constraint of his trousers, wanting desperately to be free, for him to run, to seek out the source of that heavenly smell. This was a prize egg, from some exquisitely bred bird that was fed on the finest seeds, oats, greens, and corn. This was an egg that had been lovingly produced. This was a delicacy.

He needed it.

He needed it now.

'Excuse me, sir?' A small voice called to him from the hedgerow. Alphonso waved his hand dismissively in its direction and continued scouting for the egg, his very skin tingling with avarice. It suddenly occurred to him that the nose he had cultivated so carefully was definitely more of a snout at that moment.

'Sir? If you have the time, I'd appreciate ...'

'Shut up whoever you are. I've no time.'

'But sir ...'

'Be quiet, filth, or I'll teach you to keep your mouth shut with my boot!' He kicked the hedge sharply, hoping to at least shake up whatever tramp or lingerer was in there. How he hated those who didn't help themselves. He'd fought his way out of the gutter, escaped the drudgery of the skulk, and found his way to the big city. Events had taken a turn he'd never expected and while he may have been cutthroat in grasping the opportunities that had come his way, he'd done only what he had to. Kitty had loved him, she had wanted him to be happy, for him to get all the things he had so desperately wanted. Hadn't she declared a thousand times that she would do anything for him? Was he supposed to hold back just because she'd had a spot of cold feet when it had come to the crunch? Women. He'd really only taken what she'd been offering for years, for heaven's sake. Who could blame him for taking what was offered on a plate? In a small way – a very small way, admittedly – he was her legacy. After all, he was a *somebody* these days. She would be proud that her sacrifice had come to mean so much to the world, and grasping guttersnipes like the loiterer in the bushes would not tarnish him. He didn't do charity. No one had ever felt sorry for him. He'd had to take and trade for his very soul.

Alphonso smiled briefly at the silence from the hedge before tipping his head back and inhaling once more. He didn't have much work to do; the succulent eggy aroma practically saturated the air. Working his way slowly along the street, savouring every step, Alphonso quickly noticed the scent intensify still further. He was headed in the right direction. Soon enough, he located a house with a fence to one side. Hopping over the wooden slats with a grace born of his true self, he slid into the shadows and made his way around to the back of the house.

There was no chicken coop.

Perplexed, Alphonso looked around him. The smell was so intense that he should have been able to reach out and touch the damned egg. Scanning the ramshackle garden – honestly, if you were lucky enough to own a house these days the least you could do was tend to it and its environs, he thought waspishly, peeved at not having had his own way quickly enough – Alphonso tried to locate the hidden coop. It had to be there, somewhere. Nothing. He was about to give up when a sliver of moonlight peeped out from behind a cloud and shone down on the garden, illuminating the shadows at the far end. He had assumed there would just be another fence marking the property's boundary but he had been wrong. The moonlight showed him a pathway into an improbable but very evident copse of trees. He couldn't see how far back the woods went but it couldn't be too far. They were in the city. It was a pathway to the egg, he knew it, knew it in his bones for a biblical certainty.

Following the light and trusting his nose once again, Alphonso headed into the woods without a second thought.

Soon, although he had no idea how soon, he couldn't recall how long he had been walking. The further in he went, the more crowded the trees became, preventing him from judging the time by the movement of the stars. The leafy canopy had become unrelenting, the pathway ever longer, but still he carried on because the smell was ever stronger and once Alphonso Vulpinari started a thing he finished it. His feet felt heavy but he kept putting one in front of the other, convinced that just a few more steps, a few more yards, a few more moments and he would find his prize. And it was *his* prize. No other would get there before him, take what was his …

But it's not yours.

Alphonso whipped his head around in the direction of the voice, but there was no one there. He wasn't prone to hysterics but perhaps the inexorable darkness was getting to him a little. He could admit that to himself. Being honest was not a weakness. Taking a deep breath and giving himself a stern talking to, he turned back to the path and resumed his quest. He had not taken more than a step or two when he noticed a light ahead of him. A clearing, at last. Quickening his pace but maintaining his vigilance, he was still not convinced the voice had been in his head, Alphonso made for the light. He could barely contain himself. The light grew brighter with every step he took. Finally he came to the glade he had been expecting and there, on the opposite side to the path, was a chicken coop, a finely made, exquisite chicken coop.

Surely he had never seen its equal!

Even in the now tempered light – where was that light coming from exactly? – he could see how perfectly the boards of fine wood had been slotted together, how precisely they had been nailed into place. He did not stop to think how he could spot such detail under the circumstances. The only thought that occurred to him was that if this was how beautifully whoever kept these chickens housed them, how exquisite must be the egg within? He was beguiled, completely. Caution was outweighed by desire and for the first time in many years Alphonso fell onto all fours and loped towards the coop with quite unseemly haste.

Flipping back onto two legs, he flicked up the latch and was about to slip through the door when he finally realised something was wrong. Terribly wrong. This was too easy. Too right. Nothing was ever that good. It hit him in a moment, everything his vulpine senses should have been telling him since he had first caught the scent. It hit him too late because just as he was about to take a step back, he felt a rope tighten around his ankle. His forehead banged against the door of the coop as his right leg was snatched out from under him and before he knew it he was upside down, swinging in the air.

Cursing, he hung there, caught by the snare around his ankle, feeling like a fool. He, Professor Alphonso Vulpinari, had been caught in a trap a cub should have spotted from a mile away. He could hardly believe it.

'I did try to warn you, Professor, to give you a sporting chance.' It was the voice from the hedge.

'What do you want? Who are you?' He growled the words, more beast than man.

'I wanted to see whether you were a lost cause or not, my love. Maybe I hoped you weren't as bad as I'd been told but, alas, I found you to be everything they said and everything I feared you would become all those years ago. You didn't even have to speak, I could smell the lies and the wickedness on you.'

'Who are you? I can give you money, take my watch, whatever you want, take it, I …'

'Please don't be tiresome, Alphonso. Do you really not remember me, darling? They call me Kitty Sunshine now. Some worship me and some fear me, but you already know that, don't you sweetie?' That voice. It was so achingly familiar but it couldn't be, could it? Surely not …

'Kitty? My Kitty?'

'No, not *your* Kitty.'

Finally, his assailant stepped into his line of sight. Even though he was upside down, he recognised the woman instantly. She was changed, more human than fox, but somehow she was the same Kitty. Her sharp eyes crinkled at the edges as though she found him genuinely amusing but the rest of her face remained impassive. Her hair began to glow, not exactly like sunshine, more will o' the wisp, but Alphonso suddenly knew exactly where the light that had led him to the clearing had come from. He also understood what she was.

'There is no egg.' It wasn't a question.

'No, my love, there isn't.'

'You tricked me.'

'I understand how that must feel, must I not, Alphonso?'

'I thought it was what you wanted, I thought you wanted me to be happy.'

'So you took advantage of me and stole my innocent soul to pay for your avarice and ambition. Without compunction, without a single ounce of regret. You traded me for the privilege of a human life that you have used only for wicked ends. I was never yours, Alphonso, never yours to trade and squander. You made the wrong deal.'

'I paid the price, gave what I was asked for, I don't understand why you're saying this.'

'You paid nothing, my love. I did. Unwillingly.'

'You offered yourself up, changing your mind at the last minute was an aberration; you wanted it every bit as much as I did.'

'Is that what you say to all the girls?' Suddenly Miss Kitty Sunshine's hair began to positively glow. Alphonso tried to take a step back to stop him from being consumed by that supernatural light, but he could not. He was still upside down, hung by his ankle. His eyelids were no match against her preternatural light. There was no escape because she wanted him to see, to witness exactly what was coming.

Kitty took a step towards him, her face animated now. She smiled almost benevolently at him, but her black eyes belied her true nature.

Kitsune.

He should have known, had heard the stories often enough, but he had always scoffed at superstition – except when it had served him. She was a fox spirit, a trickster, a servant of Inari, the fox Goddess he had sold her soul to for his human form, and she had waited for vengeance for thirty years.

'Alphonso Vulpinari, you have committed heinous crimes. Your human form has not disguised your actions from us. Our supplicants have made their complaint against you and it is time for you to be held accountable. There will be no reprieve. You are and have been found guilty.'

Kitty seemed to grow then, her light becoming impossibly brighter but in that moment, just as he thought his fate was sealed, Alphonso saw it, his chance for salvation.

The pearl.

A kitsune's power lay in the pearl it wore about its person. He had only to take it for himself and he would have control over this unnatural bitch. As she approached, he relaxed, ignoring the pounding in his head from being hung upside down for so long and from the bright light that had burned into his retinas. With his eyes closed, all he could see in the darkness was that pearl. It hung from a delicate silver chain around her neck. It should be easy to snatch and then she would be his once more, to do with as he pleased. To teach her a lesson. He almost laughed out loud.

Alphonso felt her near him. She was a breath away. In an instant, he opened his eyes and hauled himself up towards her, savagely tightening his stomach muscles as he threw out his hands to tear the necklace from her throat.

His hands met only air, empty space.

Laughter echoed around the clearing. No tinkling fairy laughter this, but deep fox-belly laughs. She had known, had allowed him to believe that he could take the necklace. She had wanted him to feel hope simply so she could take it away from him. He had never had a chance.

Defeated, Alphonso let himself swing back and forth from the rope, his arms dangling down past his head.

Kitty Sunshine's mouth widened inexorably, her teeth multiplying in an instant. She loosened her jaw, letting it widen to its new proportions. Saliva dripped from her maws. Hair he had not noticed before covered her skin, soft red hair that showed her true nature. She approached him slowly, almost reverently.

'This is for all the women you have raped and harassed, the people you have stolen from, exploited, manipulated, and ridiculed. This is the punishment handed down by the Old One herself. But, most of all, this is for my lost soul, for my broken heart.'

'I'm sorry, Kitty.' His contrition was real in the face of his own demise, but it was far too late and it was not enough.

'I know.'

'Couldn't we work something out?' Her sad smile raised another ridiculous flicker of hope and Alphonso became desperate. How could it end like this? His greatness dashed by a woman? 'I would make amends, work hard to give back what I've taken, help anyone who …'

'Hush my darling. Don't waste your last moments begging when we both know you would renege. Such arrogance as yours will never be tempered, so it must be ended. Now,' Kitty stilled his rocking form with one hand, 'there are those who would recommend that I savour every moment of this but in truth I seek only reparation. I do not glory in horror. Thus my love, we come to the crunch. It is time for dinner.' She opened her jaws once more and inhaled Alphonso's screams before sinking her blade-sharp canines into the softness of his flank.

Sitting cross-legged on the leaf strewn floor, Kitty sucked the marrow from the final bone of Alphonso Vulpinari's fine left leg and threw it over her shoulder onto the small mound behind her. His skeletal remains gleamed brightly in the moonlight, but there was plenty of meat still left for the local population. She needed nothing more because she was full at last. Her job was finally done. Sighing, she leaned back and looked up at the sky, the trees that had protected her little enclosure for a while having gone back to their regular business. It was a clear night and the stars twinkled merrily in the heavens above.

It was time.

Kitty pushed herself up from the floor and began to pick her way along the path that had brought Alphonso to his fate. A city fox, attracted by the scent of fresh meat, emerged from the shadows into the clearing and watched as Kitty's light receded into the darkness until finally it disappeared with a blink and, so the fox thought, a sigh.

MAGGIE AND THE CAT

When the black cat tells you to leave the house, you leave the house. Maggie didn't need to be told twice.

It had started out like any other day, the endless same old same old. Her shift at the Vet's office had started at six and ended at midday just as it did every Monday, Wednesday and Thursday. She'd come home, had a sandwich then set about her chores. The front porch had been washed, the laundry baskets emptied – colours separated from whites of course – the washing machine loaded, the previous load taken out of the dryer, and then came the task of pressing Jack's work shirts. She hated that the most. The iron was a tyrant, all steam and bluster, much like her husband. So yes, it had been a day like any other. The same monotonous tasks completed for a thankless man and a loveless marriage. Same old same old.

She looked at him tied to the chair and smiled.

One of his suits had needed pressing too and that was when she'd found it. The letter. At first she'd thought it was one of his lists – heavens, didn't the man love a list! He left them for her on the refrigerator door, reminding her of all those little things that were so difficult to forget when you were constantly being reminded of them. Like you were the housekeeper not the wife. The paper was different from the cheap lined stuff he used for his lists though. She unfolded it, prescience far away. Afterward she would feel foolish for not already knowing, for not having some inkling of what she would find. She would feel like she should have known.

It proved to be more of a note, short sharp slanted hand-writing on soft vellum. Expensive. A love note. Well, maybe not love exactly …

Darling Jack, come over after dinner on Wednesday. Tell her you have overtime to do and I'll fuck your brains out. I've missed you so much. X

That was it, her marriage dead at last in three short sentences.

Who wrote notes anymore? It was all text messages and emails these days, so why a letter? It was ironic – or was it poetic? – that her antiquated marriage would be ended by something as anachronistic as a letter. Something so decayed should have crumbled by rights, but it was the sharp *snap* of a conclusion that was ringing in her ears.

Over.

Her memory of his rescue, freeing her from the cold grey walls of the institution, had been nothing more than an illusion and it shattered around her in that instant, her eyes open and her mind straight for the first time in too long. Gratitude for her liberation fell from her like hard rain, leaving her dry and crisp. Not brittle though, not now. She had always been too afraid to ask why he'd come for her that day, why he had wanted to begin again let alone keep going for all these years, as though knowing would drop her back into the desolation of the Before – but here was as bad as there had been, she saw that now. Her illness had been an excuse for his withdrawal in the first place, so why bring her back at all? A cruel joke? Was he that much of a bastard?

Maggie laughed. She rarely swore, curse words made her flinch – her first perusal of the letter had been more focussed on that f-word than the fact of her husband's infidelity – but thinking them now made her head bubble like a freshly poured glass of cherryade.

'Bastard. Shithead. Fuckface liar.' Maggie burst out in a fresh round of laughter at the sound of her voice saying those words for real. She slapped Jack around the back of the head and more peals of laughter erupted. From her, not from him. *He* looked terrified. Which made her laugh harder.

'Oh Jack, look at you so serious.' She wasn't sure for a moment if she was ever going to stop laughing, and that jolted her back to reality. Now was not the time for hysteria – that age-old female malady of male invention – now was the time for action.

Had she already killed him?

She remembered going to the shed and getting the poison

(it was for rats) but had she made him his dinner? Time had gone a bit haywire. She should make him his dinner.

'It's your favourite, Jack darling. Spaghetti.' He hated spaghetti. Maybe she would spit in it too. The laughter threatened to return then and Maggie had to straighten up, take a deep breath and sternly quell the impulse. She had things to do.

Had she killed him yet? She couldn't remember, she didn't think so. As soon as she'd read that letter she'd felt such a rush of clarity, a clear vision of what had to be done, but now she felt disoriented and confused. Nothing seemed as substantial as it had before, as certain. What was it she was supposed to be doing?

Dinner.

She remembered now. Spaghetti.

The kitchen was soon warm from the stove's burner. She boiled some water and popped in the pasta. A frying pan for the onion and tomatoes, a dash of arsenic for (the rats) good measure. She wouldn't spit in it. It seemed too easy, too spiteful. She wouldn't lower herself to Jack's dirty (rat) level. The onions and tomatoes sizzled and spat, a tiny domestic volcano that echoed the tumult in her chest. That's where she felt it, dead centre of her breastbone, throbbing like a stubbed toe. It was pure anger; there was no sadness in there. That should have made her sad. Such a waste.

Sighing, she looked back down to the pan just in time to see a wing disappear and then re-emerge in the gloop she was cooking. A wing. She frowned even as she looked closer. Pop. A wing pinged up from the sauce. Maggie jumped, but her gaze stayed fixed on the pan. The butterfly pulled itself from the sizzling liquid, its wings stretching, flexing and then it was off, a couple of lazy circles around Maggie's head before flitting away. She watched it dart around the kitchen, surprised at how interesting the little creature seemed to find Jack. Another popping noise caught her attention. The pan. Tens, no hundreds, a thousand teeming butterflies surged up from its confines, whirling this way and that, a living blanket of undulating blue and brown. They flooded the room, covering Jack, sinking into his mouth, his ears, anywhere and everywhere, flocking into every orifice, filling him, choking him, smothering him; *cleansing him*. Somehow she knew that to be true. In her bones. They would make his flesh pure, his soul was irretrievable and she held no hope out for it. But oh, how his skeleton would shine beneath the light of the moon once they were done. She longed to see it.

By now, Jack's face was as blue as the backs of the butterflies. The plate in front of him was empty. There wasn't a smear on it. It was as though it had been licked scrupulously clean. She didn't remember giving him the plate or even dishing up the food in the first place. She did remember thousands of gossamer wings beating like a thousand tiny heartbeats, each one punctuating her husband's heartbeats until at last they both slowed to a stop. Jack's head fell forward, his chin coming to rest on his chest.

Maggie stared at him for a moment, confused.

Had she killed him?

She remembered a phone ringing. Was she hearing it now? The shrill noise persisted and she crossed the kitchen to pick up the extension that hung on the wall.

'Hello?' Her voice seemed normal. She was surprised.

'Jack, please.' The woman's voice was unfamiliar.

'He can't come to the phone right now. Can I take a message?'

'Put him on, please. I know he's there.'

'Who is this?'

'Don't you know?'

'Why would I ask if I knew?' But even as she said it, Maggie understood. This was the owner of the sharp slanting handwriting and the expensive paper. This was her husband's lover. 'Oh.'

'Yes, now put him on.'

'I can't, the butterflies took him.'

'What?'

'The butterflies. They swallowed him whole, I think.' There was a long pause on the other end and Maggie waited patiently.

'Did you say butterflies?'

'Yes. Blue ones.'

'What? Jesus, Jack said you were mad.'

'Well, he was the one who drove me there. Took me in his nice new car and then came and got me again.'

'God, stop talking. I'm coming over. It's time this was sorted out.'

Maggie opened her mouth to reply, she had no idea what she would have said, but the sound of the other end being hung up silenced her. She replaced the receiver and stared at it for a moment. What was she going to do? She couldn't let the other woman see what she'd done. Panic bubbled in her stomach but just then a butterfly fluttered past her, making her jump. Another settled on her shoulder, another on her arm. Whatever fear she might have felt about Jack's body being discovered melted away in their presence. It would be fine. Just fine.

Turning back to Jack's body – was he really dead? – Maggie considered what she should do. She nudged him gently with one finger. He was stone cold. How long had it been since the butterflies had descended? It couldn't have been very long but she could tell when dead was dead and he was as dead as dead could be.

That was when she first saw the cat. Sitting on top of the refrigerator, it was as black as pitch with eyes bluer – the same blue as the butterfly backs – than the sky on a perfect summer's day. It said nothing. It just winked at her and yawned.

Ignoring her new companion, Maggie contemplated her old one again. He would have to go down into the cellar. Would she have time to get him to the bottom of all those creaky old steps? She didn't think so, but maybe she could drag him to the stairs and push him down. That ought to do if he was dead already. She should check but time was so pressing and she was getting a headache. Resolution stiffening her spine, Maggie cast aside her dilly-dallying and marched over to the body.

The body?

Was that how she needed to think of her husband to get the job done? Whatever got her through, maybe her unconscious mind was looking out for her. Well, so it should. It was about time after all these years of confusion and anxiety. She was owed more than one apology. With one hard push, she managed to shove the body onto the floor. Walking around it, she quickly surveyed the best place to get a good hand-hold. Its right arm was outstretched as though pointing to the cellar door. An omen if ever there was one and a good place to get a grip. She bent to wrap her fingers around his wrist, the skin there oddly pallid. She was surprised to find it was clammy to touch. Maggie pulled hard. Nothing happened for a moment, but then the rather marked sound of gas – like when her dad would ask her to pull his finger – broke the silence. Maggie giggled, she couldn't help it. She pulled again, but the laughter got harder when she still couldn't move it and another gas leak punched the air. Maggie collapsed to her knees, covering her face with her hands as her shoulders shook. Weren't the strangest things funny? Controlling herself was almost impossible and finally she gave in, throwing back her head and howling like a loon.

Eventually the loud barking laughs segued into chuckling and, in the end, the occasional hiccup. Maggie sighed and looked up at the clock. How long had it been since she'd pushed the body onto the floor? She had no idea. That woman would be here soon. She looked at it for a moment and then made her decision. Fuck it – she was getting better at this cursing business – she'd leave it there, it was better than Jack deserved. What he really deserved was being ground up into mincemeat and feeding to the dogs. She'd been treated unfairly, been lied to for who knew how long, and now she was done with it, done with him.

A rumbling from somewhere deep inside her gave her pause suddenly. She tried to swallow the rising tide of ... was it nausea? She wasn't sure. She couldn't remember the last time she'd eaten. The sound grew louder, the fluttering stronger, and she was sure she was going to be sick. Maggie opened her mouth and the butterflies poured out, descending on the body, covering it, a brown and blue blanket of vengeance. She almost fell on her face, exhausted from the sudden expulsion, but she somehow managed to thrust her arms out to catch herself. She watched on all fours as they danced over the body, fussing and fretting, each one searching for a place.

Maggie felt hollow, as though everything inside her, every scrap of patience and tolerance, had been spent. She had allowed it to happen. She had sat idly by while her husband, the man who had brought her back from the dead – from the ward, from the cold glass against her face, the endless talking in a circle, the blue pills, the sharp cries in the night – had proceeded to act the hero while all the time he had been anything but that. Why had he bothered? She had asked herself so many times, secretly, at night, where no one could hear her thoughts. She didn't want to go back. Didn't want to die again. She wanted to be free.

Forcing herself to her feet, Maggie looked up at the cat.

'Time to go, Margaret. Time to take to the wing.' Maggie blinked. The day was so odd already that it occurred to her a talking cat was no more worthy of a second thought than a tin of beans at that moment, and she knew he was right.

When the black cat starts talking it's time to go.

SHOOT TO KILL AND CAN 'EM UP...

... That's it in a nutshell. There are few philosophies smarter because when the world's getting its apocalypse on you have few other choices. Best you get your head round that from the get-go.

I started shooting when I was eight years old. Air rifles mainly, but by ten I was pretty slick with a bow and arrow. Mum always said they'd make the best weapon anyway when the time came – when the bullets run out, who's going to be making new ones? Arrows, on the other hand, are relatively easy to make, plus all I've got is time, so the arsenal is pretty full right now. I can shape a bow out of pretty much any wood with decent give in it and make a quiver full of arrows to go with it in no time. I'm good at it too. Robin Hood would weep at the skill in my fingers.

And I never miss. Never.

Our bunker's pretty sweet. There's a room full of bunk beds that are more comfortable than they look, a pretty well equipped kitchen, a library, a bathroom, a canning room – my Mum's mantra is 'waste not want not' – and a big communal living area. Dad, his mate Mac, who had a heart attack two days before the event had even happened, and I suppose Zeke too, annexed and expanded the basement of the old house. It took them a couple of years or so, but they worked hard most weekends and it paid off. Speaking of Zeke, he's my brother. We were both trained in and for almost anything you can imagine: hand-to-hand combat, gas attacks, nuclear fallout, weapon making, foraging, first aid – you name it, we learned it. Sewing's my weak point, truth be told, but at least I've stopped sewing stuff to my jeans and Mum says I sew a pretty strong stitch. That's what matters.

Of course, I've not had what you might call a normal life.
Hardly a surprise, is it?

Preppers? Survivalists? Call us what you like, but we call ourselves 'sensible' – what else would you call those not blind to the inevitable? I was picked on sometimes at school, but after the suspension – and the scrum half's snapped wrist (thanks to Dad for all those self-defence drills) – I was left pretty much alone. Just the formalities, y'know? Class projects and such. I didn't go to dances, never been to a sleepover, never even sat with anyone else for lunch. I didn't have any friends and I didn't get to do any of that *normal* stuff, even less so of course when my folks finally took me out of school. Getting attached to people only makes it harder in the long run anyway, that's what Mum says. It kind of makes me sad sometimes (I've got hormones and hopes just like anyone else) but being around all those blinkered sheep just got harder as I got older and, besides, you've got to focus on what's important.

To hell with normal anyway!

Is it normal to sit and wait for Johnny Mutant to come eat your brains? To wait while the nuclear fallout burns through your guts and your brain spills out the bottom of your spine? To pretend there's hope, that someone out there's coming to save you? They're not, y'know. If you don't want to end up a splatter-fest of ex-human, then you'd better get wise, and you'd better get there fast.

There's no time for frills and fancies at the end of the world, there's only one prize and that's life – or at the very least dying on your own terms. I'm old enough to know that. The future only extends to the next hour, the next day if you're lucky. It's about survival. It's all it's ever been about, truth be told. I wised up to that the day I heard Dad telling Zeke that me and Mum were the weak link, that we were the ones who would most likely slow them down and that if he needed to get rid of us he wouldn't hesitate. I didn't understand. I was a good learner, fast, one of them self-motivators you'd call me, better than Zeke who was a lazy slob most of the time. Always had something to moan and bitch about, that boy. I was better with a bow and arrow and I could climb a tree in half the time he could. I listened and I remembered. Just because he could dig earth for longer and lift the heavier barrels, I was the dead weight? Like digging a hole and carrying heavy stuff makes the difference when the chips are down? As far as I could see, the difference that marked us out in my Dad's mind was that I was a girl and Zeke was a boy – *his* boy. I was eleven years old and from that day on I hated my Dad, hated him for deciding that I mattered less because I'm a girl, for seeing me as an albatross and not an asset. It was also the day I decided one thing –

I wasn't going to be left behind. If you're out there, if you're reading this, you've got to make sure you're not either.

Ironic really that Dad was the first to get bit. I had to shoot him; Zeke froze like he'd learned nothing all those years. Typical. So I shot my Dad in the head and then when Zeke got violent a couple of months later – the guilt and isolation got to him real bad – and went all froth-at-the-mouth crazy, I shot him too. If he hadn't tried for the door I wouldn't have had to do it. We don't know what's out there and we're not finding out until we're ready. Took the last of our bullets but Mum and me? We don't need them because we're *prepared*.

At least Zeke's death won't be in vain. Mum can pickle anything and what's left goes in the cans.

THE BACCHANAL

High heeled and crimson lipped,
Tiny-skirted thighs, barely covered nips,
Foundation slapped on pancake-style,
Eyelashes encrusted in blackest bile,
Bleached hair ruthlessly backcombed,
Another swig of the bottle and it's time to leave home.

The queue is long but VIP, son!
Strutting past the muppets, one by one,
Then it's into the club and straight to the bar
With more damned chutzpah than the Morningstar.
Necking cheap shots with toes a-tapping,
Dot dot dash, the sound of some spirit rapping.

These Maenads survey the acolytes,
Assessing the flanks of the suburbanites,
Who, like god-intoxicated worshippers,
Dance free of their worldly inertia
Beneath the merciless strobe lights,
Ecstatic eyes rolled back to the whites.

They sup from the milk and honey of the bar,
Encouraged by these parthenoi who are
Choosing, selecting, which one to sacrifice,
Whose flesh to rent and tear and slice
With their bare hands and naked teeth;
Such a venerable honour to bequeath.

The night moves on, the music thumping,
Couples debase to the bass that's pumping,
Unbridled lust spirals out of control
As lips crash together, loins bump and roll.
The frenzy builds, as they suck and fuck
Like animals down in the deep dark muck.

At last, culmination comes as the women rise,
Their fingers plunging into lovers' eyes.
As skin is torn from flesh and muscle,
The menfolk put up quite the tussle,
But this is an ancient dance of love divine,
Despite the neon-shrouded shrine.

The slaughtered bulls collapse to the ground,
As numberless female hands tenderise and pound
Meat from their chosen ones' cadavers.
Revellers barely able to stop the slather
Of digestive juices from their chops
As they harvest their sarcous crops.

They writhe and surge in the carnal mess –
Each one an exultant priestess
Ascending to commune with her lord –
A gasping, orgasmic, transcendent horde
Hurtling towards a glimpse of eternity,
A tantalising taste of perpetuity.

This, my friends, is the Bacchanal,
That habitual Saturday night cabal;
A satisfying weekend excursion
For a drink-fuelled, god-invoking perversion,
In an EDM bubble with hardcore beats
And plenty of candidates for them to eat.

TITS UP IN WONDERLAND

For the Prof

The dress was a wreck. A pouty-lipped red full-length evening gown with a thigh high split, it had been entirely embroidered with diamantes and sequins that made it shimmer and sparkle under the lights of the club. Now it was nothing more than a rag. Queenie picked it up and sniffed it, her jet-black bob falling around her face as she closed her eyes. The reek of cigarette smoke with a tang of waning vanilla – the King's preferred scent when he became The Duchess, more for the joke than the scent itself – crawled up her nose and made its way down to form a hard lump in her throat.

Someone had taken him.

God's knackers, she hoped he wasn't already dead.

The dress, the last thing the King had been seen wearing, had turned up in the mail that morning. A lovingly crafted package of black paper with a purple bow. It reminded her of the vicious Drag Turf warfare, when Big Alice and her cohorts with their big ideas and desire for monopoly had wreaked havoc on the city; but Big Alice hadn't been seen since the *Jack's Tarts* debacle and if anyone was thinking of upending the status quo or, god forbid, Big Alice had come back, Queenie would have known about it. She'd made it her business to know about every droplet of piss that swirled its way down the drains of every drag club between here and…

That rat bastard.

Clarity came hard and fast. The package was clearly meant to remind her of the Body Part Boxes that had once signalled the kind of ransom expected for a hostage, but the colours that had been used were…

That devious, pinch-faced, jealous rat bastard.

She should have realised straightaway. Black and purple. The colours of the wedding dress he'd had made for her all those years ago. She hadn't added two and two, had almost laughed when she'd seen the box, a subconsciously nervous reaction even after so long.

Funny, however, it was not.

The King was missing and she had a very good idea who had him. It was time to get the Tweedy brothers up and at 'em.

Queenie stared at the Tweedy boys. Identical great lugs, their similarity extended to their not inconsiderable stupidity. One was sporting a neck brace and looked like his face had been through a mangle while the other had gashes and bruises across the breadth of his meaty arms and chest that made his brother's two black eyes look mild. A quick recce, that's what she'd sent them over for and they'd come back looking like underdone roast beef. It was her fault of course. She'd been angry. If she was honest, she'd wanted the bastards to see the boys scoping the joint and panic. Instead, they'd beaten the Seven Holy Bells of the Almighty Sky God Kar out of them. She would have done the same thing.

They had, however, come back with a note.

My Beloved Queenie Flower,

We have your King. I'm guessing you already know this. You know what we want, still.

Your eternal champion, Mo.

Shit and biscuits. Some champion. Queenie crumpled the note in her fist and thought about stuffing it in her mouth. Maybe she'd choke to death on that shonky little ballbag's words and this nonsense would finally be over. She'd nearly lost Wonderland because of her involvement with Mr Mo, had been so smitten with him that nothing else had mattered. Of course when the King had discovered the woodland witch who'd given Mr Mo the love potion (the only rational explanation for her going within a yard of that sneaky little rat) she'd been as mad as Kar's trapped gonads. The man was a menace and she'd been hoodwinked – *her*! When he'd tried to get back into her good graces, apologising, grovelling, killing a couple of her minor enemies, she'd seriously toyed with the idea of revenge (massive unassailable sweet revenge) but the King had been the one to talk her down. He had been there for her for more years than she could remember, had been with her when she'd started Wonderland – had been the reason for it – and she wasn't about to let that little toad fuck with him more than he already had.

So it was time to play.

The Louche Lounge. What a consummate idiot. Queenie took a long last drag on her kretek, tossed the butt and ground it into the pavement with the tip of her red stiletto heel. Well, if you were going to open a shithole, you might as well call it a shithole. Big Curly was about as imaginative as a tin of shagwort meat but somehow he'd gotten in with Mr Mo and things had worked out well for them both. What had once been a spit and sawdust dive in a dodgy part of town had become a roaring success. The Louche wasn't short on oddities; indeed they catered for every kind of deviance a twisted mind could imagine. In this town, that stretched the limits. Still, Big Curly and his mob of freaks might be the face of the operation, but the brains were entirely that little shitkicker's, Mr Mo.

He'd been unbelievably patient; she had to give him that. He'd been biding his time for over six years. So why now? Had he simply run out of that legendary patience? It didn't matter why, Queenie reminded herself for the umpteenth time, it just mattered that he had stopped waiting. The thing he had forgotten, however, was that she was no longer under his spell. He might have the King but she had ways too, same as him. He was going to be chowing down on his balls come suppertime. No one crossed Queenie McCaw and no one fucked with the King.

It was time for action.

'Put it over there, then let's get out of here.' Groaning

and bitching about their aches and pains the whole time, the Tweedy boys set the bomb by the crates in the alley. It wasn't anything major, just a useful distraction. Her contortionist, Hardheart Whiplash (stage name) was already winding his way through the Louche's ventilation system, such as it was. Queenie checked her watch. By now he should be almost over where her spy had said they were keeping the King. While Mr Mo's lugs dealt with the explosion out back, Hardheart would take the duplicate set of keys Queenie had had made and get the King out – right through the front of the club. The dancers wouldn't care and the punters would be too drunk to notice.

Queenie and the Tweedys made their way carefully out of the alleyway and across the street. Once in position, she counted down the seconds, watching her timepiece like a hawk because her heart was beating so hard she was worried she might get ahead of herself.

Ten, Nine, Eight…

Hardheart should be right in position…

Three, Two, One…

Queenie hit the switch in her pocket.

A blast of white light and a bang that was surprisingly more like a boom exploded from the Louche's back alley. Firework flowers punched the air, whizzing and banging as they erupted, brightening both the night sky and the shabby district below. Glitter poured down like rain. The lugs who had been manning the front doors hot-footed it around to the back of the building, coughing and spluttering as they inhaled the sparkly air. Several others emerged from the depths of the club to assist their colleagues and they too were soon choking on the swirling sparkles. As they disappeared from view, Queenie turned her attention to the front doors. Any moment now. Any moment…

'What in the Lords of the Deeps' balls do you mean he wasn't there?'

'Exactly that, Queenie. He wasn't there.' Hardheart took a step back as Queenie's face turned a distinct shade of red

– it was the colour she always went when fury had a hold on her. Only the King could calm her down from one of her tempers. 'Whoever told you he was there was either lying or mistaken. I don't know which.'

'Shit and bloody fucking biscuits!' Queenie kicked a waste paper basket across her office, not seeing Hardheart make a quick exit as the papers in it scattered across the carpet like crumpled white wasps fleeing a kicked nest. 'I'll kill that bitch, Lanky Lottie. She'll be wearing her stilts down her lying bloody throat by the time I've finished with her.'

'Come now, darling flower, don't be angry. It was simply a little ruse to get you to come to me. One cannot stand in the way of true love. It is simply the will of the multiverse.' Mr Mo stepped into Queenie's office as though he had every right to be there.

'You! How did you get in here? How dare you ...'

'Queenie, you must not anger yourself so. I merely... *convinced* your doormen to let me in. I can be most charming when I want to be, can I not? As to why I am here, it is to bring you news.' Mr Mo settled himself in one of her guest chairs, stretching out his long skinny legs, and placing the brown bag he was carrying on his lap. He sat there waiting, a shit-eating grin plastered across his face like he was one of Kar's heavenly angels. Her fingers itched to slap it off him, but she knew it wouldn't do any good. Mo was an old hand at pain, giving it and receiving it. It was how he'd made his way in the world. Once upon a time, she had found it exciting...

Queenie determinedly shook the memory off. She perched on the edge of her desk and folded her arms.

'Okay, so spill. What news?'

'So impatient, my love. First, tell me, have you missed Mr Mo? He has missed you terribly.'

'I've missed you like a hole in the head, Mo. Now, give. What's news?'

Mr Mo chuckled. 'Dearest Queenie, always down to business. It is one of the things I love about you.' He winked at her and Queenie shuddered, not bothering to hide her distaste. It merely made Mr Mo laugh. 'Well, since you insist, the news is this—' he stood with a flourish, '—ding dong, your King is dead.' With that, he threw the bag he'd been holding at Queenie, who caught it instinctively. Her fingers squished into it, as though it were a bag full of thick jelly. Holes appeared where her fingers sank into the damp material and something red oozed out of them. Dark red. Queenie shrieked and let go of the bag. As it splattered on the floor at her feet, the bag ripped to show what was inside – a still pumping heart. The King's still pumping heart.

Revulsion and outrage coursed through her, her heart cracking into a thousand pieces along with her temper. Shattered, she looked at Mr Mo in horror... but as she did, her course became crystal clear. Preternatural calm soothed through her, making her smile. Uncertainty flashed across Mr Mo's face for the first time, pleasing her still further.

'You know, there are easier ways to attract a mate, Mr Mo.' Queenie slipped off the desk and circled behind it, keeping her movements slow and non-threatening.

'I do not want a mate, Queenie pie, I want you.'

'That is... unfortunate.' The button was easy to press, as had been her intention when she'd had it installed. With a soft click, she felt her smile widen. The door behind Mr Mo flew open, crashing into the wall. He spun around, his audacity palpably sinking into the ground at last. Had he really thought her that inept? That easy to harass?

She was the motherfucking Queen and this was *her* house.

The Tweedy boys grinned at Mr Mo, clearly eager to get their hands on him. Queenie wasn't one to tease. She waved her hand in his direction and they grabbed him, Mr Mo shouting curses and threats as they wrestled him towards the door.

'What do you want us to do with him, boss?' The Tweedy boys asked in perfect syncopation.

Sitting down at her desk, Queenie reached for the glass of Jawfoot Bourbon she'd been nursing before Mr Mo's visit, downing it in one easy motion. There would be repercussions of course, but she didn't care. Without the King her voice of reason was ominously silent.

'Off with his head, boys.'

THE FLESH TAILOR

Miss Applewhite is a patient woman. She has many virtues of course, but none more so than patience. Above all else a craftsperson must be unwearied by their task – a delicate job should never be rushed. A client will, quite rightly, be most displeased if their goods are anything other than perfect simply because Miss Applewhite was in a rush to get the commission finished. Every element of the task must be organised and arranged so that nothing is overlooked, nothing left to chance or the hurried incompetence of an ill-disciplined practitioner. Planning is the key and planning takes patience. Luckily, Miss Applewhite is possessed with an almost pathological patience. Her work is her life, and life is to be savoured, to be tasted like a fine wine, ruminated upon, and only when every facet of its flavour has been discerned, contemplated, and appreciated can it finally be emitted. Thus, only when a task has been completed in exact accordance with her meticulous planning and then tested, checked, and re-checked, can a commission be handed to the client.

The slow drip drip drip that echoes through the basement where she works may well have bothered even the most tolerant of ordinary people, the ponderously endless tap tap tap enough to drive one slowly but certainly insane. It does not bother Miss Applewhite however; indeed it does not, for she is no ordinary person. The drip merely marks the seconds that march inevitably onward, taking her closer to the fulfilment of her goals, to the completion of her projects. Besides, the work cannot be done without the origin of the drip and the work is, after all, the most important thing.

The drip comes from a tap, where else? The tap is situated atop an old enamel bath, the kind with a roll top that give the deepest, most luxurious baths for the everyday man or woman. The slow drip of the tap is intentional; Miss Applewhite is neither a careless nor forgetful woman. Every action is of course deliberate and well planned. She is a craftsman from bone to brain, through and through. The bath is where she keeps the small, non-internal organ paraphernalia - eyeballs, lips, ears, et cetera. The solution from the black tank that sits in a shadowy recess of the darkest corner of the basement keeps them nice and damp. They are discouraged from drying up into useless shrivel by a mixture of tap water and a special concoction of Miss Applewhite's own design. There are several of these baths lined soldier fashion along the farthest wall of the basement. Not all of the taps drip.

Needless to say, the items therein are not simply dumped into the baths; each one has been placed in a special container, the choice of container having been governed by the size and shape of each piece. These are then clearly labelled with unique reference numbers and these, in their turn, are all recorded faithfully in The Catalogue – a red leather bound enormity that resides on its own special shelf above the desk where Miss Applewhite does her paperwork. Everything in the workspace has its place and keeps it. Clutter is the seed of chaos, a state that must never be allowed any leeway with such delicate work at hand. The walls are lined with shelves and all manner of storage systems. Drawers and boxes are neatly labelled, books neatly alphabetised, papers filed away. The basement is the picture of organisation and preparation, in spite of the dank smell that pervades. It is – there can be no doubt – the office of a professional.

Miss Applewhite is waiting for her current client. She only ever works on one project at a time; such is the delicacy of her work. Attention to detail is of the utmost importance and she expects it in her clients as well as herself. Punctuality is a minimum, and yet this particular client is over one hour late. Miss Applewhite watches the seconds tick past on the old school clock that sits at the back of her vast work desk. She is not angry – Miss Applewhite does not get angry – rather she is anxious, anxious to get back to work (there is always something to do if one is always to be prepared), anxious that something has happened to prevent her client from attending at the appointed time, anxious that her fee will not be paid. If there is one thing capable of sending Miss Applewhite into the neighbourhood of anger it is non-payment of bills. Irresponsibility of any kind is intolerable but outstanding debts are enough to drive even this most patient of women into a fury.

Just as Miss Applewhite is about to give up on her client, one corner of the room begins to darken. The plans chest that stands there begins to lose its shape, fading silently into the blackness that seeps from the wall behind it, slipping over it, swallowing it. The brightest of stars could not penetrate the thickness of the darkness as it swirls into the room; a throat-cloying, head-spinning, bottomless emptiness swells forth from the brickwork with the merest hint of a rustle. Miss Applewhite sighs. She hates this bit the most. A woman of realities, a worker of cloth and flesh, she is not one to hold in with dramatics of any kind. The indignities of dealing with these creatures is sometimes a little hard to bare but, professional to the last, Miss Applewhite remains perched on her stool, one slender ankle crossed over the other, unmoving, a fixed smile plastered across her narrow face.

The darkness finally settles and begins to take shape. Moulded as if by some cosmic potter it becomes less of an inchoate mass and slowly, but surely, etches itself into an inkblot of what seems to be a peacock. It retains the black emptiness with which it entered the room, no features can yet be discerned – its plumage and its face are no more distinguishable than a shadow across the primordial soup. Miss Applewhite waits, ever the patient gentlewoman. She watches politely as the blackness begins to swirl, tiny specks, flashes of colour suddenly pulsing from its centre, tickling their away through the thick black nothingness, shaking it alive, giving it form. Green-blue feathers shimmer into view, legs, eyes, beak, everything becoming clear as though at once, yet it feels like the transition has taken hours, such is the intricacy of its construction. The bird bristles with some ornithological pride or other and stares straight at Miss Applewhite. She shakes her head at the creature's pretensions and spreads her smile a little wider, making it clear she will to continue to wait. The bird preens and begins to screech, the noise slicing through the relative silence of the basement. Miss Applewhite blinks, but says nothing.

The bird begins to convulse, small twitches at first, then

long, traumatic shudders that force its head down and its tail up. It becomes unsteady on its feet, dancing from one foot to the other to try to regain its balance, the effort soon becoming a manic spiral dance. Deliriously it bucks and weaves, spinning, screeching, and then it begins to grow. The colours fade as it stretches, blue gradually fading into the pale hue of human skin, green turning to pink as if with extreme exertion. The birdlike shape folds in on itself, and then spreads suddenly upwards, wings becoming arms, claws transforming into fingers, plumage to skin and hair. Again the change takes place in a matter of moments, the blink of an eye, but Miss Applewhite sees every stage, every change, and still she waits. The almost-man before her is not done yet, she knows this quite well. It wants a fuss to be made. The vanity of these creatures is simply ridiculous.

Exposed flesh becomes encased in velvet and silk, dark, dried-blood red and deepest black. A suit fit for a king. Hair sprouts from the bald scalp, twisting itself out of its trapping of skin, curling into a thick black, lustrous mane. Such a typically demonic selection, thinks Miss Applewhite. Smoking jacket, velveteen trousers, and a cravat. How unusual. The flesh tailor spreads her smile further still across her pale cheeks and hops off the chair, one arm politely outstretched to greet her customer. The new man grasps the little woman's hand, a slow, sly smile forming on his new lips.

Miss Applewhite knows that the creature's hand will be no more substantial than air, but when one deals with these creatures reality is eschewed at best. What one believes to be and what actually *is* can be two entirely different things, such is their power. However, these demons have no real control when it comes to close human contact. They may be able to turn an unprepared human to stone with one illusory kiss, make a woman infertile with one hallucinatory squeeze of her bosom, make a child convulse with a fanciful pat on the head, but they cannot hold their form or enchantments when any true intimacy is involved, so false is it to their natures. That is, after all, why Miss Applewhite and her kind are in business.

'Mr Andrealphus, how nice to meet with you again. I trust

your journey was trouble free.' Her little joke. The man, for that is how Miss Applewhite is supposed to see him, laughs briefly, pumping her hand up and down so many times Miss Applewhite loses count. In fact, the motion is so furious that she thinks for a moment she may be in danger of losing the appendage. Fortunately, Andrealphus stops in the nick of time and begins to prowl around the basement, examining the various specimens in jars, touching the spines of books, and generally doing his best, without knowing it, to annoy Miss Applewhite. She sucks in her disgruntlement and coughs quietly, but with clear meaning, one small fisted hand drawn up to her mouth.

'Do you have the merchandise?' Andrealphus's voice is deep and heavy, as though saturated with sound. It rings in Miss Applewhite's ears as if she were standing next to the greatest of bells or the oversized speakers so popular with those heavy metal types. She learned long ago not to appear disturbed by any aspect of these creatures' habits and mannerisms, and she does not allow any disconcertment to surface now. She motions for Andrealphus to follow her.

They cross the room to a curtained area in a corner of the basement. Once there, Miss Applewhite pulls the black fabric aside, the smooth swish of the silk a balm to her senses. She steps into the shadows beyond and disappears from view for a moment. Before the moment has fully passed, she steps back, a gentle smile on her face and something covered with thin, bluish plastic in her arms. Andrealphus moves aside to give her room, and Miss Applewhite turns, heading for her worktable. Almost reverently, she lays her package on the polished wooden surface and peels back the plastic, every movement a study in care and attention. She swiftly eases her work into order, making it ready for inspection, the piece exactly as she intends.

Even now, after millennia or more of this work, it brings a tear to her eye that she has been given this extraordinary gift. She is an artist of the highest order, able to recreate and even, though she dislikes boasting or preening of any kind, to improve on nature's beauty. She is honoured. Looking down at her creation evokes the pride of a mother; she is about to let her go out into the world, to be seen by all, to be admired.

'May I?' That deep voice again, this time disturbing Miss Applewhite's rare indulgence in artistic reverie. Damn these creatures. If only she did not need them as much as they need her. She nods quickly, not bothering to look up at the creature, her indulgent mood gone, leaving her wanting to be rid of both him and the merchandise.

'She's beautiful.' The awe the voice conveys is enough to set Miss Applewhite's unusually frayed nerves a good way back to rights. She turns to her customer and favours him with a flicker of a smile.

'She's one of my best. I hope you will find her perfectly comfortable.'

'I'm sure I shall, Miss Applewhite, I'm sure I shall. But, as men like to say, the proof is in the pudding. If you will just step back …' Miss Applewhite duly complies and tries not to roll her eyes as the grotesquery begins.

The suit on the table is a macramé of human flesh. Muscle, tendon, organ, skin and bone have been fused to create a wonderful original whole – a new human being. Parts have been collected and adapted to satisfy the requirements the customer outlined in his Purchase Order. Five feet and ten inches of human woman has been meticulously accumulated and stitched into place. The long black hair is that of a bareback horse rider from the Russian State circus. Miss Applewhite found her in Minsk, alone, drunk, and afraid one night after being beaten badly by her sometime boyfriend. Her kind, old lady demeanour convinced her of her sympathy, tricking her out of her life and her mane. The perfect violet eyes had been donated by a young wannabe actress who had been forced to sell herself on the backstreets of Paris to pay for both her rent and her heroin habit. The ten exquisite fingers had once belonged to a cellist from the London Symphony orchestra – beautifully sculpted fingers used after every meal to purge her of the calories that might have saved her already failing body. The skin covering the long legs was once that of a nurse from Prague, a manic depressive with an unfortunate penchant for her patients' medications. Collapsed in her apartment, near death, she had believed Miss Applewhite to be an angel come to save her. All she preserved were the top layers of her milky sweet pins. There are so many stories behind each part – it is a symphony of flesh, a harmonic cacophony composed and sewn faultlessly together by Miss Applewhite's invisible threads. No Frankenstein stitching here, no indeed. Miss Applewhite is, after all, a professional.

As the creature prepares himself for the next step, Miss Applewhite hoists herself onto another stool. Carefully, she crosses her legs at the ankles and waits, her hands folded neatly in her lap. They like to make a song and dance about this bit and she has to humour them. The basement seems to darken still further as the creature before her begins to breathe deeply – or at least he appears to breathe deeply. Demons have no real lungs; they are made of pain and hopelessness, of fear and shame, lies and filth. The fabric from which they are cut is the invisible layer of shit and sin that haunts the mortal world. They feed on it, its dark fuel nourishing their powers, sustaining them, perpetuating them and the evil they encourage. War, famine, theft and murder are ambrosia to these devils. They have no need of gods or dogma – the blackness in men's hearts is the only thing sacred to them. Of course, Miss Applewhite has seen it all before and it bothers her no more and no less than it has always done. She just wishes they would get on with it instead of always thinking they are something new and unique. Silly beggars. Miss Applewhite does not allow her sudden churlishness to show on her face.

Andrealphus closes his eyes and throws his head back. Throwing his arms up, he begins to speak in a tongue long dead in the world of man, but more or less street slang in the underworld. Miss Applewhite sniffs disapprovingly. So common. The words became incoherent as the demon begins to transmute into the blackness of his arrival. He maintains the shape of a man, but the cold darkness swallows any of the features he had created. The only thing left of him is his voice, that deep, booming voice. It rises steadily until it is an ear-splitting, indecipherable roar. Miss Applewhite rocks back slightly on her stool. The words may have been lost, but they are god-awfully loud, underpinned with such utter abhorrence that Miss Applewhite almost feels sorry for the human world. Almost. She stays where she is, watching as the blackness of the demon-thing begins to swirl in a frenzy of activity and intent. It spins upwards in a whirlwind of obscurity, only to descend, rushing downwards, piercing the skin suit, filling it, padding it, until every inch of it is infested with demonic essence, giving profane life to it. Suddenly, the darkness disappears into it completely, leaving only the memory of blackness in its wake.

Miss Applewhite waits for a moment and then gets down from her stool. She returns to the worktable where the body now lays. No longer just an exterior, the body is now a fully inflated human being. It stirs, but no breath yet fills its lungs, and no blood fills the chambers of its Bavarian flower seller's heart. Miss Applewhite taps its nose twice and whispers, 'Now'. An arc of soft white light springs from her right index finger as it hits the nose for the third and final time, seeming to pierce the soft pink tip. A sudden, shuddering breath expands the hitherto useless lungs – taken from a lonely young pop singer a little too fond of hot pants and glitter in Miss Applewhite's opinion – and the creature blinks its perfect violet eyes open to the world.

Miss Applewhite watches and waits as the body begins to move, breathe, look, see. Slowly she, for that is what she is meant to be, sits up, pushing herself into a sitting position using the cellist's fingers and the milkmaid's arms. Her shoulders, no longer belonging to a shop assistant at a Borders bookshop in Fort Worth, Texas, flex and relax, flex and relax as she tests their strength. She turns her head towards Miss Applewhite and a slow, seductive smile spreads across her lounge singer's mouth. Miss Applewhite nods in acknowledgement and crosses the room to a filing cabinet, opens a drawer and browses the files therein. She does not notice the woman get down from the table and follow her.

A ... And ... Andrealphus. Miss Applewhite pulls the file she has been looking for from the drawer and pushes it shut. She turns, file in hand, almost colliding with the woman standing behind her.

'Oh dear, I'm terribly sorry, I didn't know you were there... ahem, madam.' Miss Applewhite moves to walk around her customer, but the woman blocks her path. 'Excuse me, if you would.' But the woman simply stands there looking at her. 'I really have to get your bill in order, if you wouldn't mind…'

'Oh, but I do mind, very much.' The deep voice has miraculously, perfectly, transformed into something richly feminine, a velveteen glove of seduction. Miss Applewhite is unswayed by the newly acquired sexuality of the creature, but she is not ignorant of the menace it intends. 'Why don't you just put that down, Miss Applewhite? We could just forget about it, couldn't we.' It is clearly not a question, but Miss Applewhite is not going to be intimidated.

'The matter of the bill, madam, is to be settled here and now, as per our agreement. To renege or to waylay it would be a breach of contract and I simply will not allow that. Neither will the Infernal Court of Appeal. You must relinquish the agreed gift.' She does not allow the fear that briefly troubles her mind affect her speech. Her equilibrium remains intact, as ever the consummate professional.

'What if I don't want to relinquish anything? What if I just take this body and leave, skedaddle, split? What on earth would you do about that, Miss Applewhite?'

The room suddenly sizzles with a whiteness far too bright for the demon's eyes. The now human eyes blink once, twice, but are unable to open properly, so bright is the light in the room. She shields them with the cellist's hands as the air zings with something akin to electricity, unnatural in origin and smelling distinctly like apple blossom. The whiteness scorching the basement is reflected in Miss Applewhite's eyes – is, in fact, the colour of her eyes. No iris or pupil remains, only the icy white clearness of her sclera, twinkling in the reciprocating light infusing the room. The demon backs away from the small woman, fear radiating from her as the light radiates from what is now clearly her adversary.

'Is that a threat, madam?' Miss Applewhite's voice thunders around the subterranean chamber, rattling shelves, dislodging books, clinking and clattering glass jars. Nothing falls, nothing breaks, but disarray threatens. The atmosphere is tight with something unutterably ethereal, something even more unnatural than the demon itself. Suddenly aware of her vulnerable human form, she begins to sweat. She cowers away from the small, neat woman with the wild, milky eyes as if she is the devil themself. 'I asked you a question, madam, I would kindly request that you answer me!' The demon shrinks farther away from Miss Applewhite as she seems to expand exponentially with that final resounding syllable. Ice-white flashes of light flicker from her fingers, dancing from her extremities in sharp teasing patterns, patterns that frighten a demon that has spent their not inconsiderable existence planting terror into the hearts of men. Andrealphus had wanted to walk the earth for a while, wanted to feel for themself the conflict between fear and hope, love and hatred, experiences so unique to the human being. They wanted to feel the weakness of the flesh, to dance, even if only for a while, their dance toward death – something they have never and will never know for themself. Or so they have always believed. As she watches the flesh tailor grow in size, grow far too large for the basement that, nevertheless, continues to contain her, Andrealphus begins to fear for herself as they have never done before. Bolts of lightning flare from the once deceptively little woman, bouncing off the shelves that line the walls, flicking across the worktables, licking sharply at the demon's human skin.

'P-please,' she whimpers, 'I… I'm … I'm sorry.'

'I beg your pardon?'

'I'm sorry, t-terribly sorry, Miss Applewhite, I take it all … all of it, all back. I hereby relinquish the power as agreed.'

The bright light fades as quickly as it came. Miss Applewhite smiles happily at the cowering woman before her.

'Excellent. I hope your sojourn amongst the mortals is everything you hope for.'

The demon-woman has no idea how to process what has transpired so quickly. One minute she had been frozen to the spot, ready to squall like a newborn babe, the next she was as free as a bird. Miss Applewhite watches the creature's quandary with an objective eye. Leaning forward, she stretches out her hand, offering to pull the demon to her feet. It is the least she can do. Miss Applewhite has been in this business for centuries and she truly believes in customer satisfaction. She is, after all, the consummate professional.

LEAVE THE PISTOL BEHIND

Anne the Bone was no fool. Red Johnny Bootleg might be hung like a well-fed donkey, but he was a good for nothing bully of a blaggard and she was done with him. She'd been thinking with her cunny for far too long, acting like a sex-starved old salt when she should have known better. Talented in the bedchamber he might be, but Red Johnny was the most incompetent captain she'd ever sailed with. No sooner had they stepped on that fucking island than they'd been in all kinds of hellish bother. No treasure was worth the seven shades of shit they'd seen that day. Anne shuddered to remember all those eyes, red eyes, hundreds of them it had seemed like. All of them watching, and she knew they were no longer waiting. She could have tasted their eagerness on the air... if she hadn't been running screaming back to the boats. Now, the black spot was upon her sometime lover and there would be no running for Red Johnny Bootleg this time. He may have come within a breath of dancing with old Jack Ketch a hundred times in his cack stain of a life – if you believed so much as one of his tall tales – but Red Johnny's voyage was near its end, and the Devil was welcome to him.

Every good for nothing pirate knew Fang Sank Island was a someplace any right-minded type steered clear of, literally. Still, pirates weren't known for their restraint or, indeed, their lack of ambition when it came to riches and many had gone to the island never to be seen again. Red Johnny would be no different. More than once after they'd shaken bones together, he had told her he'd wanted to be a pirate ever since he had been a suckling grabbing for his mama's tit in one of Blind Bobba Boontang's brothels out at Carpenter's Bay, a pirate pit of villainous scum if ever there'd been one. His father had been a pirate he'd said, although Anne was good and sure Bootleg's mother had about as much clue as to any of her brats' sires as she had about what two and two made. Yet, Johnny's eyes had took a shine whenever he mentioned his father, and his voice got heavy with grit when he'd said he would do anything to make his mark to show *him*. Anything. She'd believed him too. His cutthroat ambition had been what she'd found most attractive about him after all, well, that and his big cock of course. He was going to be the most famous pirate ever to have sailed the Seven Seas and that was that. Instead, of course, he'd proved to be just another unimaginative drunk who could barely keep his cock in his pants and didn't have enough of the commons to appreciate a woman with plenty, who'd beaten her black and blue when she'd dared to question his plans about Fang Sank in front of the other men. And hadn't her own Pa taught her that lesson early on and hadn't he taught her it well? Not well enough, apparently, but this last time Annie had marked it at last. When she and the crew had cut their losses and left Red Johnny on the beach, he had begged her to leave him the pistol but she'd denied him that mercy. With her eye still black and her ribs still sore, with their men pissing themselves with fear on that godforsaken beach, she'd have been damned if she was going to let him take the easy way out. Instead of famous, he was going to end up as food. She hoped he gave those devil fucks indigestion.

Red Johnny Bootleg never backed down from a challenge, but for the first time in his life, he was beginning to wish he had because he was, quite frankly, cacking himself. Hanging by the neck until dead might once have sounded like the worst kind of end, but now he knew better. He'd rather meet his maker at the hands of a man than the terrible darkness that was racing towards him even now across the sand. Anne the Bone was a hard bitch with a decent cunny, the way he liked his women, but he'd underestimated her. He'd been too full of his own pissing importance to listen to her begging him to think twice, had struck her hard, more than once, shown her his boot when she'd insisted this trip was folly. He couldn't have the men thinking him whipped and so she had cut him loose, offered him up as sacrifice as soon as it had been clear they were no match for whatever it was this island harboured. He couldn't help but admire her for it, almost as much as he'd make her pay for it if he could, whether in this life or the next. His laughter sounded a lot like weeping.

So, this was how it was to be then, aye? Crapping in his pants and howling like a baby. Begad! He'd had such dreams, such a desire for greatness... As he watched the creatures move swiftly in on him, their devil eyes flashing in the gloom, he felt his bowels loosen and with it his sanity.

He began to scream.

They were on him too soon and, as they sank their teeth into his flesh, he knew he was still screaming but he didn't know how to stop. He felt his life slipping away, knew his dreams were all dashed, but even as they were tearing into him, eager for his blood, drinking him like they'd not seen land for weeks, his throat raw from screaming, it began not to matter. Agony turned his vision white at the edges, lifting him higher, above the carnage, above the creatures. The stars were falling down around him, silvery streaks of ether, and then he was rushing past them into the darkness beyond. He was a rush of energy, he was stardust, no, he was godhead...

... He awoke with the taste of strange blood in his mouth, another's meat pressing against his lips. For a moment he wondered if he was dead but it quickly ceased to matter. He could feel the fizzing of immortality in his veins, every tiny electrical charge that wakened his muscles, strengthening them with a fervour he had never known in life, and he knew he was reborn. What had he become? He had never seen anything like those monsters on the beach before... But what did it any of that matter? All he knew was that he was hungry, so fucking hungry. A red haze of lust came over him as he licked at the blood being forced into his mouth. As it trickled down his throat and he began to drink in earnest, Red Johnny felt its life force filling him, fuelling him, changing him still further. And then, just when he thought he would burst from the aching fullness, but cared not a whit if he did, there was darkness.

The first they knew of the attack was the clatter of a cutlass and a strangled cry for help. Anne the Bone was awake in a flash. Something was very wrong indeed.

'No quarter, mateys!' The cackling voice was gravelly, altered, but she would know it anywhere. Somehow Red Johnny Bootleg had survived Fang Sank Island and was back on board. And he was angry. In a swift sequence of movements borne out of a lifelong habit of self-preservation, Anne sprang from the bed, pulled her boots on, slipped her dagger into the left one and fixed her pistol belt around her hips. The noise was coming from the fore of the ship. It sounded an awful lot like screaming. And thudding. Bodies falling. A chill like nothing she'd ever felt had descended and she felt it right down to her marrow. There was not one thing natural about it. She needed to see what was out there and she needed to see it now. She made her way across the cabin and hauled herself up the ladder that led from the captain's cabin to the quarterdeck. Intended as an escape hatch, it was barely big enough to push a grown man's shoulders through. Carefully, Anne pushed up the wooden trapdoor and peered out into the darkness beyond. She hadn't heard the lookout boy sail ho any ships and couldn't for the life of her work out how Red Johnny could be alive let alone be back on the ship.

Scorching pain suddenly tore into Anne's scalp as she was lifted by her hair from her hidey-hole. Crying out in shock, she struggled against the talons sinking into her skull but to no avail. As she was lowered to the deck, but not enough to gain purchase with her feet, she looked up into the face of her attacker. Red Johnny, or what had once been him, grinned at her, his mouth full of teeth, more than she'd ever seen in a human's skull before. And in that moment she knew the legends about Fang Sank Island were true.

'You should have left me that pistol, Annie, love.'

THE MOST TRAGICAL AND IMPLAUSIBLE FATE OF MARY I: A DEMONIC SOLILOQUY

Veritas Temporis Filia

'Adjúro te, serpens antique…' I adjure you, ancient serpent, yada yada yada. I can't tell you how many times I've heard this old twaddle before – they just love swinging their incense thingies and bleating Latin any chance they get – and I've no doubt I'll hear it again.

Big fat yawn.

'Exi, sedúctor, plene omni dolo et fallácia, virtútis inimici, innocéntium persecutor.' Quite the mouthful that one. It means something like 'Seducer, all full of guile and cunning, foe to all that yucky virtue and persecutor of the easy-pickings innocent', and yep, you've guessed it, he means me. Yuck yuck yuck. Things is, the old boy can go right ahead and do his worst because I couldn't give a toss. Not even a hairy one. I've scored the Queen of England and he's more foolish than he looks, bashing his bishop with all that smoke and blather like a randy teenager, if he thinks I'm getting exorcised that easy. Besides, I've got the goods, the skinny, the down low, a piece of pukka gossip that should buy me the time I need to secure my payday. I can trade it for something that will finally crush this bitch's will from the inside out and get me that promotion. I'm just going to cling onto the inside of her skull and hang on for the ride. This preacher man's all hyperbole and bluster, as per. I can outlast him.

I do.

Well, of course I do. I'm not new at this. One day I'm going to be Lucifer's right hand guy, keys to the kingdom and all that shit. I've got ambition and I'm not afraid of even the darkest shadows in Hell, so some pious bore who likes to rub his wife's fabrics against his flaccid old cock isn't going to get the better of me.

I let him have at it though. I mean, who am I to deny a man his fifteen minutes? This old sixteenth century bullshit is so quaint. Wait until the twenty-first century comes along – they don't even think we exist outside of comic books. Either way, time doesn't mean anything to us. We're eternal, you finite slabs of meat, and we shine while you decay in your stinking flesh sacks. So vulgar.

The old chap demands my name and I know he's nearly done. Finally. You've got to make a play of it, though, right? Make them work a little? So I refuse a few times, let Mary's chops get another splash of holy water and a waft of that sickly incense. They think their water is holy. They think their God cares. Why would I be sitting here inside their queen, playing on her neurals like a virtuoso cellist, if their God gave two hoots about his little clay men? Deluded monkeys the lot of them.

'I am Barnabus the Breacher,' I say through Mary's chapped lips, making my voice as *plume de ma* fucking *tante* as I can, 'and I am here to smother any child from the womb of this vessel.' I know what he wants. He wants my name and my purpose. It's supposed to hoist me with my petard, to stop me in my tracks, but in truth it's the final part of a paint-by-numbers joke of a nothing ritual. Like I said though, I like to play along. If they start to think it doesn't work, the gig's up. Old Mary's got one thing right – fire does purge. Without a vessel, we demons are just smoke on the wind. If they chuck Mary's fetid carcass on the pyre to get rid of me, pretty much the only thing that will, I'd have to go through the rigmarole of finding another vessel and that's not as easy as it sounds. Demon possession is quite frowned upon, dontchaknow. Not everyone wants to make room in the old brain pan for a hitchhiker, especially one as bossy as me.

As for me being old Barnabus the Breacher (there was one once, and he was a twat, and I ain't downplaying), the fact is I'm not here to kill any babies; Mary's womb does that all on its own with its cancerous growths and malformations (she can thank her god for that). What this lot never realise, what never clicks, is that my kind is always here for the same reason, and it's real simple – we like to fuck with people. Simple as. They let us into their weak little minds and we get to play… Why are you doubting? Ok, you got me, that's not entirely true (I'm a demon, I tell lies from time to time, what do you expect?) In real terms, souls are like a sale that we get commission on. We acquire them, pass them on to the big man downstairs and our worth increases: the bigger the booty, the bigger our stock. A bit like estate agents – they, predictably, make great demons. Minor leaguers generally, but real cutthroat bastards. No offence (joke; I always intend offence). All I have to do is enslave my host's mind absolutely, get them to off themselves, and the credit's mine. As in *Credit;* infernal Benjamins, cheddar, bone, cha ching, spon-fuck-ing-dooligs. Or as near as we got to your notes and gold and coinage, better than if I'm honest. Stuff that's going to make me comfy as hell because in Hell money can buy you happiness. Oh yeah. Only problem is, Mary's utterly bonkers so the whole thing is taking longer than I'd hoped. A lot longer.

It's a good job I love my work.

Once the priest is gone, satisfied he's restored his queen, I lecture the spotty scrot of a valet for a bit, hazing him with a few power words (our skills lie mainly in persuasion rather than that laser-hand shit American TV shows like to ejaculate over), and, when I know he's totally under, I slash his throat with the hunting knife I keep close to hand. Stupid meat sack, shows how well he knew and loved his mistress if he couldn't tell there was a shit-eating demon of doom sitting right there in her frontal lobe still. I'll feed his carcass to her whiny Italian greyhounds later. That'll keep them on side a bit longer. Dogs always know when we're about. You folks should really pay better attention to them. Cats, on the other hand, couldn't give a shit but you probably knew that already.

A hearty spurt of his blood splashes into the bowl, which I rather poetically had him arrange for me earlier, with a glo-rious sound, one that makes my tummy rumble, but I can't drink. I need to conduct some business and the chap I need only does it this way. A sanguinary telephone exchange. He saw it on the telly once.

I despair, I really do.

I submit my titbit – a salacious bit of scandal that should put his main competitor out of business – and he offers me a curse but not the one I want. All he's got are strength of bond curses, but I'm already so embedded in the daft mare it would take a giant eschatological battering ram to tear us asunder, as they say. What I need is time. Time to finally get her to put her catechisms aside and take her own life. It shouldn't be so hard, but while she was easy to get into, Mary's as stubborn as a mule about her faith and suicide is the ultimate abomination to her. I say all this to my dealer, but his hands are tied, he says. Not his area, he says. Lucifer's hoary dick! Why does everything have to be such a ballache? Honestly, you…

Three sharp raps on the door echo through the room. These are Mary's private rooms; trusted guards, as far as one can trust a couple of pork chops so easily bewitched, guard the entrance. The exorcism, if you can call it that, is a secret and there should be no one to tell it. The priest is bought and paid for, one of Mary's loyal pets long before I got here, and who would get into a whole heap of parochial trouble if anyone found out about his part in proceedings. I would have had to slit the valet's throat before the night was through whatever happened, so who is that rapping and tapping at my chamber door?

The door opens. Of all the cheeky wotsits. You know, if Mary were a proper queen and not a devout maniac, intruders, traitors, and their ilk would have their heads chopped off (it's clean but juicy, and Mama does like juicy). Frankly, I think it sends the strongest message. No messing about, but Mary prefers to burn them and tries to keep it strictly to dissenters; the sight of flames licking against a heretic's skin makes the gusset of her haircloth thong sopping wet, and I'm fairly sure she jacks off to their screams of agony while praying for her sanctimonious soul. Such a bloody hypocrite. It's that type of self-deluded shitdickery that lets my kind in, you know. Just FYI for laters, son.

A woman enters. I'm pretty sure neither of us recognise her right off the bat. I might be controlling the beast, but Mary's still here, whining and moaning, clutching an imaginary rosary and crying for her poor dead mother. It's pretty wearing. A long black cloak covers the woman's face and form, but I can smell enough to know it *is* a woman. I have no idea how she could have got past the guards; to think I chose them myself!

'Who are you?' Mary's voice is gruff. She needs a throat sweet after all that demon voice malarkey, but this century doesn't do that sort of thing. They probably crush up seashells and gob in them to make a delightful balm. Peasants.

'I'm no one.' Helpful.

'You must be someone. Speak.'

'I am but a servant.' She throws back her hood.

Oh shit.

I twig just before she hits me with her fucking metaphysical stun gun. Bitch. I should have seen it coming. Grete von Schnozzle or some Teutonic sounding bullshit. Her family have been after me for eons, chasing me here, there, and everywhere, across and around the centuries. Witches. They're so bloody tenacious. This one's as doggedly aggravating as they come too. We've had some close calls, she and I. The last time we met, I only escaped in one piece because I threw her tosspot son under a passing carriage. He deserved it. For the record, witches are the real deal, but all warlocks are ineffectual ponces and don't let anyone tell you different. I do so love to see Grete's kind mourn, gives me a buzz right in the fuzzy tingle place. They tend to properly lose the plot and, in her case, the crazy really saved my bacon. Sheesh, just the memory of the wailing still makes my teeth throb.

Despite all that, I should perhaps have been more circumspect about coming back to the sixteenth century, her lot are at their strongest here – but that jizzwazz Sabnock dared me. Said I'd been trumpeting my skills for too long and that I'd never get a bounty as big as Mary's, so I could hardly give him the satisfaction of saying no, could I? I'd never hear the end of it. Besides, we're talking about the most rabidly god-fearing queen of England there ever was, good old Bloody Mary the First. The things I've made her do! It was too tempting an opportunity to pass up once I thought about it and I am going to cash in big time. Ker-fucking-ching.

I've been so hyped up on my big score that I forgot about the witch and her kin. She can cast me out like the old priest can only dream about – but she knows as well as I do it's not permanent. She's a bump in the road. If she had the goods to really finish me off I might be more worried but, as it is, I'm not that bothered. She doesn't know about fire. They still haven't figured it out but then they probably wouldn't use it anyway. You'd risk killing the vessel and all life is sacred or some shit like that. I ask you! Self bloody defeating much? While, it's true I can't move, she's already seen to that, her magic will wear off soon enough – she can only do a spurt at a time – and then, if I time it just right, I'll grab her by the throat and shake her until she's nothing but a badly dressed rag doll. She's played it badly, I'd say.

The mirror comes at me hard. I don't even see Grete's fingers move. It stops a short distance from my nose.

Ah, yes. Well.

This isn't good.

Mirrors and demons don't mix. You've seen that Terence Stamp Superman movie right? The one where he's clad in some major league black PVC? Honestly, I'd eat that man up toot fucking sweets given the chance. Anyway, it's not the same really, but Stamp is cool and it's near enough. I hear her muttering, something in German, all harsh vowels and inelegant consonants. I'm not a fan of anything but English, although of course I can speak any tongue I choose. Being a demon has its perks.

What the hell am I doing thinking about languages when that mirror is hovering right there in front of me? I can't let my concentration be shot to pieces by this bog witch's incantations… Gah! I can't stop staring at myself, I'm transfixed. Damnable mirrors! They're my kind's curse. I study Mary's face in the glass. History hasn't been kind to Bloody Mary. You can see she was a bit of a sort once, even now, rotten as she is with cancer and pious bigotry. Her deeds have twisted her memory and people only remember her as a bit of a hag.

Them's the breaks, love. All the better for me…

…Damn it! My mind's going again. Bloody mirrors. They zap your concentration and give you away. My eyes shine through hers, glowing red for anyone to see. I'm flashing my true self all over town like I'm Sharon Stone or something. Wait. Is that from some movie? One of old Wesley Carpenter's?

There I go again! Straight down the rabbit hole.

The devil pox this mirror-wielding whore!

I check across the room and realise that old Grete's ramping up for some serious shit. Seems like she's been building up her psychic muscles and I don't much like the look of it.

I'm right, of course.

The full force of the impact nearly breaks me in two. It's all very metaphorical – I'm not substantial so I can't actually break (I don't have teeth either, but you didn't think about that earlier did you, you mouth-breather) – but I feel it within me, my essence not Mary's, and it is agony. I scream, a sound I'd hoped never to hear again, not since the flea-bitten mage in the sands of Sumer made me daemon all those moons ago. So maybe I did eat his wife and spit her guts up at his feet with a grin on my face. I wasn't the nicest person in the world to be sure, but what he did to me in revenge was… unspeakable. Now, of course, I can applaud his ingenuity. Hats off and all that.

The pain subsides, but the confusion doesn't. I can't get my thoughts in order. What did she do? Where am I? The witch is looking at me from the other side of the mirror. How did she get in there?

Wait… Satan's shitting hellfire!

I can't keep anything straight in my brain for longer than a few seconds but it's suddenly obvious I'm the one trapped in the mirror. Fury and panic surge through me, and I try to scratch her cussed eyes out…

… but, finally, I feel relief.

Without that vexatious glass to cloud my mind, I realise there's nothing to worry about. The mirror thing is just another one of their half-baked theories; humans and their linear thinking, is there anything duller? Tsk. Trapping me in the mirror does fuck all in the long run, love. There is no way to kill a demon, at least not one known or easily accessible to mortals. Non-corporeal, remember? Anyway, I've heard of this before, it's nothing that can't be worked out in the end but I can't lie, it's a massive pain in the arse and it's going to properly scupper my plans. Curse her stinking witch eyes.

Hell's teats, it's so empty in here. I don't mind my own company, but it takes more than simple magicks to smudge across the borders back into the mortal plane. As Sod's Law naturally dictates it takes a lot of time and I couldn't even secure a season curse from a scumbag dealer from the wrong side of Limbo with one of the juiciest pieces of gossip I've ever snitched. It's going to take a lot of meditation and all that sort of bollocks. Man, I hate studying. I'm a talker and I like to hear myself speak, you have to if you're going to be good at this kind of work. It'd be better if I had someone to shoot the shit with, bounce ideas off, you know?

Oh no, wait, hold the phone, of course I'm not alone. To my left, a familiar woman whimpers and scratches at herself, muttering and fidgeting like she's got St Vitus' dance.

Bugger-bloody-ation!

The witch didn't, or more likely, couldn't separate us; she's thrown Mary in here too. I said our bond was strong, and it turns out I wasn't kidding. The Beast's balls. This I did not see coming. Maybe Grete's cleverer than I gave her credit for (but still not as clever as she thinks she is). I'm going to have to listen to Bloody Mary's incessant whining for as long as it takes me to work out how to get free.

Fucking fabulous.

THE HUNTER

The hunter stands triumphant as he shows his trophy to his camera. He grips the tiger's scruff tightly in one hand, its tongue lolling as one last drip of saliva falls to the ground. The arrow through his chest is a surprise, the sound of meat tearing registering before the pain. He drops the tiger's head and falls to his knees. Gasping with agony, the hunter looks around desperately for his assailant. Golden eyes shine from the bushes in the fading light of the dusk but they only watch as the hunter slowly bleeds to death. They will eat later.

MADAM MAFOUTEE'S
BAD GLASS EYE

Even with the beard, Lena was a doll. Maybe because of it.
I could have spent hours just staring at her. Those cool blue
eyes of hers made me weak at the knees and I would get the
cold sweats just thinking about them. I felt like a kid around
her and she knew it. Didn't she just.

'Mafoutee takes the eye out as soon as she gets back to her
caravan and puts it in the box. The old donah will be well
into her gin by midnight and you can grab it right out from
under her big ugly nose.' Lena winked at me; she knew I'd do
anything for her. She only had to show a bit of leg, bat those
ridiculously long eyelashes at me and I was putty in her perfectly manicured hands. I didn't care either. I should have, I
should have known better – how many times have you heard
that old chestnut? The fact was I simply didn't care.

The plan was simple. Madam Mafoutee was an old fortune teller who had been dukkering with the carnival for as
long as anyone could remember. She kept herself to herself,
except for Joey the Bipenis Boy, who seemed to be her personal slave. There were rumours that he was either her son
or her lover, but the woman had to be eighty if she was a day
and Joey was just about taking puberty in his overabundant
stride. Neither option fitted well. Still, they wouldn't be the
weirdest couple in the joint. Who would have thought that
me, Evelina Strange, Strong Woman, and Lovely Lena, the
Bountiful Bearded Lady, would have had such a connection?
Not me, I can tell you, but I digress...

The eye was the prize. Seems ghoulish, I know, but that
eye wasn't what it seemed, at least not according to Lena. Set
within its depths, she said, was a diamond bigger than the
top of my not inconsiderable thumb. How her eyes had lit
up the first time she'd told me. I'd never seen her so excited.
She said that she'd seen it before the eye had been made –

and that's the only part of her story I ever doubted. Lena had only been with the carnival for a few weeks before we started up together. I'll admit it didn't take long for me to become a smitten slave to her feminine wiles, but I'd worked this rig for just over two years and Mafoutee was here a long time before me. Still, I guess I'm not the sharpest tool in the box because I didn't question her, especially not after the look in her eye turned nasty. I might be what you might call a big girl and as strong as ten oxen, but I like neither confrontation nor nastiness. Lena amping up for a barney was a beautiful sight but the thought of the aftermath was just too much for my nerves.

'While she's out for the night dukkering those terrible fortunes of hers — honestly, have you ever heard such horse-shit? — I'll sneak into the van and slip a bit of belladonna into her gin. Not enough to kill her, just enough to knock her out.' Lena looked gleeful as she told me her plan. Everyone knew the old girl liked a bottle like a flower loves the sun, but it didn't sit quite right messing with her sauce. Sensing my hesitation, Lena slipped into my lap and put her arms around my neck, wiggling that backside of hers against my needy thighs and, like the puppet I was, my qualms vanished. There was nothing I wouldn't have done for her at that moment, nothing. Her happiness was my folly. 'Sweetling, I know you're not one for underhandedness, but needs must. We can be free of this life.' She spoke so dismissively of it, the life I'd led since I was thrown out of home at fifteen, of the people that had taken me in as one of their own, or so I thought. 'We'll run away together. Live somewhere by the sea like you've always dreamed. It will be wonderful. You do want us to be together, don't you?' Her soft little pout made my heart pound. I wanted it like I'd wanted nothing else in this world. Let me be a lesson to you, friends. Never tell anyone your dreams. They take them and twist them and use them for their own ends. I didn't know that then and hearing her talk like that made me the patsy she needed. I'll be honest; the plan made my guts quake but the thought of not going through with it made me feel even worse. Lena would be disappointed in me, she'd cast me aside, and then what would I do? I was in this for the long haul and I intended to prove it.

The night was set for the following Saturday. Lena had been watching the old woman for days and knew her routine like clockwork. The only problem was that Saturdays were my busiest time. Five performances in one day usually wiped me out, strong as I was.

'Don't worry, darling, I've got something that will pep you right up.' The white powder she gave me wasn't something I had ever tried before. I'd had a few of those mushroom things the Hurly Burly Dwarf Company liked to brew in a tea, but this was something new. The first time I tried it I knew I was going to be hooked. I was even stronger than usual on it. I loved it. It made my muscles twitch, my heart race and a grin etched itself deep into my plain old face. I had a spring in my step from the get-go – which may have been the reason for me going along with all this foolishness in the first place, or so I'd like to think now.

When the clock struck midnight on the appointed Saturday night, jacked up on Lena's powder, smiling like a fool despite my strong body being battered by that day's spots, I slipped into the old woman's caravan just like we'd planned.

I knew something was wrong ... no, I didn't. Even now I'm still lying to myself. Truth is I had no idea; I was a dupe and I didn't know it until it was too late. Everything went like clockwork, or so it seemed. The caravan was creepy inside, but that wasn't anything I hadn't been expecting. Madam Mafoutee liked dolls. She had hundreds of them in storage, Lena claimed, but kept her favourites on display where she could see them. She had all kinds of them and doted on the hokey things. It gave me the heebie-jeebies to think of a grown woman brushing their hair and choosing outfits for them. I'd never liked dolls and their too-big eyes seemed to follow me as I made my way further into the van. The old woman herself was out cold, the gin glass had rolled out of her hand onto the floor but she was past noticing. Joey was asleep in his own van and there was nothing to stop me getting to that box. It was sat in full view on the little sideboard beside the old woman. Taking it was a piece of cake. A very obvious piece of cake.

Did my foolishness end with just grabbing the box? Of course it didn't. What made me open it? Something, or maybe *someone*, made me do it, and I know that sounds stupid but truth is truth and I knew I had to open it, that nothing else mattered but seeing what was inside.

So I did.

The eye blinked at me.

No, not blinked, the damned thing *winked* at me. I would lay my hand upon a bible and swear it as God's honest truth. Without so much as a lid to call its own, the eye – the solid glass eye – winked at me. Disbelief made me pause; it couldn't be, surely? I looked again. It winked again. Suddenly, it was as though the box it nestled in was grinning at me, the gaping maw the open lid made became threatening enough to make me drop it. I had no choice. I thrust the vile thing from my hands, dashing it against the wooden floor of the caravan with a shout of disgust.

I woke the old woman. Or so I thought.

'Ha! Now, what can I suppose you're doing in here, Evelina Strange? And what have you done with my eye?' she asked. Her distinct lack of surprise was obvious even in my bewildered state. Her voice was not as heavy with the belladonna's somniferous effects as it should have been either, I could tell that too. She had been waiting. For me.

'Did you think the Naughty Man's Cherries was enough to knock me out, sweetling? You think the dose was bona? D'you really think your beardy palone was on the up and up?' She chuckled quietly to herself as she stroked the doll she was holding in her lap like a baby. Looking at her made my head pound. I needed to get out of there but I just stood there staring at the old woman dumbly.

'Now Mama, it's not polite to laugh at people, no matter how ridiculous they are.' The familiar voice from behind me was like a blow to the gut, but it broke the spell and I spun on my heel to confront the speaker.

Lena.

My Lena.

I should have known it was too good to be true. I'd fallen

for her patter like the fool that I was.

Joey the Bipenis Boy popped out from behind her as I stared at my golden haired downfall. Unable to fully comprehend this turn of events (even as I knew it was inevitable – a girl like Lena wasn't for the likes of me) I watched as, moving so quickly he was practically a blur, the boy scooped up the box, slapped the lid shut and handed it to the old woman. For a moment, without that eye staring its malevolence into the world, my head felt clearer than it had since I'd left my caravan. It didn't last long. Joey stood behind Mafoutee's chair and waited. I didn't want to know what for, but I was sure I was going to find out.

'So, my chavi has told you about the diamond, has she?' It registered then. Lena had called the old woman *mama*. Lena was Mafoutee's daughter! How could that be? I nodded even as my mind whirred uselessly, my eyes flitting between the two women. I couldn't see the resemblance, not one bit. Lena with her glorious mane of blonde hair, matching full beard and those cool blue eyes couldn't be related to the curve-backed, dark-eyed hag still slouched in her armchair as if nothing had changed. 'She's been away from me too long, that one, and I've missed her something rotten. She's a good girl, smart, knows just how to lure 'em in. She always done well for me in the past and that's not changed. Has an eye for it, you might say.' She grinned at me then, enjoying her quip, and finally I saw the whole of her face. Her empty eye socket – more a hole than a socket in truth – was deeper and darker than it should have been. The darkness within it swirled and flickered, tiny pulses of light seemed to reach out to me then retreat, teasing me, luring me in even more assuredly than Lena had. I couldn't look away. My mind quieted, my breath slowed. The van around me receded until there was nothing but those tiny teasing lights. I felt a glass being pressed into my hand and I brought it to my lips automatically. I took greedy gulps of the liquid therein, feeling the smooth rush of it travelling all the way down my gullet into my stomach. A numb sensation shot outwards from my gut, first surging through my veins, then running through my muscles, before filtering through my bones and into my brain until all I felt was sweet nothingness. The rush of it was more addictive than the drugs Lena had dosed me with. I wanted more but at the same time I was calmer than I'd ever felt in my entire sorry life.

It didn't last.

From out of nowhere, a heavenly golden glow seemed to shine all around me, from me; my body was filled with it. I had been expecting something awful to happen but instead my mind cleared of any doubts, any pain. I was free and I was light, and in that moment I somehow knew with absolute certainty that I was done for.

In the grip of my euphoria, brought on by the belladonna that should have been Mafoutee's but was always meant for me I now realise, I could hear chanting. It sounded like an insect at first but, gradually, it became more singsong, a balm to my ears. A second voice joined it, seemed to tangle with it, dance with it, elevating my senses still further. My feet lost contact with the floor and I felt how light and lithe my body had become. I was beautiful serenity. I was pounding rhythm. I yearned to join the dance, to break on the rocks of the song they sang. I was graceful for the first time in my life, no longer a thick-limbed oaf hampered by rejection and ridicule. Before was lost; now was all that mattered. Like liquid gold, I poured through the air, sleek and wanton in my need to reach out with every inch of my skin, every ounce of my being.

Lena's voice washed over me even as I felt the pull of her mother's stronger incantations. The power of the old woman's voice would have been unmistakeable even if it hadn't been licking across my skin like luscious rays of sunshine, firing my nerve endings and yet, in truth, lulling my senses to her bidding. As soon as I recognised my true mistress, everything changed.

The gold light folded in on itself, dropping me like a stone. My body hit the floor with a thud that shook the van. I felt a loss more acute than any I'd ever suffered. I yearned for the light, ached for its tendrils to hold me again. As I lay there in misery, the first cracking noise didn't bother me. I felt nothing, just my soul-shattering loss. I didn't realise it was me until my kneecaps splintered.

Then I screamed.

I kept right on screaming as my body realigned itself, the bones snapping and re-knitting, the muscles tearing and then re-hemming themselves into smaller and smaller proportions. It was white-hot agony, so pure in its intensity that it teetered on the pleasurable, but still I kept screaming.

Even as my voice box collapsed and then resurrected itself in a much smaller version, I screamed. The sound existed only in my head then. I knew that, but I didn't stop.

I began to solidify. I'm a meaty woman, I'm solid, but this was something else. It was as though I was thrust into a kiln, my skin hardening from clay to bisque in its colossal heat. I glanced down at my hands, once so clumsy but now like a doll's. I looked up at my mistress, Madam Mafoutee, and she seemed as tall as a Brobdingnagian queen. My head felt impossibly heavy suddenly and I was forced to look down, my chin dropping to my chest with a thud. At last the ache of my torn and re-rendered body became too much for my senses and I felt the sweet surety of death approaching. I welcomed it. Oblivion was all I sought. My mistakes were behind me and I would be free.

Or so I thought.

Consciousness came upon me slowly. I felt as though I should ache all over, just the memory of what had transpired – or what I thought had transpired – surely enough to make the hardest of sorts sore, but I didn't. When I raised my hand to my forehead… I didn't raise anything. It wouldn't move. Not one muscle twitched in response to my command. My head didn't turn and my legs were in no better shape. The only things I could move were my eyes. Frantic, I looked down at my body, a body that was as shiny as… brand new porcelain.

Realisation hit me like a bolt gun.

I was a doll.

I was a fucking doll! The panic was swift and, if I could have moved, I would have leapt off that table and scarpered like a fox from the hunt. Alas, I would never run again.

If I could have cried I would have, but even that was beyond me now.

The leering face of Madam Mafoutee came into sight suddenly, her nose enormous now, every hair and pore colossal. The darkness in her empty eye socket had gone. It was just a puckered useless lump of flesh once more.

'Well, Evelina. I've had my eye on you for a while. Never had one like you before, not one as strong and tall. You're beautiful and I knew you would be. Now, let me brush your hair and then we'll choose a nice dress for you. Something with frills, I think.'

As she brushed my locks, fuller and thicker than they had ever been before, she told me what would happen to me if I fell from her favour. She told me of a dark cold place where the only sound you can hear is the flicker of a thousand tiny eyelids, behind which are five hundred furiously impotent lunatic minds, cast aside by the maker. I closed my eyes and waited to be dressed.

THE DEVIL'S HAEMORRHOIDS

Wednesday 28th February 1838

This may well be my last entry. My resources have dwindled and I am no longer able to furnish myself with the drugs I require to stem the foul horror that eats away at me. My waking moments scream out for oblivion, while the solace of sleep has been denied me for more nights than I can remember. My mind and my body are in tatters. I am no longer the man I was. I exist in torment from which there is no release. I will recount my story, leave a testament to a life made wretched by the machinations of what must be the very devil himself, for no invention of man or nature could have birthed the abhorrent dreadfulness to which I have been exposed.

By profession, I am – *was* – a botanist. Young, ambitious and discontented with the mundanity of the already familiar flora of Northern Europe, I agreed to accompany a scientific journey to an island in the South Seas. Fang Sank Island was its local name, considered by the modern world to be entirely untouched. It was both an exciting and advantageous appointment. Success would surely mean a promotion within my department at the University and the information gathered would, potentially, afford the opportunity for a great many scientific papers upon which my academic reputation would be secured. My darling Clementine, the warmth of my heart since I was seventeen, only encouraged my ambitions. The separation would be long, but its significance for our future was unquestionable. We decided that we would marry as soon as I returned and I left her, the dearest girl, with the salve of bridal gowns, seating plans, and invitations to mitigate my absence.

The voyage was long but, luck seeming loyal to our endeavour, without any major incident and a complete, not to mention surprising, circumvention of pirates. We cast anchor in the bay of the island on the very day we had initially planned. I only realised later how suspicious the lack of those men who haunt the high seas really was. The delight of all was tangible, and the sight of the lush island was enough to send us all into a state of mind that, momentarily at least, impeded caution. Several of the crew, including the cook, volunteered to go ashore and scout the area. The cook was an ex-military man and claimed to have survived stranger shores than these, though where those shores could possibly have been I could not say. He argued that he would be able to replenish some of the food supplies and that he was confident in his ability to spot anything that might prove untoward to the human constitution because of his vast experience in, as he called it, the field. When I volunteered to assist him, he laughed that loud, obnoxious hoot of his and told me he would like as not be able to teach me a thing or to about my 'flowery business'. Not one to take offence with those less able than myself in the cerebral arena, I merely smiled and headed back to my room to go over some notes I had been working on in preparation for going ashore.

The first I saw of the mushrooms was at dinner that night. The cook had not consulted me as to their suitability and by the time I had stowed my papers and headed to the mess, many of the men had already half-emptied their plates.

The sight of the red-capped monstrosities was enough to make me dash the plate from the nearest man's clutches. He jumped to his feet in fury but the cook calmed him, explaining that I had come to a conclusion that was not entirely without merit. A generous concession indeed. He then proceeded to explain to me, as though to a witless child, that he too had reservations about the mushrooms at first, but that he had tested them upon his dog, a scraggy mutt who had been all but starving upon our arrival, who was as we spoke sleeping happily with a full belly before the galley's ovens. The cook then scooped a large spoonful of the agaric flesh and shoved it into his cavernous mouth, closing his eyes to demonstrate its deliciousness as he chewed.

I am not an overly fastidious man. I do not flinch at odd meats from exotic cuisines or balk at unusual delicacies such as the Asiatic continent might offer to my countrymen. I have tried many of them and not once have I wondered at the sense of it. There is, however, one thing I will not eat under any circumstances, and that is a mushroom. I do not know from whence this anathema sprang, but it is strong and I would have to be half-mad with starvation to consider them as sustenance. Their constitution is like that to the brain on which my work and life is hinged and the squalid stench of their cooked flesh is enough to clear my appetite in a repulsed heartbeat. There was no amount of seductive chewing the cook could do, had he even been able, that would have induced me into eating the red pestilence he had concocted.

I declined as best I could, giving my plate reluctantly to the man whose dinner I had knocked to the floor, and made do with the hard bread and water that accompanied the meal, such as it was. I was confident that on an island so clearly lush with abundance, I would be able to identify edible vegetables and, thus, we would be able to trace the indigenous animals that feasted upon them. The men mocked me, but it seemed in good humour and I took it as such.

The following morning, I woke with the unutterable belief that I was alone on board. The ship appeared to be as silent as the grave and, after dressing with all due haste, I hurried up onto deck to discover that I was only partly right in what I had thought an irrational assumption. At first I did not know what I was seeing. Several mounds dotted the edges and corners of the deck, I could not discern their exact shape and, I quickly concluded, only proximity would reveal their secrets. Yet, my feet would not move. Paralysed, with a ponderous feeling of dread in the very pit of my stomach, I stood, the warm breeze dancing through my hair, the sun beating down on my unprotected head. I told myself not to be a fool, that I was a man of science and as such I should be inspecting these unnatural protuberances and making an assessment of the situation rather than standing there gaping like a child frightened of shadows. I do not know how long I hesitated but, finally, I approached the nearest hump with no small amount of trepidation.

I was soon shocked to realise this wretched abomination before me had once been the young midshipman with whom I had often talked after dinner on the voyage, his thirst for knowledge appealing to my scholarly sensitivities. A burgeoning crop of mushrooms had thrust forth from the rictus scream of his now redundant mouth, while clusters of them had forced their way through his eye sockets, seemingly devouring the eyeballs, and had ripped through his death-slackened skin anywhere they could manage. I looked around in mounting horror at the tableau surrounding me, a dawning understanding that my crewmates were now the repositories of that most loathsome toadstool they had been so enamoured of at dinner the previous evening. It was a monstrous realisation and my mind loosened. I felt the crack of sanity as the intelligence I so prided myself on fled from me, and I became revulsion's quarry.

'The devil! The devil is upon us!' I spun around to face the possessor of the voice that rasped from the darkness below the overhang of the quarterdeck. Two white hands, stark against the gloom, emerged, seeking for something, anything, grasping fingers desperate. 'We are forsaken!' The cook stumbled from the darkness, his eyes rolling madly in his emaciated skull. Once a big man, he was a shadow of his former self and those dreadful mushrooms proliferated his flesh, every one a red-capped crop of despair. I backed away from him, disgust flooding me anew, but I had misjudged and stepped back into another of the mounds, my foot squelching down into the fetid remains of the decomposing midshipman's guts. A puff of some unctuous spore clouded around me and I fought the urge to cough and breathe in the noxious fumes. Hand clutched to my mouth, I pulled my foot from the foul corpse, my eyes never leaving the face of the cook. As he stumbled forward into the light, I saw the mushrooms shrink back from the rays. Of course! The mounds were all lying in areas of shadow. Mushrooms thrive only in the dark!

A rumbling groan, as though something was about to split asunder, shook me from my reverie. The cook was still coming towards me, but his steps were faltering at best. Horrified, I watched as he took one last lumbering step before toppling slowly, but unctuously, to the floor. His body hit the deck like overripe fruit, the putrescent smell that arose from it enough to send my stomach into free-fall and I managed to grab the side of the ship before vomiting over it.

When I was recovered, I went into a frenzy of activity. The fungal bastardy that had consumed my shipmates needed to be destroyed. Covering my mouth with my handkerchief, I set about ridding the deck of those dastardly mounds. I worked until my back raged with fire and sweat dripped from every pore. I cleared all of them. A cursory exploration of the dark confines below deck was all I could manage. Suddenly claustrophobic, it was all I could do to go down there, but I could not countenance the thought of leaving another alive. In the end, I found no one, although there were many mounds, all of which had grown larger than those on the deck due to the darkness in which the agaric carbuncles thrived. I settled for packing my things as quickly as possible. I gathered water from the store and some staples. Once back in the sunlight, I released one of the lifeboats and clambered down into it. I would rather have died at sea than spend another moment on that ship. The island was not a place I wished to go either. The stories and rumours I would have dismissed without a second thought the previous day were now upmost in my mind. Whatever land produced such an evil as those red caps was not a place I needed to visit.

I do not recall how many days I spent in that craft. I ran out of food and water within a few and delirium swiftly followed. I do not remember being pulled out of the boat by my rescuers but I will be indebted to them until the end of my sorry days. The debt will not be long enough.

I returned home under a cloud of suspicion. Few believed my story and preferred to think of less arcane and rather more nefarious machinations. My beloved Clementine felt she could not marry someone who had seemingly lost his wits and I cannot say that I blame her. I was a laughing stock at best, a mass murderer at worst. I lost my position with the University and it was made clear to me that no papers of mine would be accepted by any publication. It was futile anyway. I was unable to write a word other than those in this journal and they would be – *will* be – taken for the ramblings of a madman.

It was just after Clementine's desertion that I first noticed the growths. They began on my back, seeming to spread up through my muscle and sinew from my lungs. The cough I had brought back with me from Fang Sank Island was more than a cough. I should have known, perhaps I would have had my mind withstood that fateful day. I surmised that I had only breathed in a small amount of the spore whereas the others had eaten a mass of the flesh itself, thus explaining why it took so long for them to take hold and grow. I was able to hide them from others for several weeks, as reclusive as I had become it was hardly a chore, but eventually they appeared on my face. Even my purveyor of narcotics ran from me screaming and I had reckoned him for sterner stuff.

Thus it is that I have come to this. No money, no drugs to ease this pain and the fear that lies within me as blood within my veins. Now those vessels of life feel as though they are filled with dirt, the stuff the fungus thrives on. And it is dark down there, beneath my skin.

I dread to think what will become of those that have breathed air from my lungs. I tried to warn the authorities but they would not listen. Why would they? They consider me a lunatic and I was lucky to preserve my liberty. Nonetheless, basic experiments with neighbourhood cats have indicated that the smaller dose only delays the fungus from catching hold of the warmth of the body. The end result appears to be the same no matter the means of contamination. I can only hope that Professor Fletcher, my mentor and once friend, will not discard this journal when he receives it, and that he will use the knowledge herein to stem the fungi's demonic tide. I can only hope.

At the end, the least I can do is this – I can name them. *Agaricus nefandus* in the Latin, but in colloquial terms I think 'The Devil's Haemorrhoids' is more than apt. For surely they are the ruptured lining of that fallen angel's back passage and cursed be he who would venture thence.

Thus I must end my account, my eyes are sore, my lungs ache, and I can write no more.

WELL OUR FEEBLE FRAME
HE KNOWS

He sits alone in His throne room. A thick layer of dust covers the once gleaming white floors and walls, and the few furnishings left around Him show the yellowing of neglect. Enormous gilt-framed mirrors, each one finer by far than any earthly masterpiece, line the walls of the once great hall, their glorious faces covered with tattered sheets. He doesn't want to look at Himself, to see what He has been reduced to. He wants no company – which is just as well because He has no other choice. He is alone now. All of His Heavenly Host is gone; many of those that stood by Him in the face of His favourite's betrayal faded into the ether long ago. Others have been cast down to the land below by His will or are dead by His hand. Let them revel in their baseness. Let them enjoy it while it lasts.

He is an all but forgotten King, once great, once everything, but now He sits slumped on His highest of thrones and all He can do is sigh at all that has been taken from Him.

In the beginning, His intentions were only of the purest kind. His ideas were generous and loving but the nature of those created in His glorious image was not quite as He had intended. He did not understand where their wilful disobedience came from. Hadn't He given them everything? Yet, again and again He was tested in the face of the machinations and schemes His children seemed to so delight in. New messiahs were raised high and new religions, all unsanctioned by Him, were freely peddled to those weak enough to turn from Him. Their divisive natures and fickle hearts turned them against each other and their history became littered with violence upon violence. He watched on with impotent rage boiling in

His righteous veins as they argued and fought themselves to the brink of oblivion and forgot about Him.

Well, to the Abyss with them all.

They believe the world He created is beyond His influence now. They are almost right. His power over it has diminished, the power of them forgetting His truth is stronger than His sufferance for their plight and, even if they sought it, His assistance would be futile. The End has been set in motion. He is not sure He would help them even if He could. They do not want what He has to offer, even if they claim their actions are in His Name. It offends Him to hear it, to see it. Their continued existence is a bane to His and He can barely think for the clamour of their screams and tears, their desperate pleading, their curses and their barbs. All the while, the sounds of long ago haunt Him and their bittersweet cacophony is hard to ignore. He can hear the words of a song they wrote in His honour, the one He loved the best, and even now, at the end of things, it brings a soft smile to His aged lips. Praise Him, He thinks with a weary shrug of His shoulders, praise the everlasting King indeed.

To His feet thy tribute bring.

He shakes His head with a fresh shot of bitterness. What do they know? The blind eagerness with which they have rejected His authority, twisting everything to suit their whims, their indulgence in ignorance and willingness to believe anything – they know nothing. Nothing. They were His once. They were all He had allowed them to be. He had looked upon them only with His Love; indeed, they had been a source of amusement to Him, how easily they had bent to His will, how eager to love Him. Now, in the aftermath of all that has gone before, it is just another nail in the coffin that will seal them forever in the pages of His history.

His.

The tributes they had once paid and the followers who had once offered them so fervently to their most compassionate Creator are gone. He is a lonely old creature, His withered form a tribute to their loss of faith. Without them, He has nothing to sustain Him. Without their prayers and offerings He is but a shell, a ghost in the machine of creation.

Without Him, they are doomed.

Frail as summer's flow'r we flourish,
Blows the wind and it is gone.

He should have known. In truth, who could blame them? His master plan had been flawed from the first; He could admit that much at last. In His celestial arrogance He had been as blind as His children. He was omnipotent, the most high, there was nothing He could not have controlled had He wanted it to be so…

…He had believed that for a long time. He thought giving them free will was a masterstroke, a flash of His divine ingenuity. He had not for a moment believed it could go wrong, had not believed it of His children. Worse still, if they were created in His image, what did that say about Him? The worm of doubt had eventually crawled into His mind and His insecurities had started to get the better of Him.

Washing it away had seemed such a good idea once, but when it had failed He had sent an emissary in His stead. They had butchered the boy. His boy. So then He had sought to punish them by withdrawing the luxury of His grace. He chose to wait until they came to Him and begged for His succour. He would have welcomed them with promises of their hearts' desires once He had regained control. However, the dissenters had raised their voices loud and strong and His anger had been impossible to control. He had lashed out and imposed His holy wrath upon them all. Pestilence, War, Famine, and Death. The havoc His horsemen had wrought satisfied Him for but a moment, barely the space of a breath for Him, yet it was long enough in their time to drive the scourge of inconstancy from the world. His world.

But while mortals rise and perish,
Our God lives unchanging on…

Alas, at last, after the storm had cleared and all should

have been pure once more, it seemed that even His chosen, the most faithful and devout had begun to doubt. And so, He had looked upon all He had done, at the final treachery He had provoked, and He had wept.

The ravages He had wrought upon the children of His world were too much for Him to bear. He had retreated into His heavenly palace, His face turned away in shame from the devastation He had caused. The creatures He had loved so well were finally and utterly cast asunder from His love. The blackness of their souls served only to show Him His weaknesses, His self-deception.

And so now, at last, it is time for it to end.

It is time to burn it all down.

> *Praise Him, praise Him, alleluia!*
> *Praise the High Eternal One!*

He gathers Himself up, sitting straight and proud for the first time in too long. He curses the events He knows are His own making, but He has the prospect of renewal to soothe Him. He knows there will always be another time, another place for Him. He is, after all, everlasting, eternal.

> *God endures unchanging one.*

The moment has come to put this world to rest, to put them and Him out of this misery. It will be His final act of compassion. His loving mercy.

> *Angels helps us to adore Him,*
> *Ye behold Him face to face…*

Resolved, He hauls His unsteady carcass up from the divine throne, most high. It is a long time since He has stood and He takes a moment to adjust. This must be done properly. No mistakes. He wishes Himself to the great gates of His paradise, now unguarded and rusted open. No one seeks what those magnificent edifices once protected and, after all, who is there to be kept out now? Once there, He looks down onto His world, His still beautiful creation, for the last time. He will have another chance, but this is all that can be done for them. It is reparation of a kind, but it is His kind and it will be absolute.

He must do what is right at last.

> *Sun and moon bow down before Him;*
> *Dwellers all in time and space...*

He bends His head for a moment, closing His eyes as He prepares. When He opens them again, He lifts His left hand so it is flat with the palm facing upwards. In it is a tiny flame, flickering gently. It has done a service once before, but the job then was far greater than what is required of it now. Creation is more complex than destruction. The flame dances gently in His hand, growing slowly but steadily until it is no longer one flame but many, licking at His wrist, His sleeve, anywhere they can reach. He raises His arm, oblivious to the scorch marks that are already turning to flame, flames that lick along His divine sleeve, that bite gently into His skin at first and then begin to devour Him in earnest, not stopping for pity or penance.

By the time He allows Himself to fall, it is all-consuming.

> *Praise Him, praise Him, alleluia!*
> *Praise us with the God of grace.*

HIT THAT PERFECT BEAT, BOY

The whole place was covered in blood and things had gone too far. Char rested her head on the toilet seat and tried to breathe.

Calm down.

Oh god.

What the hell was going on?

There had been so much blood.

She was far too old for this shit; for the debauchery she'd been happily in the throes of and definitely for the carnage that had come in its wake. None of that mattered now though because those *things* were going to tear her to pieces and eat her too if she couldn't get out of there. What were they? Terrorists? Cannibals? Fucking zombies? The Salvation Army? Glory, peace, and J-O-Y.

Calm the fuck down.

Char closed her eyes.

The world reduced to just her and the toilet, beneath her knees the sticky floor throbbed with the bass of the music still blasting through the club. The rushing in her ears obscured the tune but the bass pumped ever on. *Hit that perfect beat, boy.* She screwed her eyes shut tighter but staccato bursts of fizzing colour pricked at her eyelids. The roll of nausea was sudden and far too much, and she opened her eyes quickly, taking deep breaths in through her nose. She refused to be sick yet again, prayed fervently she wouldn't be as everything burned sickeningly bright for a moment and then…

… the moment dragged on, her head swimming, but gradually the burning abated and finally she could raise her head from the toilet seat. She took some deep breaths, welcoming even the stale air of the ladies' loo. When her arms were steady enough, she pushed herself up from the floor, although it took more than a couple of tries to get back on her feet. Story of her life. She decided against flushing the toilet and instead dabbed ineffectually at the seat with the screwed-up wad of loo roll in her hand before giving up and pushing it into the murky depths. She straightened her dress, checked it for splashes of vomit, readjusted her ridiculously overstuffed bag, and then exited the toilet like a new-born foal. A still high and pretty drunk new-born foal who had introduced the contents of its stomach to Armitage Shanks, or whoever made toilets these days. Luckily it was only a few steps across the room to the washbasins. Behind her, the exit was barricaded as best as it could be with a tatty old chaise longue, two bins and a couple of brooms wedged through the door handle. She was lucky to have been near the back of the club when the screaming started. These toilets were situated slightly away from the main flow of the club and were used more by the staff than customers.

Char leaned heavily on the black porcelain of the sinks. Once upon a time they'd been the height of fashion but now they were as faded as the rest of the place and most of the people in it. People who had likely suffered terror and agony in their final moments. It was probably no more than any of them deserved because really? An Eighties night? Filled to the rafters with middle agers intent on reliving their sad little glory days, dancing to a mixture of anything from Five Star to The Cure, The Smiths to Rick Astley – a combination that would never have seen the light of day in the way back when. If they were anything like her, and judging by most of what she'd seen before the killing had started they were, then they'd been desperately pretending their teenage years hadn't been the start of an endless desert of wasted opportunity, regret, and bad memories. Char for one had made some Very Bad Choices. Lost in misery, she'd sunk ever deeper, clutching hold of anything around her, and everything around her had proven to be quicksand. She wished she could get that time back. She wished she'd worked it out sooner, that there had been someone to help her, to tell her she was worth so much more. Instead she'd languished in self-hatred and fear, blaming herself for so long... but not for as long as she would wish that dismissive, unrepentant bastard got gangrene of the balls. If wishes were horses…

Hit that perfect beat, boy.

She was supposed to be turning over a new leaf, getting her shit together but, as Char wiped her mouth on the back of her hand and looked up into the mirror, she wondered if she would ever be anything but the same scared little girl she'd always been. Forty-five years old and still as chicken as shit. Despite the make-up, she wore her years on her face for everyone to see. Had she been hoping the angle would help? If she had, she was sadly mistaken. Her reflection was a good match for the pockmarked surface. Pinpoints of red freckled her nose, matching the streaks in her eyes. Her face and neck were blotchy; detracting somewhat from the décolletage she'd taken such pains to display. With her boosted assets and perfectly done make up – for once! The Holy Grail! – her trusty old Doc Marten's on her feet once again and the little black dress she'd never thought she'd get into, she had really truly felt like this was her night. She'd told herself she was going to go out there, have a good time, maybe even meet someone decent, start over. Have. Fun.

The irony of a horde of violent psychopaths – because there was no such thing as zombies and vampires were from wank bank books for bored housewives and teenage girls – derailing her night was not lost on her. Char closed her eyes for a moment, trying to block out the moment she'd seen her friend Dani being thrown aside, headless and limbless, by the big bald woman with the long stripe of bright hair running down her muscular back, right from crown to arsehole. Naked as the day she was born, or maybe something like her was hatched from a fucking dinosaur egg, she had prowled proudly through the club, full breasts bouncing wildly in and out of her arm pits, picking off victims and feasting on their still twitching bodies with every other step. Green was not a human colour and she was not human. So much for your wank bank vampires.

The shots had been a huge mistake. All five of them. Especially as they'd come after a couple of large glasses of wine that definitely could not have amounted to more than a whole bottle, and then there'd been that cotton candy stuff that had tasted like the death throes of her stomach lining. Char's stomach rolled again at the memory, but she swallowed hard against it, clamping it down.

'Pull it together, Charlotte.' She had some coke in her bag, a friend had laughingly dropped it in there earlier, reminding her that life was made for living and... well, some habits were hard to shake, no matter what promises she made to herself. The fact was a line of the old Baltic would settle her. If she was to have any chance of getting out of there alive, some Dutch courage, or in this case Peruvian, was sorely in order.

The minute she got the little baggie of white powder out of her bag, she felt better. Her faithful Charlie boy, the only loyal friend she'd ever had, burned along the insides of her nose like Incey Wincey Spider drag racing up her drainpipe, and it didn't take too long to hit her brain. She whooped with the rush of it, feeling the shakes ebbing swiftly away. She rubbed away the blood that trickled from her nose with the back of her hand, trying to pay it no mind because suddenly and surely – one hundred per cent, Ma – she was ready. Felt ready. Yeah, she was! To prove it to herself, she showed out with some splendid Rocky moves, laughing wildly when she caught sight of herself in the mirror. Oh yeah. The edge had been taken well and truly off and clarity was back on. She was indestructible. She could do this.

She needed a plan. Maybe there was some sort of air duct system in the ceiling, like in movies. Maybe she could Breakfast Club her way out. Or maybe there was a hatch in the floor – a boobie hatch! – connected to roughly hewn tunnels made by the bare hands of prisoners from a World War Two internment camp, maybe Pele would score a winning goal and she could escape in a gymnastic horse thing. Maybe she could hop on Steve McQueen's bike and have him slide in behind her, speeding them both toward safety this time, Nazi bullets falling futilely behind them.

Char realised she was facing a wall. How much time had passed? However long it had been, she'd been sweating for every minute of it. She remembered why she'd given up coke in the first place. What had she been thinking? Had she been thinking? At all? *Start now*, said the little voice in her head, the one that had been getting stronger of late. She looked up and suddenly saw her chance. A window.

The window was of course stuck. Char pushed at it once more with feeling before giving up. She was no match for a dozen layers of emulsion and years of surreptitious cigarette smoke. Which gave her an idea as she slid back down to the floor, snagging her tights and ripping a ladder down her left thigh. Well, fuck-a-doodle-do. Wasn't that just the cherry. And speaking of cherries…

The first acrid tang of smoke in her lungs was dirty sweet, which was how she liked it. The slight rush compensated a little for the steady dip in her coke high. Char settled herself on the floor, back against the wall, legs stretched out, all sense of urgency gone as she enjoyed her cigarette. There'd not been so much as a tap on the door so far, not that she'd noticed, and Char felt quite philosophical about it. They either didn't know she was in there or they were planning to storm in and rip her limb from limb. As there wasn't much she could do about either scenario she took another drag and then blew out a perfect smoke ring. Pleased with her accomplishment, she tried another and choked on the smoke as someone stepped into the room. Through a door she'd not noticed. Nice one, Char. Standard nonchalance.

'Hello.' He was short – at almost six feet tall she was used to looking down on most people and short men seemed to have a real thing for it – but he was eerily handsome, the kind of handsome Dracula might have been happy with. Especially if he liked his skin tinged with green. His black eyes flitted about the room restlessly, as though he was nervous about something and yet his demeanour didn't seem urgent. Char wiped her mouth and ground out the cigarette on the floor next to her, her movements measured. She didn't want to startle him. She watched him carefully, her heart pounding so hard she was sure he'd see it. If he was one of those things, and there could be no doubt he was, she had nothing to defend herself with… or did she? Slowly, she reached up and touched her backcombed, crimped to buggery hair. Hair like that needed maintenance. Hair like that needed spray.

'Hello,' Char said as cheerfully as she could. Her hands

were in her bag and she tried to look nonchalant as she rummaged. Her new companion didn't seem to notice anything amiss as he came further into the room, head twitching, dark eyes never still. The door snickered shut behind him and he jumped at the noise. A bit more nervous than she'd thought then. Good. The last remaining dregs of her high had joined forces with the adrenaline pumping through her veins and were soldiering on together. Char tried to keep her breathing steady, and it suddenly felt as though she was being controlled by someone else – if she wasn't a cynic she might have said it felt like some higher force. Thankfully, however, she was a cynic and knew a spot of fight or flight when she saw it. That it was fight not flight was a pretty big surprise. She'd been a coward for so long she'd figured her blood would have been purest yellow by now. She tightened her grip on what she'd found in her bag and waited as the man-thing came closer.

'Sorry, I hate to be a bother, but I really should get started.'

'On what?'

'On your flesh.' He was across the rest of the room in a flash and was almost on her by the time she had pulled the small can of hairspray from her bag, swinging it in front of his face and pressing down on it with one hand even as she rolled the flint wheel with the thumb on the other, igniting a stream of lacquer directly at the man-thing. He reared back, a high-pitched wail piercing through the flames, and Char pushed herself to her feet, pushing past him and running for the barricaded door. As the man-thing screamed, clawing at his face, Char grabbed one of the mops she'd jammed through the door handle, pulling it out in one fluid movement, spinning on the balls of her feet, and charging at the thing, wooden handle pointed straight at its head. The shaft punctured through the flames and into the thing's eye socket, popping the eyeball as it went. With strength borne from thirty something years of cowering, she pushed it right through the skull and then pulled it back out again, kicking the thing hard in the stomach so it fell backwards as it began to sink to the floor. Turning, she made for the door she'd missed on her way in, shoving the mop through the door handle and pushing the remaining piece of furniture, a badly abused armchair, in front of the door to block it. She leaned with her hand against the door for a moment, waiting to see if anything out there had noticed the commotion, as though she would be any match for any kind of horde, praying the toilets were tucked far enough away for it not to have been.

The place stank. Chargrilled man flesh was one thing, but there was something else. Char steeled herself as she turned around to examine the room. It was no wonder she'd missed the other door, it stood in a dark corner she had assumed was dead space, practically hidden beside what must be a cleaning supplies cupboard. Her head was pounding. The adrenaline had subsided and she felt weak. As she peered around the toilet cubicles, she took a breath to stop herself from crying out or anything else needlessly melodramatic but, as she did, she inhaled the stench the man-thing had made. It was definitely a thing and not a man. Even her worst decision of a boyfriend hadn't smelled like that.

The good thing, however, was the whatever-it-was seemed to be well and truly dead. It was now an ex-whatever-it-was. Char chuckled and then winced at the smell again. It was less pungent this time, she noticed. There was even something sweet amid the putrid, frazzled stench. Something lingering, something almost attractive. Something… delicious. Char inhaled again, this time on purpose, and the room around her suddenly filled with the most perfect light, sparkling and refreshing. Its warmth tingled its way right through her, stronger than any drug she had ever snorted or smoked. Its effect was immediate and intense. The bones in her spine stiffened, lending the supporting muscles vigour. She inhaled again and felt her flesh become plumper, the blood, running hot and swift through her veins, rushing to its aid, strengthening every sinew, binding with every cell, every atom of her. Her soul rushed upwards and around the room, swooping and twisting in the fetid air, seeking out the nooks and crannies, examining, glorying in its many seeing eyes and its heightened senses, wondering at its power. Great Gods! She felt amazing!

All of a sudden, thrust from the fury of the wild spiral in a single heartbeat, Char's mind torpedoed sharply and her course of action became clear. She threw back her head and laughed.

Heart still pounding with exhilaration and reaction, mouth suddenly very dry but her thirst oddly quenched, she headed back to the supply cupboard. As she opened the carelessly unlocked door – she hadn't ripped it from its hinges, the thing had been flimsy at best - she hit paydirt. *Told you so.* Aerosols, bleach, hundreds of tiny bottles of hand sanitiser, it was a veritable arsenal of potential. Char grinned the grin of the triumphant and stepped into the cupboard for a closer look.

One good long rummage and a holy communion with the goddess Google later and Char was pumped and ready for action. She hadn't felt this excited in so long and it felt like coming home. This was what she had been made for. She breathed deeply as she worked, the heady scent of the man-thing jiving those atoms, rocking those synapses, moulding her to her fate. A large portion of the cupboard's contents had been commandeered for the cause. With two fully loaded lighters in her bag she was as good as Ms Rambo, thank you very much, fully locked and loaded and she was going to save the fricking day, son. Those miscreant motherfuckers were going to get what was coming and she was getting out. Alive and a heroine to boot. Power fizzed and popped through her entire body, her mind sharp even as it crackled at her magnificence. She was everything, anything she wanted to be, and she was going out there to take names and... Char stopped for another deep inhalation, letting the still pungent fumes take her up yet another notch, rocketing through her in a spume of sparkling grit; she was effervescing from her scalp to her toes, she was in the zone, tapped into the loop, sparky and spunky, like a vessel of some holy warrior-spirit destined for victory. She was a Viking! A Valkyrie! An Amazon, a goddess divine! And she was about to bring down a blaze of righteous pain upon those unholy vipers out there. Her sacred judgement would be cast upon them and they would be found wanting. They would cower at her feet, subjugated and debased before she ground them beneath her bootheel.

Her stomach growled, the rumble echoing around the room. Char tried to ignore it but hollowness gnawed at her insides, increasingly insistent. It seemed to reach through her body and seize hold of the power she'd harnessed from the man-thing. It knew it, greeted it happily like an old friend, and tried to rip it out of her by the roots. Char's neck arched backwards, her jaw cracking as she tried not to scream in agony, her arms thrusting out in front of her, hands scrabbling at the air for purchase, for help. And then, just as suddenly, it was gone.

Focus, she told herself. Breathe in. She did.

Char ignored the green tinge that seemed to flush the skin of her arms. It was a trick of the light.

She'd found a tabard with a huge pocket in the cupboard, loaded it with the aerosols and hand sanitisers, all of which had been stuffed with jay cloths and pages ripped from the stash of porn mags she'd found stuffed right at the back, jagged strips of pink pantie peppered delicately against the brown check of the overall. She had her lighters and knew they kept matches behind the bar to the right of the toilets. If she couldn't get to them her holy fire would sustain. She would slip outside and into the throng before they knew what had hit them. A couple of toilet brushes were jammed in the belt that tied the apron together at the sides. One quick jab in the eye with one of them once the creatures were alight, and the suckers would be on their way back to hell. They would know her and they would tremble, her name a malediction on their lips when they sang their chthonic lamentations in those infernal halls.

But gods, the hunger was back. That persistent insistence rising in her stomach again, twisting her insides, screaming at her to feast! To eat! Oh please! Feed me! It clawed at her, wedged its demanding feet in her craw and refused to leave. It popped at her joints, buckling her knees, and driving her to the floor. She gasped as the heat of purest greed almost choked her.

And then it was gone, just as quickly as the first time. Breathless for a moment, Char stayed where she was on the floor and gasped air into her lungs. The man-things essence was fading now though, and while it was enough to get her to her feet again, she knew it would not sustain her for long. She needed more. She wanted more. She would have more.

Char strode to the door, ploughed through her makeshift barricade, and threw the door open.

She plucked one of the toilet-made cocktails from her pocket and set the lighter to the end of the dry cloth sticking out of the plastic bottle, raising it over her head in salute, tears of ecstasy sliding down her cheeks as she embarked upon this, her holy crusade. Carpe diem.

'Hey Motherfuckers!' She threw the bottle and watched it arc through the air. The screaming started.

Hit that perfect beat, boy.

FRESHLY BAKED CHILDREN

An Invitation

Demelza Greenwood cordially invites you to a Tea Party.

*Please come prepared to eat well and hearty
So we may give thanks to the great goddess Astarte.
Come cloaked in darkness and please dress to impress,
Be here by midnight and I'll lay on the rest.
There'll be hot cakes and fancies, grilled wolf and ham,
Biscuits and crepes, and all kinds of jam,
Roasted pheasant and phoenix and mouthfuls of wren,
Eggs of all sizes, from dragon to hen.
And sisters, be assured, the pièce de resistance will of course be
A pie of freshly baked children who hath offended thee.*

Friday October 13th

The Candy House, Dark Oak Grove, Forest of Endless Gloom

Regrets Only

THE HOLY HOUR

Elise closed her eyes and waited. Waited for her atoms to catch up and band together, waited for them to do their job so she could be whole again, so this could be over. The feeling did not come. Yet again. Time after time she had let herself believe it would be different but here she was, still stuck with her grief, still alone. All people ever seemed to say was that she should try. Try, try, try, try, try. Well, she had tried hard and she had tried often but every time she was left with the same conclusion – it would never happen; things were never going to be right again. Sighing, she opened her eyes and stared at the mantelpiece, still covered in condolence cards, thick with dusty regret and thankful grief – thankful that it had happened to her, not them. She knew what friends she had left sympathised well enough, empathised even, but it was a long time since she'd seen any of them and, besides, they were old with troubles of their own. Anyway, none of them could know what was happening to her because none of them had loved *him* as she had. None of them knew this particular flavour of wound. They knew their own but not hers. Anyone that said otherwise was a fool.

The room was cold, the house empty. Every movement she made thundered, but dully, an echo of the emptiness inside her. Greying light added to the sombre mood, night falling again, another day done, another day lived without him. Elise knew all the advice about not wallowing, about remembering the good times, but all she could recall at times like this was his pale drawn face as he had lost the battle, as he had finally slipped away from her, gone beyond her reach. The memory played over and over in her head. What she wouldn't give for one more moment with him, for one more glimpse of those sweet hazel eyes.

The bark snapped her out of her reverie and almost into a heart attack. Elise jumped up from her place on the sofa, one hand to her chest as she cried out. The bark came again.

Wait. Florence?

But it couldn't be. Could it?

As the sitting room door swung open slowly, Elise's heart froze in her chest, her entire system ringing with alarm bells, but somehow she waited. For a moment there was nothing, the door swung to a halt, and the whole room seemed to wait on her shaky exhalation.

Dog claws tippy tapped across the wooden floor in the hallway, happily scuttling their owner's way to the sitting room. A white nose appeared around the door, then that face, so achingly familiar, so loved.

'Flo!' Elise's breath rushed from her lungs and she couldn't stop the grin from spreading across her face. Before she knew it, she was across the room and hauling her beloved dog into her arms. Dog smell filled her nose, the warm body in her arms the surest sign of love fulfilled. She buried her face in the white fur, inhaling frantically, deeply, hardly believing she had forgotten about Florence in her grief.

'Oh, Flo. It's so good to see you. You have no idea. I wish you knew.' Not wanting to, but knowing she should, Elise bent to put the odd little white dog back on the floor. As she did, she saw something achingly familiar in her dark brown eyes. Grief. Sorrow. Sadness. That hateful melange. Of course she would know, of course. Had it been so long that she'd forgotten how much Florence had loved him too? Dogs felt loss, didn't they? Felt it just like she did. If there was anyone who had an inkling of what it was to lose him, it would be her.

Florence trotted away from her and over to the French doors that looked out into their garden. She whimpered softly, pressing her wet nose against the glass and staring into the fields that backed onto the house. It was an old familiar habit, one she had not seen in far too long. Flo wanted to go for a walk. Elise smiled, the muscles in her face aching with the unaccustomed usage; it felt as though it had been forever ago since she'd had anything at all to smile about, it had seemed impossible she ever would again.

'Hold on a sec, Flo, let's go find your lead.' She crossed the room and headed for the kitchen, the sound of Florence's pursuit echoing through the otherwise silent house. It made her feel warm for the first time in ages and Elise could feel those atoms of hers beginning to swirl into place at last.

Finding the lead was not as easy as she'd thought. Where had she put it last? Rummaging through drawers and boxes, Elise was reminded of the life she had shared with him. They'd had no children, had very little other family who concerned themselves with them, but they'd had each other, not to mention Florence and her predecessors. Unconventional but happy, they had grown more in love with each passing year. People wondered at it, had said as much to her, to him, but the only thing that could explain it was that she was her and he was him and together they were them. What else was needed? As she searched for Florence's lead, Elise found her breath catching at every forgotten photograph, newspaper clipping, and ridiculous memento – there were rocks, feathers, tiny plastic children's toys - from a thousand different adventures, a million moments encapsulated. The smile on her face did not fade. How lucky she had been. How lucky to have loved and been loved so well in return.

In her grief she had forgotten, had seen only her loss, but now with fate forcing her hand, she remembered. Tears spilled over her lashes and down her cheeks, but she paid them no mind. The memories kept coming fast and hard as she sat on the floor sorting through them. It was the sort of thing that should have been a release, that was what all the bumf she had been given on grief and grieving had said, but she found it had the opposite effect. The more she saw, the less she could contemplate finally saying goodbye. Catharsis be damned, she thought.

Then, *that* photo. How she had always loved it, remembered so clearly the day they'd taken it, standing together at the cliff's edge, daring each other to get closer and laughing like children, and they had been a long way past that by then. She had kept it in her handbag for years. How had she lost it to the wasteland of the kitchen drawers? His face, smiling, happy, carefree, looking at the camera, at her, and every ounce of love he had for her shining through the old forgotten lens into her present day soul.

Catharsis be damned indeed.

Oh, how she wanted him back, wanted him now, in her arms, in her kitchen, in her life. She wanted him where he belonged. His loss was not fair, it wasn't right. How dare he be taken from her? How dare he leave? Elise felt her old friend Anger burn through her, felt it take hold, making her muscles shake with the force of it. This was all too much; she felt the balance shift, felt despair waiting for her. She had lost everything, why should she be reminded of that so brutally? It wasn't enough to remember and smile. God damn all of it. God. Damn. It. She had tried grieving, had tried hard, but it wasn't working. She didn't want to say goodbye, she didn't see why she should. Who was to say what they'd had was enough? She had said forever and she had meant it.

The balance tipped finally and she threw the drawer she'd taken from the dresser hard, the contents spilling from it mid-air, photos, half burned birthday candles, balls of string, and ancient takeaway menus scattering to all four corners of the room and then, finally, the crash of wood smashing against the wall. The sound should have been shocking in the quiet house but all Elise could hear was the wailing that was coming from her own mouth. She could not stop, could not make it stop. Clapping her hands across her face, she tried to quell it, but the sound kept coming, cranking up to a high pitched keening noise that could have shattered glass.

The bark shocked her out of it.

Florence.

How could she have forgotten?

That damned lead, where was… There. On the table, as though she'd placed it there on purpose, was Florence's lead. Bright red against the pine, it waited. She felt it waiting, felt Flo behind her waiting too. Walkies, that was it, it was time for a walk.

Elise grabbed the lead and shoved it in the pocket of her jeans. She found her wellies, still encrusted with mud from that last walk together a thousand years ago, in the bottom of the cupboard by the sink, and wedged them on her feet. Her old wax jacket, a bottle green cliché, was still hanging by the back door and putting it on after all that time was like coming home; ironic considering she was leaving. The rush of fresh air as she threw open the back door was invigorating, solidifying her resolve. It pinked her skin and made her nose tingle. The scent of spring was in the air – odd because it was December – and it was intoxicating. Suddenly, Elise couldn't wait to get out there, to stretch her legs and run, run far from this empty place and the memories that taunted her.

'Come on, Flo,' she said, patting her leg as she called to her, just like she always had. The dog came running, just as she always had.

They flew down the steps together, Elise laughing, Florence barking. They ran across the grass, away from the festering frustration of memory, and through the gate that led to the fields beyond. Euphoria had taken hold and they were both embracing every moment of it. The grey evening light was much darker now, but somehow she could see her way, only losing sight of the white dog in the gloom every now and then. She always came back though. That's a dog for you. They always come back and they always bring you home.

They walked and ran for what felt like hours. Elise threw sticks and Flo chased them, almost bringing them back. Almost, just like always. They walked farther than Elise had for a good while, but she felt almost as though she was young again, energy seeming to pour through and out of her, warming her against the chill night air as it came on.

Dark woods bordered the fields about three miles from the house. Elise was surprised to see them. Had they really come that far? It was hard to believe, but then the day just seemed to be that way. For the first time, she felt trepidation. She'd never walked through the woods without him, had always been a little afraid of doing so. Did she dare? Flo barked, as though to remind her she was not alone. She would be okay; Elise smiled to herself, of course she would. Taking a deep breath – she'd always been good at saying the words she wanted to hear, less so at believing them – she followed Florence as the dog charged into the thickets ahead, displaying a typical lack of canine concern. She didn't want to tear her trousers in the thick undergrowth, but carried on after her anyway. In for a penny and all that.

Soon, she saw there was a path, could thankfully see it as

soon as she stepped into the gloom. Small white pebbles had been laid either side to show the way. She'd never noticed them before. Maybe it had been so long ago since she'd seen them, she'd simply forgotten. Or maybe not. As her foot came down on the track, she felt a little better, as though the pebbles somehow formed a barrier against what lurked in the darkness beyond. Lord, she hoped they were something of the sort, because as soon as she could no longer see the fields behind her, when her passage had been all but subsumed by the gloom, Elise began to hear noises. The soft cracking of twigs at first, the rustle of dead leaves half-mulched into the floor. Then came the wind through the winter-stripped branches, creaking and groaning like a woodland banshee. The sound sent a shiver down Elise's spine, the portent of death ringing in her ears. She remembered the stories her mother had told her when she was a child, stories from the old country, how those women of the barrows keened when someone was about to die. She remembered how, as a teenager, she'd researched the mythology and found that a possible explanation for the phenomena was the screech of the barn owl and how, despite the enlightenment, it hadn't seemed any less frightening for that. She'd been scared by an owl in these very woods, years ago, a ghostly apparition that had sent her scuttling home. There was no turning back now, however; she could feel it in her bones. Her atoms were set-tling, fixing fast and at long last on her course, and she was committed. To what she did not yet know but her feet kept carrying her forward, following the small white dog as she ran ahead of her, weaving in and out of trees away from the path, digging holes and sniffing everything in sight. It was as though she was saying there was nothing to be afraid of and Elise felt better for it.

Despite the forward impetus, every step was hard. Her feet would feel like they weighed a thousand pounds one step, the next they were feather-light, keeping her equilibrium reeling. She felt lightheaded, like the time she'd given blood and, just after the needle had gone in, she'd passed out, slipping from the chair and hitting the floor as she'd lost conscious-ness, the moment before impact bright with giddy wonder.

Everything had seemed so clear in that moment, so perfectly lit and full of sensation, then nothing. Passing out was not an option now, however. She had a destination, she felt it in the air around her, felt it in the impatient glances Flo shot her way every time she paused to check her mistress's progress, as though egging her on, ever on.

The wind was stronger now, having gathered pace without her registering it before. Elise pulled the edge of her jacket around her, her fingers suddenly too numb to contemplate tackling the zip. The banshees keened louder, the branches snapping and swaying angrily in the rising breeze. The dark night was making itself felt and the unease that had trickled through her earlier now etched its way down into her flesh, chilling her to the bone. She kept watch around her as best she could, head snapping to and fro in a neck jerking spasm. She felt like she was closer, to what she did not know, but she knew she was nearly there and she would not stop walking. There was a place, she knew it, a somewhere to discover. It was a journey worth taking, worth the fear and uncertainty, worth the cold and, now, rain. It fell in sheets, as though the sky had split like overripe fruit and could no longer contain its slick contents.

And still she walked. Still, she followed the white dog.

Then, suddenly, there was an opening in the trees. Elise couldn't see the clearing properly until she had stepped out into it, a surprise considering there was a faint glow of light emanating from the small building set at its heart. It was barely there, but it should have been enough to pierce the dark night beyond the vague boundaries of the clearing. Perhaps the incessant fat drops of rain had obscured it but, as Elise surveyed the small structure, she instinctively under-stood that the light was only for those who entered it, not for those who stayed outside. To access its comfort you had to make a choice.

Florence was standing a few feet from her, tail wagging and tongue lolling as she panted happily from her exertions. She seemed content with their progress and was now waiting while her mistress decided on her next move. It was tiny, a church perhaps, old, white, and wooden. It didn't belong to the architecture of the area, she could tell that much even in the gloom. It wasn't unfriendly but it didn't seem as though you were being encouraged to enter either, unusual for a church. Frowning, she scanned the building, trying to work out what was making her uncertain. Suddenly, she laughed at herself. She'd walked for miles through the deep dark woods and now a building worried her just because it wasn't sounding bells and blowing whistles at her coming? The wind had picked up, that was all; there were no banshees heralding death, no oogie boogies or serial killers waiting for her inside. Why not go in and light a candle for him? She wasn't a devout woman, but she believed in something, that there was another place beyond this one. Maybe she was here to say goodbye... no, she wouldn't say that yet. She would *never* say it. She had set her course and she would stick to it.

The church bell rang out suddenly as though heralding her decision, but it was not cacophonous in the gloom. It was as though it supported her choice, as though this was indeed the holy hour and she had come to the right place.

Resolved, and more than a little comforted, Elise started towards the church. She would go in, sit a while, light a candle, ask for guidance maybe – who knew, maybe she would even get a miracle. A second coming. Smiling to herself, she reached out to grasp the brass handles of the doors, noting how surprisingly shiny they were in the dark, and hauled them open. The wind whistled past her, streaming into the church as though some giant had bent to inhale on the other side of the building. Elise felt as though she was sucked through the threshold, rather than pushed, and fell to her knees on the floor, her palms coming down hard on the stone beneath her. The sting and shock of it robbed her of breath and it took a long moment for her to gather her wits. She was not young, had not been for a very long time, and she wasn't used to this sort of exertion. It all came flooding back to her, onto her; the weight of her grief, the effort of the walk, the fear of the darkness ... In the sudden silence that followed her entrance, a surge of everything she had and should have felt shot through her – shock, denial, bargaining, guilt, anger, depression, hope. All seven stages. All at once.

It was the last, however, that stayed with her, that buoyed her back to her feet. Hope. That old scoundrel, the number one tease. With one hand on the pew to her right, she swung around to look into the body of the church proper. The nave.

Quiet bodies were scattered amongst the pews, heads bowed in prayer. As each raised their head, having finished their particular invocations, they rose and slipped away into the night, not through the door, but into the air, their bodies evaporating like mist into the ether. Elise blinked as one supplicant faded and another took their place. Once they had appeared, they would sink to their knees and kiss the ground before settling themselves onto the wooden pews to pray. She did not understand at first what she was seeing but somehow she found herself sitting amongst them, towards the back of the nave.

That was when she saw him. At last. He was sitting alone in the middle of a pew a few rows in front of her. She would recognise the back of his head anywhere. Tears smarted at her eyes, but she blinked them away, not wanting to ruin this impossible sighting. Hope. Again. It was irresistible and she could not stop herself, could not hold back. Standing, she ignored the sudden shaking in her legs and walked out of her row into the aisle, heading forwards, making her way to him.

The air was soft around her, the candlelight, which could not have been candlelight because there were no candles, guiding her on her way. A few small steps and she would be there with him, beside him.

At last.

The sound of children laughing behind her, of them playing long forgotten games with nothing but their imaginations rather than the technology that ruled the younger generations these days, did not deter her from her path. She knew they were there, knew they were the souls of those lost too soon. They were no threat to her. They were merely waiting for their people, for when the time came for them to say their prayers and be together again. Her heart ached for them, for those waiting to be with them, but still she walked on. Those few small steps seemed to last forever.

And then…

He turned to look up at her as she approached him, the warmth of recognition lighting up his familiar face. How she loved that face, how lost she had been without it and now it was there in front of her, *he* was there in front of her and coming home had never felt so wonderful. He did not speak; just smiled that beautiful smile of his. Her heart swelled to bursting and she went to him, her hand outstretched to grasp his as soon as she could manage it. His touch was thrilling, like the first time he had touched her when they had read Shakespeare together for her college course an eternity ago. The frisson of excitement she felt was more real than anything she had experienced since well before his funeral, since she had watched them all say goodbye to him as the curtains had closed and he had gone into the furnace beyond. She had slept with his ashes ever since, not telling anyone lest they thought her crazy. It had been months. Nothing in the house had been touched since that day; the cards still sat on the mantelpiece, the teacups in the dishwasher doubtless consumed by mould. Her friends' patience had been the only thing to change. She wasn't sorry to lose touch with them. So utterly lost in her grief, why would she have been? She had longed only for him and now here he was in front of her, his hand in hers, his eyes on her face, his smile only for her. She had promised him a thousand times or more that she would never leave him. She kept her promises.

'Hello sunshine.' She whispered the familiar endearment, not wanting to raise her voice and break whatever spell this was. His smile deepened and he pulled her towards him. As she sat next to him, their hands still clasped, Florence joined them, nestling between her feet, her muzzle resting on her knee. Elise reached out with her free hand to touch the wiry white fur. Florence belonged there as much as they did, she knew. It shouldn't have been a surprise. The urn containing her ashes had sat on the mantelpiece long before the condolence cards had joined it. It had sat there for five years, four longer than the cards. Such a long year, but now she was here it didn't matter. She had waited long enough. They were all together at last. Resting her head on his shoulder, she closed her eyes and smiled.

*

The rumours concerning the discovery of Elise Harper's body spread like wildfire through the town. How could it not? It wasn't a place much accustomed to anything happening let alone a suicide. It was the next best thing to a murder. Not many people had known the old woman well, although many knew her by sight. She'd kept to herself for the most part, even more so since her husband had died the previous year. Few of their friends were left now and those that remained had not spoken to her for some time. Isolated herself, they said, couldn't come to terms with his death, they said. Marie Travis at the Post Office reckoned she must have been planning it for a while, saving the painkillers for her arthritis to go with the expensive bottle of brandy she'd bought from Wilmington Wines, the one Bob Wilmington had thought he'd never shift. She couldn't, however, explain why Elise had left the back door to the house wide open so any Tom, Dick or Harry could just stroll in and take their pick. Mind you, it was anyone's guess as to who stood to inherit it all. No one could decide why she had chosen that day to end it. She'd lost her husband less than a year ago and they'd been married in May not December, so it wasn't an anniversary as far as anyone knew. Of course, no one could say for sure if it had special meaning for her or her husband – they'd had virtually no family, just each other, and their secrets died with them. Most of all, however, no one could explain the red dog lead she had been holding in one hand.

ALL THINGS FALL

There is a cottage that sits at the edge of the world. On one side stands a thick forest that stretches for a hundred leagues or more. On the other lies a garden rich with vegetables and a lake with water fresher than any mountain spring. Beyond that, there is the end. Sheer cliffs slash down into the blackness of Below bringing the world to a halt. The fecundity of the garden and the purity of the lake's waters belie the irrevocable nothingness so close at hand. They call it an ocean, the sea that rings the world, but that is to keep the nightmares at bay.

The white horse grazes quietly beside the lake as the lush green woodland behind her darkens with the dying of the light. As the day passes into night, the horse changes too. Soft white hair turns to pale skin, muscled hindquarters to strong legs, the hard hooves to soles used to going barefoot. The change is not conditional upon the close of the day. It is merely her habit to run through the surrounding woodland at twilight, stopping to take a long drink from her lake before returning to the prison of her human form.

The man waiting in the shadows knows this.

He has been watching her for days.

The woman, sky clad with only hair the colour of winter snow to cover her, moves gracefully through the tall grass. Her keen ears and eyes keep a check on her surroundings but no one ever comes to her grove and perhaps she has become a little complacent. He watches her, his mouth dry, the heat he feels low down something he hadn't felt for a long time before he first saw her, before he heard her song. He can hear it now; her soft tones drift across the water towards him, caressing his ears, his heart. He has lived a long time and has travelled through many lands, but he has never heard anything quite so beautiful.

Alas, he knows it for what it is – a siren's song.

And yet it still calls to him. *She* calls to him. He waits.

Her skin itches, it always does. The bath is running; it's not the lake but it will do. Besides, what else is there? She wraps the silk robe around her, cinching it in at the waist. She is impatient to feel the water on her skin, it would be heaven to slip into the lake beneath the rays of the crisp white moon, but she cannot take the chance. Night is lit by fire and fire is her enemy.

As it so often does, the window that looks out onto the lake catches her attention and she wanders over to it, sighing at the sight of the moon-bathed waters below. A flicker at the corner of her vision surprises her and she turns towards it, straining to see past the gloom into the dark forest beyond. There is nothing there. She has had a feeling that something is coming for days now. She tries to tell herself that it is nothing but the anxiety of this constant waiting, but her voice is less sure with every telling. The forest has settled back into stillness. She waits for a few minutes, senses strained, but there is nothing more.

With a sigh, she takes one last look at the lake before turning away from the window. Another long night awaits.

They come in the night. Red haired foxes that glow in the cold fire of the moon. They devour the crops and damage the small levee that channels the water from the lake into the cottage's supply so that the gardens are flooded. Years of work are ruined in a matter of moments. The man watches on. There is no satisfaction in overseeing such a thing, waste is always unappealing, but needs must and he needs a way in. He watches his charges frolic in the moonlight, envying them their freedom even as he pities their frailty.

All things fall.

The morning light is harsh as the breeze whips sharply around the side of the building. The last building at the end of the world.

Nyx flinches at the unusual brightness of the day as she steps onto the porch. It is usually marred by the endless darkness beyond the cliffs; only her skill and what lies at the bottom of the lake keep the garden growing. The light at the end of the world is not the stuff of summer days but it is far brighter than that which the rest of the world has begun to labour under. She is sent a bird once every turn of the moon. The news is never good and yet receiving it has maintained her hope. The most recent bird is overdue. It is ominous; the sense of impending doom haunting her cannot be written off for much longer because she knows the truth of it.

It is all coming to an end.

She takes comfort in the smallholding that sustains her. The practicality of everyday work, the feel of the earth beneath her hands, and the faint sunlight on her back all serve to make her appreciate the moment. What will come will come. Despite what her mother told her, she has never believed that her task will be indefinite; she has always known the frailty of the hope she carries because all things fall.

It is only when she steps down onto the path in front of the cottage, as her bare feet slip in the watery mud that should not be there, that she sees what has been done. The garden is a mess, her work ruined. Hitching her skirt, she slips and slides as she runs to check her crops. What isn't gone is half eaten. The shock of it makes her skin tighten against her bones, her eyes smart with tears she refuses to shed. What could have done this, what could have... her ears prick at the sound of what can only be a footstep. It cannot be. She has not seen another living soul for so long that it must either have been her imagination or whatever lives in the forest playing tricks on her.

No. Another step breaks a twig under foot.

Quick as a flash, Nyx grabs a pole that was once a spine for runner beans and hurries back to the porch, sliding quietly along the side of the cottage. It is coming from the other side of the building. Someone is going to walk around the corner and she will...

Stare.

She will stare – is staring – at him. She can't seem to do anything else.

A man. Broad and tall, stronger than any she has ever seen before, with thick black hair that hangs wildly down to his shoulder blades and eyes that are so bright they glow amber even in the glare of the unnaturally harsh morning light. Like fire waiting to ignite. *He has a beard* is her only coherent thought as he takes a step onto the porch towards her.

Neither says anything. He does not come any closer and Nyx doesn't back away. Something about him is… inevitable. No.

Finally the alarm she should have felt straightaway sounds sharply in her mind and Nyx whips the pole up, holding it like a bat, ready to strike.

'Who are you?' Her voice sounds strange to her ears. She hasn't spoken, only sung, for the longest time. She watches as the man blinks, hiding those eyes for a moment, and her alarm becomes sharper. 'I said, who are you? And what did you do to my garden?'

'My name is… Sam.' She knows a lie when she hears one, but Nyx motions for him to continue. 'I didn't do this to your garden; it was like this when I got here. I need shelter, I swear that's all.'

'And you thought you'd find it here? Nobody comes here, least of all for safe harbour. Walk back through the trees and you'll find a hut about five leagues from here. I don't know if anyone lives there now but at least it will offer you the shelter you seek.'

'Five leagues? That's so far. Please, I can see you need help, that your garden is flooded, your crops ruined. I would gladly sleep in your shed, if you'd only give me a little water and a blanket, in return for helping you.' His voice is deep, all velvet and chocolate, designed to tempt the weak, to get him what he wants, but she is not weak. She has a purpose. She hasn't so much as contemplated letting him inside, letting him touch her, wondered about the feel of his mouth on her skin… Enough. He must go.

'You'll have no more mattress than the dirt floor in there.' The words come of their own volition, surprising her as much as they do him. His eyes flare and something inside her answers. She turns away before she can run to him. 'I'll fetch you some water and that blanket, then I will show you where I keep my tools.'

'Thank you.' That voice, it is so familiar to her. She can't place it but it has settled upon her with the certainty of something more than acquaintance. It is right.

She must be out of her mind. She knows a trap when she sees one but damned if she can send him on his way. This is his destination. She feels it. Stepping into the house, she quickly pulls the front door closed behind her and locks it. She thinks about sliding the bolt across too, but is it to keep him out or to keep her in?

He waits on the porch, determinedly not thinking about having her so achingly close to him. He has wished for it for too many days, dreamed of it during the endless nights, but still he had not been ready. It was her scent that bewitched him, he tells himself, the scent of fresh woman and open pasture, enough to drive someone who has lived like a monk for so long to distraction. He knows the lie for what it is. The soft paleness of her flesh is a sharp contrast to his rougher, darker skin. He aches to feel the balm of her beneath his callused hands, to have his burning fever assuaged by her cool lushness. He is going to scare her away if he does not keep himself in check.

They work together in the gardens all day. It is back breaking work and yet each of them toil as though their lives depend upon it. Nyx tries not to stare as Sam removes his shirt; the sight of the hard corded muscles of his torso glistening with sweat almost enough to bring her to her knees. She digs on in a frenzy of purpose, determined not to succumb.

Sam tries not to notice when Nyx splashes water on her face to cool down, the resulting rivulets trickling down her neck onto her chest, dampening her pale blouse, making it see-through. The baseness of his desire shocks him even now and he ploughs on with vigour. By the time the light begins to darken, they are both exhausted but neither wants to stop. What is certain to come next is too much of a temptation. They shouldn't.

'Would you like a bath?' The words are out of her mouth before she can stop them. 'To clean up, I mean. After all, you have worked so hard and it's only fair, it would be nice for you to...'

'Yes, thank you.' His simple answer cuts through her babble and she is grateful.

She leads him into the cottage and up the stairs, the scent of his sweat slicked body almost more than her senses can stand. Opening the door to the bathroom for him, she fights the urge to throw herself at him, to beg him for whatever he wants to give her. Steeling herself, she does no such thing. He squeezes past her in the small confines of the cottage's landing and he can smell the fresh air on her hair. It makes him wonder what her skin tastes like, if it tastes like sunshine and rain. His desire for her heats in his veins, making his eyes glow brightly in the darkening light, his breath comes quicker, his chest tighter than he has ever felt it.

He cannot – will not – fight it any longer.

Nyx turns from him before she is swept away, but he reaches out for her, takes her by the wrist and swings her around to face him. Nyx gasps, but as Sam pulls her to him and his mouth comes down on hers, she welcomes him. His hands on her skin are like fire, the heat echoing through her veins, licking across her skin as his tongue slips between her lips and makes her want, makes her take, everything he offers.

All things fall.

Their days pass in isolated bliss. It is as though they are the only two lovers in the world. Neither one had expected to find the other and now they are together it is as though it has always been this way. This is meant to be.

The bird still does not come and, despite the happiness that has swollen her heart to near bursting, Nyx cannot shake her anxiety. If anything it is worse. The world around them seems alarmingly bright sometimes, the wind sharper, crueller, and yet the salve of his lips against hers, the scent of him on her skin, his strength bearing down onto her softness all serve to make her forget for a while.

Nyx wakes in the night, wrapped in Sam's arms. She is not sure what has woken her, does not want to leave the warmth of their bed and his embrace yet she is drawn to the window. Slipping out from under his arms, careful not to wake him, she crosses the room to look out at the lake. That is what has woken her.

The light.

It glows from the bottom of the water, a warm orange radiance that frightens her. She knows perfectly well what it is. Her heart aches, even as she knows it could never have been stopped. Tears gather in the corner of her eyes and spill down her cheeks, splashing onto the windowsill where her hands grip the wood in agony.

'Nyx?' His voice, that deep seductive voice, is heavy with sleep and concern. She wants to go to him but she holds herself back. This time there can be no indulgence.

'Go back to sleep.'

'Come back to bed. We can…' The orange light is suddenly stronger; it illuminates the room now, reminding Nyx of fire. Her enemy. She looks over her shoulder at Sam and her heart stops. She did not want to see it before but now it is so clear she wants to scream at her own flagrant stupidity.

His eyes are aflame.

He is fire.

Hissing, she backs away from him, edging slowly towards the door as though he's a wild animal bent on her destruction. She almost laughs at that. That is exactly what he will be soon enough. Not taking her eyes from him, she edges towards the door.

'Nyx, please, I'm sorry. I should have told you.'

'No.'

'Please, I…'

'I know!' She shouts the words, her wilful blindness angering her too late. Sam tries to rise from the bed, but she calls the change upon her before he can reach her. The tidal wave of transformation rips violently through her body in a push that affects every cell, from her heels to her head, in an incessant fizz of activity. Sam can only watch for the short moments it takes. As the white horse pushes back with its muscled legs, Nyx's face disappears in a flourish of long shaggy muzzle. Only her eyes remain. He wants to beg her to stop this, to plead with her to just listen to him, to do all the things it is in his very nature not to do.

'Please Nyx, no…' But his words are too late. Fired by the change, she charges for the window, leaping through the glass with no regard for sharp edges, landing on the ground below with a heavy thud but, keeping her hooves beneath her, Nyx thunders on towards the lake. As she lets her legs fly, her hair streams out behind her, catching the moonlight. He watches her for a moment from the broken window, torn between what must be and what he desires. He has come a long way for what he seeks but now he has found it, he finds he wants something else far more.

He wants her.

He cannot have her.

All things fall.

With a roar of anguish borne of a frustration that has existed for as long as there have been lovers, Sam feels his own change begin. His muscles pulse with growth, his bones throb, and his head pounds. His body, so large but graceful as a human, swells relentlessly, his cells splitting and reforming over and over in a fury of expansion. His weight becomes intolerable for the small cottage and his legs burst through the floor of the bedroom, thrusting down into the living room below. He screams in agony as his arms smash through the walls of the bedroom, as his back tries to push up through his skull, the unrelenting growth a torment that burns him, stretches him from the inside out, outside in. As he bursts through the roof the tiny cottage pulses in a final stab of resistance before it explodes, sending splinters of wood and brick shooting across the grove.

Nyx looks back at the sound and stops. Terror grips her at the sight of the giant Sam has become. Who he always was.

Surt.

Ruler of the land of fire.

He has come for what is his. For what must be done.

All things fall.

Defiance rages through her and she ploughs on, heading for the lake.

'Nyx!' The giant's bellow makes the earth tremble. The

very roots of the trees shake in fear at the sound. Waves form upon the surface of the lake, disturbing the peaceful mirror moon, making it more dangerous to leap into but leap she does, ignoring his demands, ignoring the tremors upon the land. There is nothing left to lose. She must try.

As she leaps, Nyx changes again, soft white hair and foam flying from her mouth changing to pale skin and red lips once more. She arches over the water, reaching out as far as she can, wanting only to make headway, to evade the giant. He could crush her so easily, level the area and destroy the lake, but he needs her to bring him what lies at its bottom and she will fight to protect it.

The cold rush of the water thrills her as she breaks the surface, plunging into its depths with a cry of joy. It is a balm to her muddled senses, to her righteous fury, and as she swims, her body undulating along with the water, caressing it, she feels more hope than she has felt for a long time. It fuels her, pushes her on, makes her faster. The light is the key. It hurts her eyes but she heads for it, its pulsing frenzy a beacon. The water swirls around her as the giant steps closer, washing her further than she wants to go, surging up her nose, stopping her breath. She has to fight to the surface. She is not a fish; her lungs need air. As she breaks through the water, she sees the world around her has turned to fire. The giant's anger has been turned loose on the woodlands and the land beyond, his scorching fury impossible to contain. He stands over her lake, staring down in its depths desperate to catch sight of her. Of course he does. She is the one who must hand him the sword. She must give it to him of her own free will.

She will never do it.

Taking a deep breath, she ducks back under the churning waters once again, kicking hard to go deeper, to get to the bottom. She does not know what she will do but she knows she must reach it first. One of the giant's hands plunges into the water, trawling along the bed of the lake to find either her or the sword. He makes the water wild, it froths and eddies against her, and she has to fight the demented current he has created.

As she gets closer, the sword gets brighter, its fiery orange glow all but blinding her. All she can see is fire but she carries on, feeling her way towards the prize. She reaches out with her hand, willing the sword into its grasp. For long moments, her long legs kick harder and harder, her oxygen gets lower and lower, panic settles in her gut and grows. Despair mocks her but desperation stretches her… and finally she feels the hilt of the sword against her palm. Quickly, she curls her fingers around it, gripping it tightly. It is hers. Relief soothes her overworked muscles and she allows herself the luxury of floating to the surface.

It may be the last indulgence she ever knows.

As her body is carried upwards, the water tossing her gently in its embrace, her mind works frantically. She has no idea what she is going to do, what she intends. As she breaks through the water once more, she is disoriented but one gasp of air quickly rights her. She looks up into the face of the giant. It has the same face as the man. It grips her heart like a vice. For a moment, they simply stare at each other.

The eye of the storm.

'I'm sorry.' The giant's rumble is the saddest sound Nyx has ever heard. She closes her eyes against the tears that threaten. She tells herself that this is not the time for her to pity her enemy but, when she opens her eyes to look at him once more, her throat thickens with those unshed tears. It had only been for a brief moment in time, a speck in the grand scheme they are trapped in, but she loved the man that wore that face. She wants to touch him again, to feel his rough skin beneath her smooth fingertips, his darkness to her light. She remembers the way they laid together, the way he had made her understand her human form, to take pleasure in it. Frustration and regret almost steal her breath away.

'I love you.' She doesn't realise she has spoken the words aloud until the light in the giant's eye dims and one huge tear gathers in its corner. It does not fall, but slides slowly down his cheek, petering out as it nears his chin. The lid closes slowly over the eye Nyx stares into and a great sigh almost blows her out of the water. The trees shake and the ground trembles, but nothing falls.

The giant slowly straightens up and takes a step back from

the lake. Treading water, Nyx watches as he begins to contract. The process is quicker, but no less painful. She can see the strain the change takes on him, the veins in his muscular forearms and the side of his strong neck popping and convulsing with every beat of his surely overtaxed heart. He is Surt, he is Jotnar and he is the bringer of All-Fire. His fate will be to destroy the land of men and her soul aches with the inevitability of it, she must do something but…

The stories her grandmother told her come to her in a rush as she faces the giant. Her mother's dictums, to hide the sword, to protect it and keep it from the Fire Bringer, the scourge of man and gods, ring pointlessly next to the other memories she had all but cast aside under her mother's tutelage. She sees the truth of them. She is the girl at the end of the world, but this will not be the end of all things. The world has run itself out; it has been brought to the point of irrevocable destruction. It must be cleansed, but it must also be reborn. What does love matter in the face of that? What is love if not that?

With the sword slung over her shoulder, Nyx kicks out for the shore. Despite her tired limbs she swims quickly, reaching land as Surt's form finally reverts back to Sam's. He is not Sam, she reminds herself. He is Surt. He will set fire to the land, the realms will battle and the world will be destroyed. Yet, that is not the end of the stories her grandmother taught her. Two will hide within the world tree's branches. They will emerge after the fighting is done and theirs will be the charge of repopulating the world. It is a cycle. It is not for her to stand in its way.

She throws the sword at Surt's feet. She will not kneel before him and offer it to him. However great the necessity of allowing the world to turn, she cannot stomach the thought of the violence to come. She is complicit but she will not condone it.

Surt stares at the sword at his feet. Finally, his beloved sword. Lost so long ago to thieving Nixie hands. Their intentions were good, he can see that, has always seen it, but they were misguided. It must be done.

All things fall.

AFTERWORD

At a reasonably young age, my grandfather had all his teeth taken out in order to avoid any future dental problems. I know, it *does* sound mad. Of course it does! Doesn't it…? Anyway, the very idea, even at such a young age – Granddad died when I was eight – absolutely fascinated me. I'd ask him about them, his teeth, maybe tease him a bit, knowing full well what was coming, and sure enough he'd pop out his dental plates and chase after me with them, slapping his gums demonically and shouting 'We all have teeth, dear!' I'd run as fast as I could, laughing so hard I could barely breathe. At least that's my memory of it and it probably explains a lot about me.

Which is to say, the thrill of the weird and the downright horrifying was all mixed up with the absurd and, I have to admit, joy inside me from a very young age. I knew I was safe; my grandfather adored me and would never hurt a hair on my head, although it was always possible he might singe them a bit. He was mischief incarnate and I loved him all the more for it. Mischief. That's my genre, I think. It's why I named this collection, and the drabble that kicks it off, for him.

If you should ever end up in Hell, you'll likely meet Granddad; I've long been convinced he was and is the devil himself. Say hey and mention my name. He's Raymond. You can't miss him. He'll probably chase you with his teeth.

THANK YOUS

I'd like to thank the mighty Fox Spirit Books for publishing an entire book of my guff! You are always a joy to work with and we will forever be Skulk. Daz Pulsford and Gavin Pugh, you are such loves and always so patient with me, thank you. Vincent Holland-Keen, one day they will make a mega-meta-bot out of our brains and we will ruin the universe. Of this I am sure.

To Adele Wearing, the Cap, you have always believed in me and championed my work from the start. Frankly, I don't know where I would be without you. You're a powerhouse, #HardFact, and I am proud to call you my friend.

To Kate Laity, the Prof, who always inspires, encourages, and grounds me. I am lucky to have you as a mentor, whether you want the moniker or not, and even luckier to have you as a dear friend.

To Alasdair Stuart, my full Jarreau buddy and the Cookiest of all humans. Thank you for your unflagging support and kindness. I couldn't have asked for a better brother from another mother.

To Mairead Chammartin, my constant reader. You make me feel like a writer at times when I feel anything but.

To my Mum and Dad, you showed me the stars as a kid and I have never lost the wonder you instilled in me. I love you both so much.

And finally, to Yates, husband mine. I find it so hard to believe in myself but you have never done anything but believe in me. YOU WEIRDO. I'll never be able to say it enough, but thank you, Pinky. I love you, always.

NOT EVERYTHING YOU READ IS TRUE...

Noir Carnival

For many years Chloë toured the world with J.B. Lansbury's Travelling Circus Company as Scheherazade The Sibilant Snake Woman from Beneath the Hot Sands of Zanzibar (although no one is quite sure why as she is, in fact, from Kent). It proved an excellent cover for her real role as an operative for the Skulk, an elite band of ninja foxes. Forced into hiding after a routine job went bad, she embarked on establishing a new life. After extensive and excruciating epilation, Chloë turned to writing for comfort... She is suspicious of dolls.

Girl at the End of the World (Vol. 1)

Leaving the rotting carcass of her alien pod far behind her, Chloë Yates defied her xenomorphic Queen and took to the open road, refusing to be held down by 'the man'. Mixing metaphors and confusing pop culture, she has trailed a blaze of defiance in the post-apocalyptic landscape of both Slough and Grenoble (neither of which she's been to). Catch her in Chalmun's Cantina at weekends, where she plays her harp made from the skin of mutant managerial staff – but don't accept a drink from her; she was once a pupil of the renowned Catherine Deshayes. She writes accounts of her prophetic dreams and expects another Apocalypse toute de suite... She's available for most things of a writerly persuasion. Bring your own gloves.

The Mouse and the Minotaur

Brought forth from that most holy union of the juice of Hera's golden apples and the shimmering hair of a demi-god's nut sac, Chloë Yates's mind sometimes takes a dark turn, but never on a rainy day. While she is a fan of both mice and Minotaurs, she could never eat a whole one... of either.

Eve of War

Imprisoned, for a crime she more than likely committed, deep beneath the majestic Alps in a treacherous network of caves, the Right Reverend Chloë Yates chisels her work by candlelight and then hoists the inscribed tablets topside via a complicated system of ropes and pulleys, achieved only with the assistance of her rodent bandit army. No one knows what she looks like, both because it is dark down there and the last known portrait of her was painted by that infamous forger of the seventeenth century, Count Shen A. Nigan...

Drag Noir

It is entirely anecdotal that Chloë Yates was the inspiration behind the infamous and redoubtable adventurer and lover, Giacomo Casanova, though one can understand why this story has endured. Neither is it true that she was Da Vinci's original choice of model for the Mona Lisa, but refused to shave her beard for the sittings. It is also but a rumour she once masqueraded as the Spanish Infanta in a Channel Four 'reimagining' of Dashiell Hammett's lost work *They Only Hang You in Spandex,* and had the credit for her discovery of the fossil *Fabulosa Sequinus* stolen by The Duchess of Duke Street in 1785. It is true, however, that she writes odd stories. She does insist you bring your own gloves.

Fearless Genre Warriors:

Fox Spirit Sampler

The (not at all or in fact) Reverend C.A. Yates is the dynamic yes-all-mens hero of your worst and possibly dullest nightmare. Not particularly strident about her political and social mores, she exists purely to kick rote-reeling minds right in their smelly creases. Generally surprising, sometimes a bit leaky, she has been writing for Fox Spirit for a number of years, in which time she has also failed to climb any mountains or search high and low. Don't even ask her about fording streams. Most of this is lies. Adjust yourself and wash your bloody hands.

The Jackal Who Came in From the Cold

C.A. Yates – the fiendishly veiled pseudonym of Chloë Yates – graduated top in her class at the Howard Marks Menagerie of Abstract Espionage in 1947. Specialising in infiltrating Post-Nazi Scientific Research laboratories she, as part of an initiative now considered legend, headed the team responsible for the successful liberation of the Bubaline Obstinacy from the clutches of the infamous madman Professor Venedictos Von Holinshed in 1967. Unable to prevent the mad scientist's escape, however, Yates felt compelled to finish the job and alas her determination turned into a lifelong obsession. Driven mad by her failure, although some say Von Holinshed's disappearance during the Intergalactic Scourge of the Sororal League in the 1980s – disguised as a series of Jeff Goldblum movies to protect the innocent – should have been the end of it, Yates's career culminated catastrophically in the total decimation of the vegetarian frozen food compartment of a Lidl in Crewe. Witnesses reported seeing a white haired woman screaming 'AND YOUR LITTLE DOG TOO, YOU BASTARD' at the Brussels sprouts while trying to fit as many vegan Magnums down her knickers as she could.

Yates now lives in the Swiss Alps, a patient at the über-pleasant, maximum-security psychiatric facility known as Die Boobie-Luke. She spends her days crocheting effigies of Von Holinshed and singing to the moon.

Respectable Horror

Coddled within the coterie of Contessa Cadenza Crimpildi's College for Cultured Young Ladies in the temperate cheese forests of a forgotten Swiss canton, C.A Yates, as she is currently known within certain hallowed circles, perversely cultivated a curiosity for all things respectably macabre during her early teenage years. Although frequently cited for insubordination and flagrant contempt, she eventually excelled in all her studies, most notably in Comportment, Gracious Conduct, and Finger Boxing (Heavyweight). By the end of her education, even the Contessa herself, had she not some years previously become ill-advisedly dead at the hand of her erstwhile Bavarian paramour, Colonel Dandy Von Nichols, would have been proud of how very respectable Ms Yates had become. Should you wish to follow her continued pursuit of excellence and, of course, respectability, you may visit her most courteous web presence at www.chloeyates.com or follow her, @shloobee, on the tawdry garden path that is Twitter.

PUBLISHING HISTORY

WE ALL HAVE TEETH The Sirens Call, Spring 2020, Issue 49

GO FORTH IN THE DANCE OF THE MERRYMAKERS Holding On By
Our Fingertips, Kristell Ink, Grimbold Books, 1 May 2018

TUNA SURPRISE! Under the Waves (Fox Pockets Vol 5) ,
Fox Spirit Books, 27 April 2015

TONIGHT, YOU BELONG TO ME Unpublished

A TREACHEROUS THING The Jackal Who Came In From The Cold,
Fox Spirit Books, 19 January 2019

PINS AND NEEDLES Unpublished

HOW TO BE THE PERFECT HOUSEWIFE Wicked Women,
Fox Spirit Books, 26 October 2014

THE SWEETNESS OF YOUR SKIN Fox Spirit Books website, Nov 4 2019

PROFESSOR VENEDICTOS VON HOLINSHED VERSUS THE
SORORAL LEAGUE OF BAZOOKA-BIKINI-WIELDING DEMONIC
DIVAS FROM OUTER SPACE (DENOUEMENT)
The Evil Genius Guide (Fox Pockets Vol 9) Fox Spirit Books, 31 July 2016

KIKI LE SHADE Drag Noir, Fox Spirit Books, 28 Oct 1014

THE CITY IS OF NIGHT, BUT NOT OF SLEEP In An Unknown Country
(Fox Pockets Vol 7) Fox Spirit Books, 7 Feb 2016

EMMELINA IN LOVE The Sirens Call, Spring 2018, Issue 38

A KICK IN THE HEAD Weird Noir, Fox Spirit Books, 29 Oct 2012

A CACKLING FART Tales of the Fox and Fae (Bushy Tales 2),
Fox Spirit Books, 9 Dec 2018

MAGGIE AND THE CAT www.Terranullius.It June 2013

SHOOT TO KILL AND CAN 'EM UP The Girls Guide to Surviving the Apocalpyse, www.ggsapocalypse.co.uk, 4 July 2012

THE BACCHANAL Unpublished

TITS UP IN WONDERLAND Missing Monarchs (Fox Pockets Vol 4), Fox Spirit Books, 18 Dec 2014

THE FLESH TAILOR Unpublished

LEAVE THE PISTOL BEHIND Piracy (Fox Pockets Vol 1), Fox Spirit Books, 25 June 2013

THE MOST TRAGICAL AND IMPLAUSIBLE FATE OF MARY I: A DEMONIC SOLILOQUY Reflections (Fox Pockets Vol 10) Fox Spirit Books, 2 Oct 2016

THE HUNTER Unpublished

MADAM MAFOUTEE'S BAD GLASS EYE Noir Carnival, Fox Spirit Books, 4 July 2013

THE DEVIL'S HAEMORRHOIDS Things In The Dark (Fox Pockets Vol 6) Fox Spirit Books, 15 Dec 2015

WELL OUR FEEBLE FRAME HE KNOWS Guardians (Fox Pockets Vol 3) Fox Spirit Books, 3 March 2014

HIT THAT PERFECT BEAT, BOY Unpublished

FRESHLY BAKED CHILDREN Unpublished

THE HOLY HOUR Resepctable Horror, Fox Spirit Books, 6 March 2017

ALL THINGS FALL Girl At The End of the World Vol 1, Fox Spirit Books, 29 June 2014

Printed in Great Britain
by Amazon